THE SHE BOSS

A WESTERN STORY

ARTHUR PRESTON HANKINS

1st WORLD
LIBRARY
Literary Society

The She Boss

Arthur Preston Hankins

© 1st World Library, 2007
PO Box 2211
Fairfield, IA 52556
www.1stworldlibrary.com
First Edition

LCCN: 2007923756

Softcover ISBN: 978-1-4218-4239-4
Hardcover ISBN: 978-1-4218-4141-0
eBook ISBN: 978-1-4218-4337-7

Purchase *"The She Boss"*
as a traditional bound book at:
www.1stWorldLibrary.com/purchase.asp?ISBN=978-1-4218-4239-4

1st World Library is a literary, educational organization
dedicated to:

- Creating a free internet library of downloadable ebooks

- Hosting writing competitions and offering book
publishing scholarships.

Interested in more 1st World Library books?
contact: literacy@1stworldlibrary.com
Check us out at: www.1stworldlibrary.com

1st World Library Literary Society

Giving Back to the World

"If you want to work on the core problem, it's early school literacy."

- James Barksdale, former CEO of Netscape

"No skill is more crucial to the future of a child, or to a democratic and prosperous society, than literacy."

- Los Angeles Times

Literacy... means far more than learning how to read and write... The aim is to transmit... knowledge and promote social participation."

- UNESCO

"Literacy is not a luxury, it is a right and a responsibility. If our world is to meet the challenges of the twenty-first century we must harness the energy and creativity of all our citizens."

- President Bill Clinton

"Parents should be encouraged to read to their children, and teachers should be equipped with all available techniques for teaching literacy, so the varying needs and capacities of individual kids can be taken into account."

- Hugh Mackay

CONTENTS

CHAPTER I

BEAR VALLEY'S DRONE

Spring was manifest in the vast big-timber country of Mendocino County. "Uncle" Sebastian Burris felt the moist warmth of it oozing from the slowly drying road as he trudged along. The smell of it emanated from the white, pale-yellow, and pink fungi that flourished on the soaked and ancient logs along the way. He heard the voice of it in the soft murmuring of the South Fork of the Eel, which went twinkling down Bear Valley through firs and redwoods straight as telegraph poles; in the caress of the soft south wind soughing in the tree-tops. Chipmunks and gray squirrels darted across his path.

A quarter of a mile from Wharton Bixler's store he turned off on a narrow road which led into the deeper forest. He passed through groves of redwoods which towered three hundred feet above him, and whose girth was over sixty feet. A half mile more the old man trudged on sturdily, muttering occasionally to himself. Then he struck a cross trail which paralleled Ripley Creek, and this he followed into the sunshine of an open spot.

Across this, through thickets of whitethorn, manzanita, alder, and bay he limped along, following deer trails. The deeper forest was left behind in the lowlands. A grass-grown bark road, which he eventually found, followed the creek, ascending sharply through shade and sunshine, crossing and recrossing the creek on wooden bridges, twisting, always climbing.

On one of the bridges Uncle Sebastian Burris halted. A great snarl of bleached driftwood had collected just above the bridge, and through it the clear water roared in a dozen tiny cataracts. Beyond the drift Uncle Sebastian had caught a glimpse of some living, moving object. He wiped his watery blue eyes with a red handkerchief, looked once more, then crossed the bridge and wound through a thicket of huckleberry bushes till abreast the drift.

A little later he was peering down a steep bank into the boulder-studded bottom of Ripley Creek, where lay a fine young specimen of the genus homo idly tossing pebbles into the crystal water. A smile half sardonic grew in the features of Uncle Sebastian as he stood looking down at him.

The youth, unconscious of the presence of another, kept on idly tossing the pebbles, recumbent on one elbow. His long sinewy legs were incased in slick jean trousers of stovepipe lines and stiffness. He wore no coat. A faded blue shirt covered his barrel of a body, and his slouch hat was off, exposing long, light, wiry hair and a freckled neck. His lean jaws were covered by a two weeks' growth of beard. About him drooped hazels and alders. From one end to the other Ripley Creek was beautiful; there was no lovelier spot in all of California.

"Hello, Hiram!" Sebastian Burris called at last.

The youth started perceptibly and sat up. He turned his head over his left shoulder. Big, bulging blue eyes laughed back at Sebastian. The good-naturedly twisted mouth that grinned at him was suggestive of a sluggish drawl. The long legs twined themselves, and Hiram Hooker flopped over on his stomach, facing his friend.

"Why, hello, Uncle Sebastian!" he cried in a tone which bore true welcome. "What're you doin' 'way up here? Come on down an' look at the young trout!"

Without remark, Uncle Sebastian, grasping roots and

low-hanging branches, clambered stiffly down the bank. He sat down by the side of Hiram Hooker and glanced at three old, dirty backless magazines that lay on the pebbles and smiled.

"Ain't seen ye down to th' store at stage time in I dunno when, Hiram," he remarked, surveying the handsome young Hercules with admiration.

Hiram skimmed a flat piece of slate across a riffle.

"I never get any mail, Uncle Sebastian," he drawled.

"They's a heap o' us don't go to Bixler's fer th' mail, Hiram."

"Heaven knows there's nothin' else to take me there," and there was just a shade of bitterness in the twist of Hiram's good-natured mouth.

In place of tossing pebbles, Uncle Sebastian chose to pick up a redwood splinter on which to whittle. He took out a slick-handled jackknife, blew a clot of pocket lint from the springs, opened a whetted pruning blade, and began shaving the brittle wood. His watery blue eyes were far-off and thoughtful.

"Jest come from there," he resumed. "We was talkin' about ye down there, Hiram. Put me in mind to come up an' see ye. Hiram, ye ain't any too popular in Bear Valley—d'ye know it?"

"You know I do," promptly replied Hiram.

"D'ye know what they're sayin' agin' ye?" Uncle Sebastian continued after a long pause.

"Don't know as I'm carin'."

"Yes, ye are, Hiram," said Uncle Sebastian positively. "Don't tell me that. Ye c'n tell yerself ye don't keer, Hiram, but ye're lyin' to yerself. It ain't in human nature not to keer what folks thinks about a fella. Gosh! where'd we be if it wasn't so?"

Hiram flipped a pebble. "I reckon you're right, Uncle Sebastian, and I reckon I know you're aimin' at somethin'. You came 'way up here to spring somethin' on me, didn't you? Well, le's have it."

"Ye're right, Hiram—I did. In the first place, then, they're sayin' ye're the laziest fella in Bear Valley."

Hiram laughed mirthlessly. "There's nothin' new in that, Uncle Sebastian. They've said the same since paw died. I reckon I am, maybe."

"Hiram," patiently persisted the old man, "I didn't walk 'way up here to listen to such talk. I tell ye, ye're playin' insincere, Hiram. Down in yer heart ye know as well as anythin' it makes ye hot to be talked about an' called th' laziest man in Bear Valley. I'd druther see ye hoppin' mad ner takin' it that a way.

"Now, Hiram, listen to me: I've known ye sence ye was knee-high to a duck, ain't I? Yer paw an' me was thicker ner molasses. Yer paw would 'a' made a brilliant man, Hiram, if he'd 'a' had th' chanct. You've inherited yer paw's brains.

"When ye was a kid ye was a little devil, I'll admit. Still, givin' myself credit fer a set o' brains a leetle above th' average o' Bear Valley, I made allowances. Ye was mean because yer head was full o' ideas; an' in Bear Valley they's so blamed little to use them ideas on that ye jest naturally had to turn to meanness. Ye wasn't really bad; ye was jest alive. All yer life ye been hankerin' fer sumpin that Bear Valley couldn't give, but ye didn't even know what 'twas ye was hankerin' fer. How could ye? A man's gotta taste olives before he c'n tell if he likes 'em, ain't he? Yer paw taught ye to read." Uncle Sebastian glanced once more, half pityingly, half resentfully, at the backless magazines. "Readin's put notions into yer head an' set ye to hankerin'.

Arthur Preston Hankins

"Then as ye grew up th' Valley folks begun to shun ye, didn't they?" he continued. "They called ye queer. Then when yer paw died they dropped ye altogether. It hurt ye, an' ye jest drew aloof an' went to shakes.

"D'ye know, Hiram, sometimes I find myself not blamin' ye like I oughta. They called ye no good before ye really was so, an' practically driv ye to it. Then ye was too proud to brace up an' give 'em th' satisfaction o' thinkin' their treatment o' ye had made ye turn over a new leaf. If they'd gone on treatin' ye decent ye'd likely come out all right o' yer own hook. Hiram, pride's put a heap o' men in th' penitentiary. Pride's stubborn, Hiram. But layin' aside th' root o' th' trouble, an' lookin' at th' matter through *their* eyes, it's really a shame th' way yer paw's place has gone to ruin—th' way you've gone th' same route. I'd druther see ye plumb bad ern so all-fired no-good all round. Ye had jobs a number o' times drivin' eight an' ten on jerkline, freightin' tanbark from Longport. Ye're a good jerkline skinner, Hiram—no better in the country—but ye won't stick no more'n a month or two outa each year.

"But I'm makin' allowances fer ye—I always have—I'm th' only one that ever has. I been watchin' an' waitin' fer ye to right yerself an' get at sumpin; but this mornin', down to th' store, it come over me that ye'll never do it in Bear Valley.

"Consequently, Hiram," Uncle Sebastian resumed, "ye've gotta move."

Hiram glanced at him with wide-opened eyes. "Move! Where to?"

"Out into th' world, Hiram, to strike yer gait. Ye gotta hit th' hard places an' git experience. Ye gotta taste olives to see if ye c'n stummick 'em. Ye'll get an awful batterin'-up, I reckon, but ye'll likely learn if they's anything in ye. At first ye'll probably go to th' bad an' get a heap worse ern ye was in Bear Valley. That's neither here ner there. Th' point is, if they's a gait in ye ye'll eventually strike it. If not—well, then, what's th' difference? I'm goin' to pay up fer ye down to th' store an' give ye enough to land ye in Frisco. Then th' good Lord an' what He put into that head o' yers must look after ye. I'm gonta foreclose on ye, Hiram."

Hiram was not looking at Uncle Sebastian, but the old man saw his slight start and the red creep down his columnar neck as the last sentence came out. One great toe protruded from the upper of one of Hiram's shoes. Uncle Sebastian saw it twitching.

"You're foreclosin' on me?" The words came slowly and with a hollow gulp.

Uncle Sebastian's lips went straight and hard. "Unless ye'll deed th' place to me, Hiram."

Another pause, while the low wind whined in the treetops and Ripley Creek went gurgling and sucking through the latticed trunks in the pile of drift.

"What did you tell me when I gave the mortgage, Uncle Sebastian?"

The reproach in Hiram's voice did not move the arbiter. "I know what I told ye, Hiram. I told ye, ye needn't worry—that I wouldn't foreclose—that I wasn't speculatin' when I lent th' money on th' place. Jest th' same, Hiram, I'm foreclosin' on ye."

Uncle Sebastian eyed the young man keenly. The first shock past, Hiram seemed now to be turning the matter over with just deliberation.

"I reckon I know what you're up to, Uncle Sebastian," he said at last. "We've talked the matter over too many times for me to misconstrue your motives. You're thinkin' that I'll amount to somethin' if I get away from here."

"I reckon ye've said it, Hiram." Uncle Sebastian voiced this with great relief.

"And you're foreclosin' on me to force me to go."

"Eggzackly, Hiram. I'm proud that ye interpret my motive."

Hiram was silent another long minute. Then, with a hollow laugh: "I reckon you'll be tolerably disappointed, Uncle Sebastian. There was a time when I'd 'a' looked forward to leavin' Mendocino. I've had hankerin's, and I've got 'em yet—but I'm scared. I've never been outa the country but once. What c'n I do away from here? What d'ye expect of me, anyway?"

"Ye c'n certainly do as much out o' here as ye're doin' here, Hiram."

"I don't know about that. It don't take much to live here. I've got about all I want, I reckon. If I had more books to read I'd be pretty near content. There was a time, as I said, when it was different; but now I don't reckon I care. But what particular thing d'ye expect me to excel in, Uncle Sebastian?"

"Excel's a tol'able big word, Hiram. I can't tell ye any more. Ye've wanted to be a poet, an' ye've wanted to be an officer in th' army, an' this an' that an' th' other—ye've wanted to be pretty near everythin' ye read about last. When ye git in touch with these things, Hiram, ye may be able to choose—though they's a heap o' 'em ain't that's in constant touch. I know ye've got imagination. I know it's wasted here in th' backwoods; an' I know ye gotta git."

Uncle Sebastian had risen to emphasize this ultimatum. Now, standing and looking down, he finished:

"Whether ye'll bless me or curse me remains to be seen."

Hiram made no reply—he did not even look up.

"So be down to Wharton Bixler's by stage time to-morrow, Hiram, an' be ready to take th' stage to Brown's Corner. I'll go with ye that far, an' ye c'n deed me th' prop'ty before a notary, so's I won't be obliged to foreclose. Then I'll come back an' pay yer bill at Bixler's, an' ye'll have one hundred dollars to take ye down to Frisco. Will ye be at th' store at half past nine?"

A wait, then a short nod.

Uncle Sebastian half turned, paused, cleared his throat, and for the first time lost his high-handed control of the situation.

"Hiram," he said in a lower tone, "I reckon I'm a fool, but I hope ye ain't holdin' anything agin' me. So help me, boy, I believe I'm doin' ye a turn. Do—d'ye believe it or not?"

"Wait'll to-morrow, Uncle Sebastian," came Hiram's pleading voice. "Le'me think it over all to-night. You've plumb knocked the props from under me."

Without another word, Uncle Sebastian climbed up the bank and strode off through the huckleberries.

CHAPTER II

OUT OF THE WOODS

For over an hour Hiram Hooker lay perfectly still at the creekside. His wide-open eyes stared dreamily into the water. His mind was stunned by the present situation. Feverishly and against his will his thoughts went hurrying back over the years which had led up to this momentous climax.

A woman moved frequently across the picture—a bent, tired, work-warped woman—his mother. The pitiable leanness of the life of Hiram's mother had been appalling. One word stood for the tenor of her days from sun to sun—nothing. She had never seen a piano or a typewriter, or even a washing machine. Silent, unmurmuring, she had given her life for nothing and gone.

Swiftly came in the picture the likeness of Hiram's father— tall, bewhiskered, strong as an ox, soft-voiced, and easy-going. Nothing but kindness had emanated from the father to his wife and child. Foster Hooker, too, had slaved his life away for nothing. The rocky land had claimed him and held him down. They had had enough to eat and to keep them warm—beyond that, nothing. Now he lay with Hiram's mother between the big bull pines on Wild-cat Hill.

There was in Hiram's thoughts no bitterness against his parents. They had been always kind and had given their best to him. The rocky land had held them chained. It offered sustenance, and of the big progressing world beyond they had lived afraid. In the early days they had buried themselves in the big woods to make their fortune. But the fortune was not there, and old age crept on. Old age told them that the world outside had passed beyond them, and they were afraid.

After all, had they given Hiram nothing? In his bitter moments he had thought so, but to-day his thoughts were mellowed. He was on the eve of leaving everything that held memories of them. Had they not given him of themselves a love for the grandeur of these woods which touched no other soul, save Uncle Sebastian's, perhaps, in all the valley? Hiram saw more in a redwood tree than the natives did; saw the beauty of contrast in the open spots in the forest, where the others saw only grazing ground for cattle; saw wonders in the rioting streams without a thought of miners' inches. His father had taught him the love of books, but there had been so few to love. He had taught him to think. Hiram was weird, queer, a "leetle cracked" to the others of Bear Valley. Uncle Sebastian alone had understood him—had sympathized with him and helped him.

Now, though, it was over. He was leaving forever. One hundred dollars! He had never possessed so much in his twenty-six starved years! An exultation seized him which beat throbbingly in his temples and fired his soul with recklessness. He was bound out into the Great Unknown, where the promises of his dreams would be fulfilled. He would do great things, live great adventures, then come back to scoff at them!

He sprang to his feet, collected the backless magazines, and climbed the bank. With long strides he hurried along the bark road which wound round the contour of the hills. An hour later he was trotting down a manzanita slope to his cabin, nestled in the cup of the hills, surrounded by the whispering firs.

Just within he paused and looked about as if seeing the sordidness of his home for the first time. All the way up the hill the exultation of impending departure had thrilled him. It thrilled him still, and a new feeling of contempt of what he saw came over him.

A panther skin hung on the rough, unpainted wall above the black and cheerless fireplace, three sets of antlers surrounding it. Near the fireplace lay an unsightly pile of wood and chips. The doors of the cracked and rusty stove were gaping wide. The remains of his breakfast were on the clothless, homemade table. His rifle, the only thing well kept, stood in a corner.

He passed through into the other room, separated from this by a thin board partition. There, in oval walnut frames, hung the pictures of the two who lay between the big bull pines on Wild-cat Hill. A slight sense of depression seized him. The bed unmade, brought a sparkle of anger to his eyes. He was disgusted with himself, but it did not last. The thought of the adventures that lay beyond and beckoned came uppermost once more. "The girl" beckoned, too.

Yes, there was a girl. Hiram had seen her only in his dreams. She was not like Bear Valley girls. She was large and sturdy and strong, and her hair was of such dark brown as to seem almost black, her eyes dark and large and lustrous. She was a queen among women, this girl of his dreams. About her hung some great mystery, and adventure followed in her footsteps. Out there somewhere beyond Bear Valley she stood beckoning him to come!

He went to bed early, to toss for hours and at last to drop into fretful, torturing dreams. The scream of a panther awoke him once.

He was up before sunrise, cooking his bacon and coffee and frying slices of cold biscuit in the bacon grease.

The east was pink when he left the cabin, carrying the rifle, which he meant to give to Uncle Sebastian. Everything else he left behind. He took a short cut over Wild-cat Hill. On its crest, between the two bull pines, he stopped before two graces.

The red sun was peering through the saddle of Signal Hill. Cold mists rose from the forest. In the air was the breath of the morning. Weirdly the early wind moaned through the needles of the tall bull pines. Up from the canon came the roaring of Ripley Creek as it raced to the sea.

A lump came in Hiram's throat that he could not down. At his feet lay those who had lived and starved for him through the countless denials of this wilderness. Below him lay the cabin which he had known as home for twenty-six long years. About him stretched the grandeur of this untarnished land. Scalding tears burst from his eyes. Some monstrous ogre had arisen to crush him. They were driving him from his home, from the land of his birth, from the spots he loved! No bitterer period ever came in Hiram's life than when he stood that misty morning and watched the sun rise on the turning point of his career. Blindly he stumbled down Wild-cat Hill and took up the long road to Bixler's store. They were driving him, like Hagar, from all that he held dear, and there was hatred in his heart.

CHAPTER III

SAN FRANCISCO

The train that carried Hiram Hooker to San Francisco was late. Thirty miles from the bay it began making up for lost time. Through the falling dusk it roared toward the metropolis. Slowly the landscape faded. Vineyards and chicken ranches and orchards and rolling hills studded with live oaks gave place to the electric-lighted tentacles of the city. The lights blinked by at Hiram. They helped depress him, for they were a part of the modernity that he feared. Suburbs grew to a continuous stretch of lighted streets and houses. Always those lights blinked on every side. There was witchery in all of it—in the smell of the city close at hand, in the cold salt air from the bay, in the *chunk-a-lunk, chunk-a-lunk* of the speeding locomotive.

Hiram sat forward on the seat, eager, shrinking, exultant, always straining while he shrank. He tried to plan, but could not. Night closed in, and all that he saw now were the blinking lights that raced astern. Off in the black sky to the southward a rosy light suffused the night—San Francisco.

"Saus-a-lito! Everybody change! Don't forget yer baggage!"

Hiram was swept out with the crowd, swept through the chute to the ferryboat, swept aboard. He followed the crowd forward and stood in the bow. Black as ink the Bay of San Francisco stretched before him. Like fireflies the lights of vessels scurried through the blackness. Beyond the black water blinked the countless eyes of San Francisco, above these the rosy glow which had beckoned since the fall of dusk.

The boat had started before Hiram was aware. Smoothly it slipped along toward the beacons on the other shore. Hiram breathed the keen salt breeze in gulps and looked steadily and curiously at the world that waited for him. Somewhere there, perhaps, the girl of his dreams was beckoning, and begging him not to be afraid. The boat nosed into her slip and the crowd swept him ashore, swept him through the Ferry Building, and, as it went its thousand ways, left him stranded, staring unbelievingly up Market Street.

Ten minutes he stood there. Thousands pressed by him. The laughter and grumblings of life buzzed in his uncomprehending ears. No one noticed him. The continuous *clang-clang-clang* of the street cars grew to a rhythmic roar. Strange odors filled his nostrils. What held him most was the lights— the myriad lights that blinked away in perspective up Market Street, clusters of them, pillars of them, wheels of them, stars and squares of them. They all blended into a shower of diamonds and held him spellbound. Then the clang of the street cars, the clatter of hoofs on cobbles, the crunch of wheels, the raucous toots of automobile horns and the purring of the engines, the ceaseless laughing and murmuring of the crowds, the unfamiliar odors all blended with the lights, and Hiram Hooker was breathing life, and knew that it was warm, knew that he loved it, and was unafraid!

At last he sighed and began warily crossing the street from the Ferry Building to Market Street. He had read of country boys in the city. He knew enough not to stand in the street and stare. He wisely kept with a crowd while crossing, and made their experience in braving the dangers of traffic protect him. He reached the other curb in safety and started up the long, broad street.

Hiram Hooker will never forget that night. Not once after

leaving the water front did he know his location, and it would have mattered little if he had. He walked on and on untiringly through an entrancing dream. He was alone in a great museum—the other human beings were not fellow spectators, but specimens on exhibition.

The beauty of the women fascinated him. Never in his wildest imaginings had he fancied such forms and faces. The most beautiful girl in Bear Valley bore the face of a gargoyle compared with the soft, creamy faces he saw that night. The flashing, long-lashed eyes, the red lips, the coils on coils of fluffy hair, the swishing silk, unfamiliar furs, sparkling jewels, and the slender French heels were stupefying.

He was growing hungry. He had not eaten a bite since early morning, and now it was eleven o'clock at night. It appalled him to think of entering a restaurant and being confronted by one of those white-skinned, slim-formed divinities he saw flitting from table to table. He did not know what to order nor how to order it. Even the smallest places looked imposing with their myriad lights and fixtures of gilt and white and glittering glass. But he knew he must screw his courage to it.

There seemed to be a restaurant nearly every other door in the locality he was now passing through. Not only that, but many electric letters blazing down the street notified him that he would have no trouble in finding rooms; rooms by the day or week; rooms and board; rooms 15 cents and up; lodging; rooms with or without board; beds 10 cents and up. He was on Kearny Street, he knew, but he did not know where Kearny Street was in relation to the rest of the city.

He strolled along, staring through the windows at the appetizing displays and searching for a restaurant where none of those creamy-skinned beings that caused him so much uneasiness were employed. At last he found one where, it seemed, only smooth-faced men in short black coats and low-cut vests were serving. His abused stomach goaded him to slink through the doorway and seek a table.

Just within the door he paused. The place seemed crowded. He was about to slink out again when a woman's voice said in his ear: "This side, please—all full here."

He turned quickly, with a gulp, to see a slim, black-clad girl, with one of those appalling piles of fluffy hair topping her head, whisking past behind him. Now he noticed that the restaurant was divided in half by a screen which ran the length of the building, and that one side—the side he had seen through the window—was for men, and the other for women. The tables on the men's side were filled. The girl stood beckoning from a table on the women's side. Other waitresses he had not seen before were working here. Hiram could not back out now. His legs trembled as he obeyed the girl's beckoning finger.

He reached the table and stumbled noisily into a seat. The girl, now holding out a menu card, was looking at him curiously, he felt. The blood rushed to his face; he dared not look at her. Fumblingly he took the card and straightway dropped it on the floor.

Together they bent over to regain it. Their bodies touched. Hiram grew sick. She recovered the card and was standing erect when he crawfished up from the floor. He was burning up with shame. Again he took the card, but his glazed eyes could not read a word.

Suddenly he knew that she was speaking.

"I think you'd like a ribber, medium," she was saying, "with French fries and a dish of peas."

Hiram's head nodded without command. He knew she was leaving the table, and something forced his eyes to her. She was turning, but her eyes were looking back into his. In those eyes, big and brown beneath dark, arched brows and long lashes, there was a look that thrilled him to his soul. She was more beautiful than any woman he had seen through all the

Arthur Preston Hankins

splendor of the night, and she had flashed to him a spark of kindness in a maelstrom of misery! Was this the girl who had been beckoning him on?

She was coming back. She paused beside him and placed a napkin, silver, bread and butter, and a glass of water before him. He tried to look up, but could not. He felt her close to him as she arranged the things before him.

She was speaking again, low, soothingly.

"Awful crowd to-night. We don't usually put single gentlemen on this side, but I guess you won't mind. Your ribber'll be here in a minute."

She was gone again. He saw her brown hair bobbing toward the kitchen. He watched the swing doors, eager for her return.

They burst open at last and she came forward and placed a big platter before him, on which steamed an enormous rib steak, beside this a dish of French-fried potatoes and a dish of peas.

She glided away once more and did not again come near his table while he ate. He kept his eyes on her throughout the meal, and continued to lower them when he thought her about to look toward him. His "ribber" was good, and he ate the last scrap. Then he paid his bill and hurried out.

Through the window he looked back for her. She was nowhere in sight.

In a miserable hallway on the second floor of a dingy brick building, he obeyed the legend over a button in the wall, which read: "Landlord—push the button." The result was that a squint-eyed man came from a door marked "office" and yawningly asked him his business. Hiram wished a twenty-five-cent room, he said. He was taken to one, which was not a room at all, but a stall—that is, the thin board partitions did not connect with the ceiling by three feet. The bed was a single one, and the sheets had brought the proprietor many a twenty-five-cent piece since coming from the laundry. The additional furnishings of the "room" were six nails driven in the board wall to hold one's clothes. From all over the floor came lusty snores and the mutterings of world-worn men.

With the city smells still in his nostrils, the buzz of city life still in his ears, and the countless lights twinkling in a frame about the white face of a brown-haired, red-lipped girl, he fell asleep from sheer fatigue. But with unaccountable perversity his dreaming mind dwelt not upon the beautiful vision he had come to love in fifteen seconds, but on the whispering firs and twinkling streams of Mendocino, and on a plodding ten-horse jerkline team hauling tanbark over the mountains to the coast.

CHAPTER IV

TWITTER OR TWEET

Hiram Hooker washed in the community lavatory in the hall next morning. Then he sought the squint-eyed landlord and paid a week's room rent in advance, thereby saving fifty cents.

He wished to strike out at once after breakfast to begin justifying Uncle Sebastian's faith in him, but so far he had not laid a plan. He noticed lettering on a door in the hall which dignified what lay beyond as a "lounging room." The door stood ajar, and he saw that the room was empty. He decided to go in and think. A thousand and one wonders awaited his curious eyes, but they must wait. His hundred dollars had dwindled perceptibly; it was time to give his future a practical thought or two.

In the "lounging room" were a long plain board writing-table, ten yellow kitchen chairs. Hiram took a seat by a window overlooking Kearny Street.

He could not plan, he found, for his ideas of seeking employment were of the vaguest; he did not know where to look for it, nor what duties he should state that he could perform. Dreaming of it up there in Mendocino County, climbing up in the world from the bottom rung had seemed so easy.

He began feeling a little lonesome. He had resolved to brave the fascinating eyes of the girl of the restaurant again, and perhaps speak to her if occasion offered, when the door opened and three men came into the lounging room.

Two of them scraped chairs to the table and from a drawer took a dirty pack of cards and a homemade cribbage board, with headless matches for markers. The third took from his pocket a folded newspaper and sat down at the window opposite Hiram. He at once began reading, and seemed not to be a companion of the other two. Hiram took note that he perused the want-ad sheets.

Hiram studied the two at cards. He resolved that he did not like their unkempt looks, so turned his attention to the man with the paper.

In dress this man was in a class with the other two, though perhaps a little better groomed. But a careful observer would have taken note of certain finer characteristics in the face. It was the face of a man in the thirties, robust and good-natured, with bushy brows, slate-blue eyes, and a nose that would have been termed Grecian if it had not been for a semiconical twist to the left. He was of stalky build, carefully shaved that morning, and wore a dingy turndown collar. His shoes, though scuffed with wear, were polished.

In the midst of this scrutiny the man suddenly lowered the paper and leveled his eyes at Hiram. The look almost said "What do you want?" in a disinterested though not antagonistic way. Hiram was caught unawares. He felt the question and had answered it, to cover his embarrassment, before he knew the words were coming.

"D'ye find any jobs in the paper?"

The two at cards looked quickly at Hiram and shrugged, and the game went on in silence, as before.

"What d'ye follow?" asked the man with the twisted nose in a

Arthur Preston Hankins

sort of rollicking voice by no means unpleasant.

"D'ye mean what c'n I do?"

The man with the paper nodded.

Hiram scraped his chair a foot closer. "Why, I don't exactly know. I'm willin' to do anything—that is, try."

The slate-blue eyes quizzically studied Hiram a little longer, then settled on the paper once more.

A few moments they scanned the column. Then:

"Maybe some o' these'll look attractive ol'-timer. 'Wanted three bushelmen; one coat-maker; first-class pants operator; shoe shiner; two farm carpenters, Arizona, four dollars a day, fare refunded; two carpenters, city, five dollars a day; one hundred muckers, New Mexico, two-fifty day; one trammer, three-fifty day; one hundred laborers, New Mexico, three dollars day; porter in bakery, city, must be sober; boy, sixteen years old, make himself generally useful in pickle plant; two jerkline drivers—must be good, southern California; cooks, waiters, teamsters, muckers galore. Call and see us. Morgan & Stroud, Four-hundred-and-fifteen Clay Street.'"

He lowered the paper and once more fixed the slate-blue eyes on Hiram. "There you are, ol'-timer—pick yer road to wealth and prominence."

His smile brought Hiram's chair closer.

"How d'ye get any o' these jobs?" he asked.

"Part with two dollars to Morgan & Stroud for the address o' the advertiser, then beat the other fella to it," was the reply.

"But they wanted a hundred muckers, you read."

"Oh, that's different. They ship you out for two dollars to where the job is. The contractor deducts your fare from your first month's pay and refunds it to the railroad company, or sticks it in his pocket if he's wise. Le's see—where they shippin'?" He glanced at the column again. "N' Mexico, eh? Yes, they'll ship you down there for two dollars, and you c'n go to work and grow up with the country. C'n you drive a team?"

"Sure," said Hiram. "I c'n drive eight or ten, or even sixteen jerkline, too. You read something about jerkline skinners."

"Then I'd go as a jerkline skinner at—what is it?—fifty-five and found. Found means board, you know."

"And you're sure they'll send me down to southern California for two dollars and gi' me a job drivin' mules?"

"They'll be tickled to death to do it. Where you from?"

Hiram heaved a sigh. "Mendocino County," he replied.

"Hittin' the trail for the first time, eh?"

The questioner evidently knew it, so Hiram did not reply.

"M'm-m! Fine big country—Mendocino. You oughta stayed there. That country'll go to work and come out with a loud report some day."

"You've been there?" asked Hiram eagerly.

"Been everywhere."

"What do you follow?" Hiram used the new expression almost unconsciously.

"I'm a promoter and capitalist."

"A promoter and capitalist," Hiram repeated vaguely.

"Yep. At present, though, I ain't workin' at the capitalist end. But I'm always a promoter."

Hiram was growing uncomfortable. He had been warming toward this genial stranger; now he felt he was being ridiculed. He kept silent and looked out the window.

The other nonchalantly resumed his paper as if the conversation were over.

But Hiram did not wish it to end here. Despite the stranger's fantastic statement, there was that in his bearing which told Hiram he meant what he said, and that, furthermore, it was with him a matter of indifference whether any one believed him or not. He wished the two tramps would leave. He felt that then he could talk to the other man with less reserve.

As he sat there silently thinking, this wish was granted. A third unkempt individual thrust his head in at the door and remarked, "Hey, youse!"

The cribbage players looked up.

In explanation the man in the door held up a quarter between a calloused forefinger and thumb.

A broad grin broke on the face of one of the players as he scraped back his chair and rose. "Cheese, Thumbscrew, where'd youse glom it?" he gasped ecstatically.

"Never mind w'ere I glommed it, Scully," was the retort. "De point is, are youse guys in on helpin' me lick up a growler?"

The other tramp had risen, and spoke for both as he strode toward the door. "Lead us to it, Thumbscrew," he swaggered portentously; "lead us to it, ol'-timer!" And the door slammed behind the three.

Hiram glanced back at the man behind the newspaper. He had

not so much as slanted a look toward the door.

Hiram's chance had come. After a silent minute he essayed:

"But I didn't come to the city to leave it right away and go to drivin' mules. I came here to get a start."

The other politely lowered his paper. "What're you doin'—breakin' loose from home to make yer fortune?" he asked.

Hiram nodded and smiled.

The man surveyed him for the first time from head to foot. "Been a farmer up in Mendocino?" he queried.

"Sorta," Hiram admitted. Then in a low voice: "To tell the truth, this is my first time in a city. I got in last night. I've never been out o' Mendocino County but once before."

A few wrinkles of puzzlement came between the other's brows. "How old are you?"

"Twenty-six," was Hiram's meek confession.

The stranger studied, a whimsical smile twisting his lips, a far-away look in the slate-blue eyes. With a little jerk he emerged from reverie and asked:

"And what d'ye expect to take up here in Frisco?"

Hiram scraped his chair still closer. "I don't know," he acknowledged. "To tell the truth, I'm pretty green. I don't know anybody here and don't know where to begin."

"Don't say green," corrected the other. "That's obsolete. Say raw, or that you're a hick, or a come-on. Well, what d'ye want to follow?"

"I thought if I could get into some big man's office and work

Arthur Preston Hankins

up, I might reach—"

The other man raised his hand protestingly and his face assumed a sick expression.

"Forget it! Forget it!" he cried. "Say, that's the biggest mistake a fella like you could make. Your feet are too big for an office. Say, take this from me: An office man is always an office man. He knows the figgers—nothing else. The fella out on the works is the lad that knows the fundamentals of the job. Take this railroad-construction business, for instance: When the contractor wants a new general superintendent he don't make him out of an office man. He goes out on the job and gets him. You get offices outa your head, and get out and learn something." He was thoughtful a minute, then finished with the question: "How long are you on cash?"

"I haven't got much," Hiram confessed—"sixty some dollars."

"M'm-m," the other said musingly. Then, after another thoughtful pause: "Say, I suppose you're a little shy about bracin' these employment men, ain't you?"

Hiram nodded.

"Then I'll tell you what I'll do: You go to work and dig up my fee, and I'll go down to southern California with you on the jerkline job. I been wantin' to get outa Frisco for a week, but couldn't raise the price. Anywhere'll suit me, where there's a chance o' makin' a little stake. That's what you wanta do—go to work and make a stake. Then look about for something you c'n float for yourself. There's nothin' in working for somebody else. Work for yourself if it's only running a peanut stand. Southern California'll do. What d'ye say?"

"D'ye mean you're broke?"

"Broke! I'm ruined!"

"How did you lose your money?" Hiram asked innocently.

"You're askin' for the story o' my life. What d'ye say, now? Le's go to work and get breakfast, then enter Morgan & Stroud's in our usual graceful manner and tell 'em we've decided to accept their kind offer and let 'em ship us south. You'll probably learn a few things on that trip."

"Are you a jerkline skinner?"

"I dunno. Maybe I am. I never tried. But if that's what you wanta hit—me, too. Say, what's your name?"

"Hiram Hooker."

"That's a peach, all right. They sure labeled you for the part. Mine ain't much better though. They call me Twitter-or-Tweet."

"What!"

"Proves I'm a bird, don't it? My name is Orr Tweet. Can you beat it? So they call me Twitter-or-Tweet, or just Twitter—or sometimes Playmate. I'm gregarious. I gotta have a partner all the time. I'll play with any o' the little boys so long as they're nice to me."

He handed Hiram a card. It read:

ORR TWEET

REPRESENTING THE CUCAMONGA
DEVELOPMENT COMPANY
Cerro Gordo, Mexico

THE HOMESEEKERS' PROMISED LAND
OF MILK AND HONEY

"That Cucamonga Development Company and the

milk-and-honey business is passe," explained Mr. Tweet, "but I've got no other card. They pinched the owners, and I flew the coop before they could lay it onto me. Crooked deal."

"What was it?" Hiram asked vaguely.

"Banana plantation," Tweet replied lightly. "At least they called it that—I never saw it. I was just promotin' the deal. Well, what d'ye say?" he persisted. "I'm broke and I need a little cash. But I'm a money getter! You tide me over this little depression and I'll remember you. We may strike somethin' that'll look good anywhere between here and there. If so, we'll drop off and look into it."

Hiram did not know what to say. He had no experience in reading human nature, and Mr. Tweet would have appeared as an enigma to many more astute than Hiram.

"What do you want me to do?" he hedged.

"Hold me up, if your coin lasts, till I hit the ball—that's all. You'll never regret it." Tweet sat pulling his twisted nose from side to side, as if trying to straighten it.

"But I don't understand. You seem to be—that is, you call yourself a capitalist, and you're only—I mean it seems funny—"

"I get you. I talk like a millionaire and travel with tramps." Tweet sighed. "Well, my faculty for breedin' confidence in others is one o' the big secrets o' my success. Success, I say— get that? If this faculty won't work on you, then I lose this time. I'll say no more. Think it over."

He yawned, rose, and started for the door.

"Are—are you goin' down on the street?" Hiram asked timidly.

"Yes, I thought I'd stroll about a bit."

"I—I guess I'll go with you, if you don't mind."

"Sure not—come on."

Hiram rose quickly and followed him out. Even though he were to distrust this man, in the end, the thought of losing him now was appalling.

Down on the street he thought of breakfast and paused before the restaurant.

"Have you had breakfast, Mr. Tweet?" he asked.

Tweet stopped and looked at him soberly. "Are you invitin' me to dine?" he said quizzically.

"Well, kinda that way," admitted Hiram with a foolish grin. "I haven't eaten myself, and—"

"I haven't eaten myself either, nor anybody else since yesterday mornin'. I accept."

And promptly Mr. Tweet pushed ahead through the swinging doors.

CHAPTER V

A RIVAL

The restaurant was all but deserted at the late breakfast hour when Hiram Hooker and Mr. Tweet entered. Hiram timidly wished that the men's side were filled, so that he would be obliged to eat on the ladies' side again. A waiter was beckoning them to the men's side, however, and Hiram meekly led the way, though casting a quick, expectant glance down the long row of tables beyond the screen.

Waitresses were dallying about, but he did not see the girl with the cords of fluffy hair. He was halfway through breakfast before it occurred to him that, as she was at work at eleven the night before, he scarce could expect her at nine in the morning. He was glad she was not there to tantalize him, and at the same time deeply disappointed.

Hiram's new acquaintance changed perceptibly as the food began to warm him. Mildly loquacious before, he now became voluble.

"I wanta tell you this," he remarked finally, "you're in luck to strike me when I'm crippled for cash. A week from now, perhaps, you'd never met me at all. And if you had, there'd 'a' been nothin' to connect us. But right now I'm up against it and forced to sleep in a twenty-five-cent lodgin' house. Therefore we met and found out each of us had somethin' the other wanted. You're lucky, Hooker—that's all there is to it.

You'd 'a' drifted about for years and never got the chance to hook up with Twitter-or-Tweet. And here you are, right from the backwoods, makin' yourself solid the first crack outa the box with the original money-getter. Stay by me till I get a toehold, and I'll make you."

Hiram was at a loss how to take him. He had not agreed to tide him over, had not even made up his mind that Tweet was not a rank faker; yet Tweet seemed to be taking it for granted that his case was won, and that they were to go from the breakfast table to Morgan & Stroud's to enter the road to competence.

As if answering his thoughts, Tweet said:

"I'm a mystery to you, ain't I? I don't use very good grammar, but I talk sense. I'm talkin' about makin' piles o' money, and I'm gettin' my breakfast off o' you, ain't I? If I really was the heavy hitter I'm advertisin' myself to be I wouldn't condescend to take you on, would I? That's what you been thinkin', ain't it?

"Take those hobos up in the lodgin' house, for instance. Curiosity's eatin' their hearts out in regard to me. They know I ain't a tramp, yet they see me float smoothly along among 'em and never strike a discord. I don't seem to mix with 'em, neither do I seem to keep aloof from 'em. I'm there and I ain't there—see? If they only knew it, I've tramped miles to their feet. Yet I never was a regular tramp.

"On the other hand, when I'm hob-nobbin' with the upper class I keep them guessin'. I talk kinda crude, yet what I say seems to be worth listenin' to. I go into a flash hotel or cafe and never stumble over anything, or knock the carafe off the table, or order corned-beef hash when the menu card looks like an advanced lesson in *parlez vous*. They take me to the circus to amuse me, and I come back at 'em with grand opera.

"So that's the way it goes, and you'll savvy more about it when you see more o' me. At present I'm goin' to take you away from Frisco and, if somethin' turns up, give you a start. I'm doin't this principally because I need your little roll to tide me over till I get a workin' stake. I'm frank about it. But I may learn to like you. You appear to be sorta bright."

Tweet pushed back his chair. "Now we'll go down to Morgan & Stroud's and get out where we c'n go to work and do somethin', and have a chance to look about and think."

Protestations died on Hiram's lips, and he dutifully rose and followed.

There was a cigar case on the cashier's counter, and Tweet leaned over it, looking down at the contents, while Hiram laid his check beside the cash register and fumbled for his pocketbook. He produced a dollar and laid it on the check, then looked about for some one to receive them. The space behind the counter was empty, but from a little inclosed portion of the window came the slow, labored clicking of typewriter keys.

"Tap the dollar on the show case," suggested Tweet.

Hiram tapped the glass.

Instantly, in the window room, the clicking keys were hushed. Hiram heard the squeak of a swivel chair. He heard the swish and caught the gleam of a white skirt. The next moment she was standing before him.

His breathing checked itself, and his knees began that sickening tattoo. He was instantly so miserable that he longed to die. Yet he faced her big eyes, brown and good-natured and smiling with recognition, and dumbly pushed the check and the dollar across the counter.

"Why, hello!" she said lightly.

"Hello," came a quavering echo.

The drawer of the cash register shot out with a metallic clang. Hiram's dollar jingled in among its kind. The girl's slim fingers were suspending a quarter to be dropped into his palm, suggesting to Hiram's abnormal mind the fear of contamination. He feebly put out his hand, and she dropped the coin.

"Thank you," she acknowledged in a light, professional tone, raising her voice on the "you."

She was turning away, when Tweet looked up from the cigars.

"Since when, Lucy?" came his rollicking voice. She turned back, smiling. "Oh, since just this morning," she replied. "The boss fired the cashier just before I went off watch last night. He said he was going to call up the employment agency and get another the first thing this morning.

"'What's the matter with giving some one here a chance?' I says. 'That's the way with you fellows,' I says. 'A girl can work her fingers off for you for years, then when the chance comes for something better, why, you telephone an employment agency and give it to a perfect stranger. You give me a pain!' I says.

"'But you ain't a cashier—you're a waitress,' he says.

"'I'm not speaking about myself in particular,' I says. 'I'm speaking about all of us who are working for you. Then,' I says, 'how do you know I can't make change? When there's an opening for better pay and easier work,' I says, 'why don't you come to us and see if any of us think we can hold it down? You know us and can trust us, and instead of giving us a look-in, you go and hire an outsider.'"

"Good stuff!" commented Tweet. "And he fell for it, did he?"

She flipped out her palms in a little gesture. "I'm here, ain't I?

Waited table from seven to three last night, and came behind the counter here at five-thirty this morning. The boss'll relieve me at twelve o'clock. Guess I'll sleep some to-night!"

"Fine business! Makin' good, eh?"

"I'm not fired yet, am I?" Her white teeth flashed.

"But c'n you keep the books?"

She sniffed. "I certainly can. I haven't been a waitress all my life. These books are nothing."

Here the gigantic Hiram caught his lower lip sagging and resolutely lifted it to dignity.

"Well, I like your style," Tweet was telling her. "Tell 'em about it, every time—that's the way to get a toehold. But you're not much of a stenog, Lucy—was that you peckin' away in there?"

A shade of pink swept her face.

"I used to operate a machine a little with one finger of each hand," she explained, "but I'm all out of practice. I don't have to use a typewriter on this job though. It's an old one the boss took for a bill."

"Just practicin' up again, eh?"

"Ye-yes," she hesitated. Again her skin grew faintly pink.

"Good business! Go to it! Every little bit helps. Well, congratulations, Lucy. So long! C'm on, Hiram."

"Thanks." Lucy laughed, and went into her little room.

Hiram sighed boyishly, upset the toothpick holder at his elbow, and fled in Mr. Tweet's wake.

"Pretty nifty little kid," Tweet remarked, as Hiram joined him.

"You know her—wh-what's her name?"

Tweet turned and looked at Hiram's red face in mild surprise.

"Wh-what's wrong with you?" he queried.

"Nothin'"—sheepishly.

"Well, I'll be dog-goned if I don't believe you're gun shy on the female question!" was Tweet's conviction. "These frisky Frisco pullets goin' to your head, Hooker. A little paint and a little powder and a frowsy topknot seems to sorta touched some new funny bone in you, eh? Heavens, I remember how I fell for it years ago!"

Hiram closed his lips tight. He hated Tweet.

Tweet slapped him on the back and laughed.

"Forget it, Hiram," he advised familiarly. "It ain't like me to roast anybody when I see it hurts. Why, le's see now—I don't know the kid's name. I've heard the men call her Lucy—that's all. I been eatin' there right along—that is, up till yesterday mornin'. She seems to be popular with the fellas. Not a bad little kid, though, I take it. Got some savvy, at any rate. Ain't content with her lowly lot—and that's my kind. Oughtn't to make customers have to call her away from that typewriter, though—I don't like that. Well," he switched abruptly, "what you been thinkin' about our little deal?"

"Nothing," Hiram retorted resentfully.

They had been slowly walking down the street. Tweet stopped short and looked at him.

"That means what? That you don't care to consider it further?"

It had meant just that when Hiram said it. There was now in Tweet's question a tone of finality. Hiram felt that his reply would end the matter. Swiftly his mind grasped for a judicious rejoinder and settled on "No." He could not bring himself to part with this semblance of friendship just yet.

"All right, then," Tweet returned. "You're just not through considerin', eh? Well, I'll tell you: We'll break away and give you a chance to think. There's a man down California Street I wanta see before I leave and I'll stroll down that way. You think it over, and meet me at eleven-thirty up in that disfiguration old Squinty calls a loungin' room. So long."

He turned abruptly and strode away.

Hiram watched his erect figure and firm step till the crowd hid him, then followed more slowly in the same direction. His feet were carrying him toward the restaurant, and he was guiltily permitting them. He saw a shining drab automobile drawn up at the curb before the restaurant door. He walked slower and slower as he neared the door, paused, and looked within.

Lucy was leaning on the counter negligently collecting scattered toothpicks, and conversing laughingly with a carefully dressed middle-aged man with a handsome face and curly brown hair. His hair and Lucy's fluffy topknot were almost touching. Hiram saw him grasp playfully at Lucy's hand, saw her jerk it away with a flirtatious laugh.

Then Hiram bolted, half blind with pain.

CHAPTER VI

THE FIRE

Hiram did not take note of much till he was three blocks from the restaurant. There was a dull pain somewhere within him, but when his thinking apparatus began shaking off its stunned condition he found it difficult to analyze this pain.

The girl had done practically nothing. In fact, but for her laughter, her attitude toward the well-dressed man would have showed righteous displeasure. The thought that this might be a common occurrence did not enter his head. He was distressed now; he found, only with a keen feeling of utter alienation, he was one lone backwoodsman against San Francisco, scorning him, ready to trample him under foot.

A sign over the window of a store cleared this mystery. Hiram stopped and stared up at it. In a flash he knew what was the matter with him, and that he hated the stranger for his clothes—that he hated everybody because this man wore good clothes. He squeezed his pocketbook and read and reread the painted words in their painted circles:

"O'coat, $40, no more; Coat, $20, no more; Pants, $5, no more; Hat, $3, no more."

His mind was adding twenty, five, and three. The total was twenty-eight. He could get along without an overcoat, though in San Francisco, even in summer, an overcoat is comfortable

Arthur Preston Hankins

at night. Should he or should he not? His rusty old clothes were torturing him. Twenty-eight dollars! And perhaps only four or five more for extras—a tie, collars, suspenders, and—oh, yes! shoes. He had forgotten the shoes. His were brogans. He must have shoes, too. Perhaps five for shoes. He had barely sixty-seven dollars. Should he? Was it foolish, or—

Reflected in the show window he saw a drab automobile flash behind him. At the wheel he saw, erect, forceful, jaunty, and well-dressed, with a black cigar gripped in his teeth, the man who had snatched at Lucy's hand. Clinching his pocketbook, Hiram entered the store.

A half hour later he came out, poorer by some thirty-eight dollars, but rich in the self-esteem which the bright, stiff garments gave him.

He left his bundle in his stall at the lodging house, criticized himself before the cracked mirror in the hall, and went down on the street. He bought three five-cent cigars and lighted one. He gripped it in his teeth and let it protrude from the left-hand corner of his mouth. Then he started for the restaurant.

Long before he reached it panic was upon him. He had absolutely no pretext on which to enter. It was then only ten-thirty, and he had breakfasted at nine. To enter boldly and begin a conversation with Lucy—which he had all along boastfully promised himself he would do—he now knew to be the last thing on earth he would dare.

Besides, though the garments he wore were new and bright and stiff, those two brief glimpses of his rival's clothes now tardily showed him that there was a difference. His coat, for instance, seemed a bit angular—there seemed to be corners he had not noticed in the store. It did not snuggle down to his neck and shoulders just right. Hiram thought that perhaps the linen collar was a trifle too large.

Thus criticizing, and walking slower and slower, he neared the restaurant. Now it was impossible to take another step without coming abreast of it. He stopped and looked in a jeweler's window next door.

He stood there fifteen minutes. Time and again he nerved himself up to entering the restaurant, only to feel cold sweat break out on his forehead as he lifted his foot. He would return to the lodging house, change his clothes, and see her when he ate at noon. He would never let her see him in those now hated new clothes. He had squandered thirty-eight dollars for her, and he had only twenty-nine left.

Down the street from the heart of the city came a sudden clangor. Vehicles were rushed close to the curbs. Up a side street a new jangle of bells broke out. Never had Hiram seen a city fire, but at once he knew that such was happening.

A hook-and-ladder company rattled past with clamor and gongs and clatter of hoofbeats. People poured from the doors of buildings to watch. Men rushed to the curb and looked after the firemen; the women stood near the buildings, under the awnings, shading their eyes and standing on tiptoes. Quickly the sidewalk filled. A chemical engine passed, clouds of black smoke rolling in its wake. Across the street a pillar of black smoke burst from a third-story window.

"It's across the street! Across the street!" shouted the crowd.

A hose cart rumbled up. The men on the curb grew frantic, yelling and pointing to the smoke. The hose cart was stopped.

A little later the chief's automobile came. Then the apparatus that had passed down the street came back. Flames and smoke were bursting from three windows now. The street and the sidewalk were filled with the crowd.

Hiram had not moved a muscle. People elbowed him on both sides, but he paid no attention. The rapid operations of the fire fighters held him spell-bound.

Arthur Preston Hankins

"Oo-oo-oo! Look there!" suddenly came a shrill familiar voice at his side.

A sputter of sparks had shot from the roof of the building, and a man had emerged from a trap-door, it seemed, and darted from sight. But the fire and every new phase of it had lost all holding power over Hiram Hooker. Pressed to his elbow, wedged in by the crowd, stood Lucy.

"Oh, I love a fire!" she was ecstatically informing some one on her other side—a waitress.

Hiram stood there sick with her proximity. She had not recognized him—she was engrossed with the clouds of black smoke, the intermittent red gleam of blaze, and the crackling streams of water. Her tongue was wagging rapidly, and she seemed not to care to whom she spoke or whether that fortunate person were listening.

Suddenly, through the scurrying firemen in the street, a big red automobile came slowly. It was filled with men and women. Its horn was honking perpetually. Besides the fire apparatus, no other vehicles were allowed in the street, yet no one seemed to interfere with this machine.

"Oh, it's the Samax Company!" exclaimed Lucy, dancing up and down. "They're going to take a fire picture. Look, Minnie! There's Mr. Kenoke—the director! I never thought of it—right here at my very door, too! If I only could see him, Minnie. What a chance for the fire scene in 'The Crowning Defeat!' Oh, why didn't I think of it, Minnie? Mr. Kenoke! Mr. Kenoke! Oh, dear, he wouldn't hear me in a thousand years!"

She was waving over the heads of the crowd at some one in the red automobile, it seemed. There seemed even less likelihood now of her taking note of Hiram. He watched her furtively and wondered.

"Oh, I must see him!" she went on excitedly. "Say, mister"—she suddenly turned a flushed face to Hiram—"won't you—Why, hello!" she broke off. "I didn't know it was you. Oh, you will, I know! You're big—you can do it! Won't you try to get to that heavy-set man in the machine for me? Please—won't you?"

She was looking eagerly up at him. Hiram rose to the situation like a man. For her he felt he would have cheerfully entered a beehive should she command him. Was not this the adventure girl of whom he had dreamed?

"What'll I do?"

"Oh, will you? Good! Listen: Tell him to have Mr. Blair carry Miss Worthington out the door. And listen: Miss Worthington has fainted—see? Mr. Blair faints then, and staggers and falls down with her. Then Mr. Speed rushes up and takes a letter from Mr. Blair's pocket and runs out of the picture. And listen: Mr. Blair and Miss Worthington still lie there. Tell him there's no makeup. And tell him Miss Lucy Dalles wants him to do that, and that he won't regret it. Tell him I said it was a peach—see? But listen: Don't say anything about me being in a restaurant, though. Oh, can you? Will you?"

Hiram was stunned. Had the girl gone crazy?

"Go on, please, before the fire's out! I can't explain now—wait. I'll tell you later. He'll know, though. Go on, now—try!"

Without the faintest notion of what it was all about—with only the thrilling thought that he was serving her—Hiram's big figure began pushing through the crowd, dazedly repeating her queer message and the names.

He was tall, strong, and angular. Shoving this way and that, he fought his way to the curb. Here he encountered a rope stretched lengthwise of the street. The crowd was now confined to the sidewalk. Hiram crawled under the rope. A policeman shouted at him and started toward him. Hiram ran, tripped over a slippery hose, caught himself, and plunged on through the knots of struggling, dripping firemen.

The automobile had stopped. The occupants were clambering to the wet pavement. One man was hurriedly setting up a peculiar-shaped camera directly opposite the entrance of the burning building. Another, a heavy-set man, was bobbing about, shouting orders to men and women, who listened, then ran toward the door.

Everybody was crazy, it seemed, but this had nothing to do with Hiram in carrying out his mission. He ran up to this heavy-set man and cried:

"Are you Mr. Kenoke?"

"Sure! Get out the way! What d'ye want? Now, Miss Worthington, run for the ladder. Hurry up, girlie! Come on, Blair! Quick! Quick! What d'ye want—you?"

Hiram gulped and searched his brains. "Miss Lucy Dalles says to tell you to have Mr. Blair carry Miss Worthington out of the door. She's fainted, she said, and then he faints and falls. They lay there, and another fella—I forget that name—takes a letter from Mr. Blair's pocket and runs away. Mr. What's-his-name and Miss Worthington still lie there. Mr.—er—let's see—there's no makeup. And it's a peach, and you won't regret it."

"Humph! All right; I get you. I'll take a chance. Lucy Dalles, you say? Thanks. Get that, Collins? 'Bout ten feet, I guess. After this. Now, out of the way, please. All ready, there! Let her go! Now, up with that ladder, deary! Get in there! Get in the picture Worthington!"

Hiram stepped back. The man with the camera began turning a crank on one side, and a low whirring noise blended softly with the roar of the rushing water. Hiram saw dripping men and women dancing about like maniacs before the smoking door.

He did not wait for more. He had done his duty, and he hurried back for his reward.

"Did you do it? Did you see him?"

Lucy Dalles, with parted lips, was straining toward him as he cleaved his way back to her.

Hiram nodded.

"Oh, what did he say?"

"He said: 'All right. I'll risk it.' He said a lot more, but I guess it wasn't to me."

"Well, you're all right," she said, with a beaming smile. "D'ye hear, Minnie? Mr. Kenoke's going to take it!"

Minnie, a freckle-faced girl, was busily chewing gum and watching the spectacle. She indifferently replied, "Yea," and craned her neck away to focus some new development in the fire fight.

Lucy at once ignored her.

"Say, that was great, all right! I'm much obliged, I'm sure. That'll mean something to me." She was looking straight at Hiram. Now she hesitated, then, a bit flustered, concluded, "That was all right."

Hiram grinned and bobbed his head.

She looked at him in confusion a little longer, then turned to Minnie.

Arthur Preston Hankins

"Goodness! I must get back in," she said hurriedly.

Still Minnie gave no heed, and Lucy faced Hiram once more.

"I said I'd tell you about it, didn't I? Well, I will—that is, if you care?"

Hiram bobbed his head again.

She looked through the jeweler's window at a small brass clock.

"Gracious! Can that clock be right? It's after eleven! Say, listen: I'm going off watch at twelve. If you'll be here I'll tell you then."

"Yes, ma'am—I'll be here."

"All right. Good-by. Much obliged, I'm sure."

She squeezed back of Minnie, and scampered through the restaurant door.

Hiram stood watching the streams of water—that is, he looked that way.

CHAPTER VII

HIRAM, THE BUTTERFLY

"Mother, I've come home to die!" gasped Playmate Tweet.

He was seated in one of the yellow chairs near a window of the lounging room. He had dropped his newspaper and was staring at Hiram Hooker as he strode through the door.

Hiram seated himself on the edge of a chair and grinned uncomfortably.

The ordeal of appearing before Tweet in his new clothes, at first poignantly dreaded, had been absent from his thoughts for the past hour. Standing there before the jeweler's store after Lucy Dalles had left him, tingling blissfully in every vein, the mundane thought that Tweet was probably awaiting him in the lodging house had obtruded itself and hurried him up the street. As he opened the lounging-room door he thought once more of his clothes.

Tweet rubbed his eyes and looked again. "Christopher Columbus!" he added in an undertone. He blinked his eyes three times, then threw himself back and laughed uproariously.

For a half minute he shook in his chair, then got up, wiped his twisted nose with his handkerchief, and came over to his half resentful charge.

"Well, Hiram," he said with a chuckle, "how much did they set us back?"

"Set us back?"

"I mean, how poor are we now?"

"How poor are *we*?"

"Sure—Tweet, Hooker & Co. pays the bills."

"I guess I c'n do what I want to with my own money, can't I?"

"Sure—sure! Don't get your shirt off. I don't mean to insinuate that you're not capable o' judiciously handlin' the firm's money. I just want you to read me the balance sheet."

"Well, then, I spent thirty-eight dollars, and I've got twenty-nine dollars left."

"Stand up."

Hiram did so.

"Turn round."

Hiram wheeled slowly.

Tweet studied him from every angle, and as Hiram turned he noted the twinkles which came and went in his slate-blue eyes. Without another word Tweet left him standing there, went back and sat down, and hid his face behind his paper.

Hiram waited a minute, then slowly sank to the edge of his chair. After a little he asked pleadingly:

"Ain't they all right?"

Tweet's paper trembled. A bit of this, then Tweet lowered it and presented a countenance which seemed never to have known a smile.

"Hiram," he remarked, "I don't wanta hurt your feelin's, but the part o' true friendship calls for me to use the surgeon's knife. Hiram, I wouldn't wear that outfit to a funeral. D'ye get me?"

Hiram's blue eyes blazed. "Yes, I get you," he began coldly, then curbed a threatening outburst. "I know they're not the best in the land," he concluded sensibly, "but I feel better in 'em."

"There's somethin' in that," Tweet propounded sagely. "There's a whole lot in gettin' that feel. Good clothes kinda brace a fella up and give him the nerve to buck on in the big game. Hiram, if your new outfit gives you the *feel*, it's the goods. When you get next a little it'll cost you more money to get that feel outa clothes. After all, now, when that tin-roof look wears off of 'em you won't appear so whittled-out in that suit. But now, layin' all jokes aside, are they just the thing for drivin' old Jack and Ned on the railroad grade? And didn't this sudden lavishness kinda set the company back on its haunches?"

Hiram looked out the window. "Did you see the fire?" he asked absently.

"Yes—walked round the block to get outa the crowd. But—"

"I just had to kinda spruce up a bit, Mr. Tweet. I felt so kinda—well, kinda countrified and—and lost, you might say."

"What's the fire got to do with that? And call me Playmate, too."

"Nothin', I suppose."

"Right across from the restaurant wasn't it?"

Arthur Preston Hankins

"Yes."

"M'm-m—I'd 'a' made a good lawyer, wouldn't I, Hiram?"

"I don't know—why?"

"Why, talkin' about sprucin' up, as you call it, you drift to a fire that occurred across the street from the place where there's a frowsy-topped waitress that's got you goin'. Well, le's foget it. Do we go to southern California together, or not? Our pile's dwindlin' on account o' this butterfly life you're leadin'."

"I—I'd like to, but—Well, I left home to get a start in the city, and I think I oughta—Really, I wanta go, but—" Hiram gave it up, and his lean face flushed.

"Go on—I didn't interrupt you."

"Well, I—that's all. I want to go to work here."

Tweet laughed with a little snort. "Now looky here," he said, "I think I savvy you pretty well. If I was to go to work and tell you outright that you couldn't win Lucy, you'd get bull-headed and try to show me. But le'me tell you this: You ain't goin' to win her till you get next to yourself. Now, Lucy's a pretty popular dame with the fellas about the restaurant. I've seen her joy-ridin' with fellas I know are there with the coin, and savvy more in a minute than you ever knew. Now, wait a minute!—don't get excited. All this ain't your fault. It's the fault o' your past environment. You're a hick, and you can't help it. You get out and learn somethin' and gather up a few beans. Then come back and, if you still want the kid, go get her.

"Now, you see this Lucy this afternoon and tell her you're bound out into the Great Unknown to make your fortune, but that you're comin' back to see her. Put emphasis on who you're comin' back to see. Then flee from temptation. Come now—le's swallow this awful pill like a man."

Hiram thought a long time, looking out the window. In the midst of this Tweet resumed his paper.

The sensible thing to do was for Hiram to sacrifice love to the friendship that promised him a start, in order to gain love back more conclusively in the end. Yes, he loved her—he loved her madly!

Boiling the present situation right down to facts, he had little confidence in Tweet's boasted powers. He could not reconcile Tweet's present impecunious condition with his hints of past affluence. But he liked him instinctively, which, after all, is more human and satisfactory than liking a person after analyzing him and weighing his good qualities against his shortcomings. So it was the thought of Tweet's friendship which finally prompted him to say: "I guess I'll go with you."

"Good!" Tweet dropped his paper. "This afternoon?"

"No—to-morrow."

"Not on your life! This afternoon."

"Well, I'll tell you in an hour or so. Now—now it's about noon. You wait here a little, while I go down in the street. Then I'll come back, and we'll go eat."

Tweet looked at him long and steadily. "Got a date with Lucy, eh?" he said at last.

"Ye-yes—I saw her at the fire this morning. She said she wanted to see me when she went off watch at noon—I'll be right back—probably."

Tweet frowned, then laughed. "Go ahead, Hooker," he relented testily; "go ahead. Got a date with her, eh? I thought maybe you'd just go down there and gape at her through the window. Go to it—but don't forget!"

Arthur Preston Hankins

Hiram hurried out.

Again his feet seemed palsied as he neared the restaurant. Was he to suffer such pangs of stage fright always when about to meet her?

He had not long to dwell on the query. Before he knew it he was face to face with her. She had been looking in the jeweler's window while she waited for him, and had turned as he came abreast.

She was smiling. "You're a minute late," she scolded, pointing to the jeweler's brass clock.

"Yes, ma'am—I was kept."

"Oh, don't look so serious. A minute's nothing."

"No, ma'am—not much."

Silence claimed them for a time.

"Well, what'll we do?" she finally asked a little petulantly, and turned her back on him to look into the window.

"I dunno," he began; then a sudden wild idea struck him. He had seen along the curbs automobiles bearing signs which read "For Hire—Four Dollars an Hour." It was worth it, if only to break this humiliating situation. "We might take a little spin in a machine," he finished with a tottery tone of indifference.

"Oh, I'd like that," she said instantly. "But I gotta dress. We'll get a car and ride 'round to where I room."

They walked to the corner, where was a taxi stand. Hiram engaged a car by the hour, and they entered. She directed the driver to her rooming house, and they were off.

The car presently drew up to the curb, and the driver swung

the door open for his passengers. Into a dark, musty little parlor the girl led Hiram of the butterfly life.

"Sit down," she invited; "and excuse me a minute."

She went back into the hall, and Hiram heard the tattoo of her feet on the stairs.

It was a grand parlor, Hiram thought. There was a piano, a phonograph, a whatnot filled with specimens of quartz, and four cloth-covered cushion rockers. With rattlesnake fairness the one Hiram chose squeaked a warning before it tried to land him on the back of his neck.

Hiram sat there round-eyed and dreaming, while outside the hired car purred on, indifferent to the flight of time.

Twenty minutes later Hiram's dream was broken by the clatter of Lucy's high heels on the stairs. Lucy entered, dressed in silk and furs and wearing a large picture hat. The savings of many months were on Lucy's back, and Hiram felt further removed from her than ever.

"Where'll we go?" he asked miserably as he clumsily helped her into the car.

"Golden Gate Park, Mr. Hooker," she said.

The driver, having heard, touched his cap, and they rolled away.

"How'd you know my name?" The burden of keeping this question had been overriding Hiram's bashfulness since she had spoken it.

Lucy laughed. "You didn't think I'd go so far as to invite you home with me if I didn't know you, did you? At least kinda know you?"

"I hadn't thought about that at all, ma'am. But when you said 'Mr. Hooker' it gave me a jolt."

"I'll bet it did. Well, didn't you stand in front of the jewelry shop for over a quarter of an hour before the fire this morning?"

"Yes, ma'am."

"And you didn't see your friend come out of the restaurant while you were there?"

"Who, Tweet? No, ma'am—I didn't."

"Well, he did. He'd been in talking with me. I didn't know his name, though. Is that it? Tweet? Heavens above! Say, he's a funny guy. Well, he'd been in talking about you. He said you were out in front of the jeweler's shop and wondered if he could get out without you seeing him."

Hiram only stared and waited.

"He told me your name was Hiram Hooker, and that you had just come from Mendocino County. That's how I knew."

For quite a time she was silent. Then she said:

"He appears to be sort of butting in, it seems to me."

Hiram waited again.

"He came in and says: 'Say, Lucy, your lifeline and mine are getting tangled. You're crossing my path and frustrating my plans.' You know how he talks!

"'How d'ye get that way?' I says. 'Spring it.'"

"'Why, your many charms are leading my business partner from the path of duty,' he says.

"'Go on,' I told him, 'and talk sense, if you've got anything to say.'"

"Then he told me that you two were partners, and were going down to southern California together to 'get a toehold,' he said; and that you were keeping the thing back by—by—by wanting to hang around Frisco. He said you two had a good thing and that you were spoiling it, and that you were nearly broke and getting more so every minute.

"I kind of like him. He's funny, but I'll bet he's right. And he said for me to give you the cold shoul—well, what he meant was for me to advise you to hurry up and get out with him.

"But now listen: If I'd intended to do that I wouldn't have told you that he told me to, would I? Of course not. I wanted to see you about something else. Two things: First, I promised to tell you about the moving picture you helped me with this morning. Then the other thing is Mendocino." She leaned forward and lowered her voice. "Listen, I'm from Mendocino County," she finished. "I've been away three years. I'm nearly dying to talk to some one from up there!"

CHAPTER VIII

LUCY'S AMBITIONS

Learning that Lucy Dalles was from Mendocino County was startling, but surprise over this took second place in Hiram Hooker's thoughts. He was stricken with consternation to think that all the time he had been before the jeweler's window, trying to nerve himself up to enter the restaurant, she had known he was there.

"After your friend left the restaurant," she was saying, "I thought I'd go out and tell you about me being from Mendocino. Just as I left the door the hook-and-ladder came by. Then I stood by you watching the fire, you know, till the Samax people drove up. Then I forgot everything but getting the picture for the fire scene in 'The Crowning Defeat.' I asked you to see Mr. Kenoke for me, and you did—and it was dandy of you, too. Now I'll tell you about my scenarios; then I want to talk about nothing but Mendocino County.

"Well, I write scenarios for moving-picture production," she went on. "That's one reason why I wanted the cashier's job— so I could have the use of the boss' old typewriter. I've been paying a public stenographer fifty cents a thousand words to copy my work, and it cuts into the profits when you get so little for a scenario.

"I've been writing them a year now. I've sold ten. That's not very many, is it?—when you know; that I have written over fifty. I've sold most of mine to this Samax Company, through the mail; and one day I went to their Western studio, here in the city, and told them who I was and got acquainted with Mr. Kenoke. He's their best producer, I think.

"As it happened, I am now working on a play that calls for a big fire scene. I was worried about it, because they send so many of my scenarios back with the comment that they are too difficult to produce. It's a dandy plot, and I hated to give it up just because it would require a burning building. They would hardly buy a building and burn it down just to please me, you know.

"But when they hear of a fire they get right to it, if they can, and take rescue scenes, and so forth, then have their contract writers work up a scenario in which the scenes can be used. But that's hack work. Mine is different, you see. My scenario called for a fire, and couldn't be produced without it. Quite different from having a fire call for a scenario.

"Well, now you know. I couldn't explain then, you see. There wasn't time, and, besides, I was too excited. I doubted if you would have understood, either—you just from the country.

"Now don't think I'm making fun of you. But it's the truth, isn't it? And it was certainly great of you to go the way you did, not having the least idea of what you were up against."

"It wasn't much," Hiram said in his unassuming way.

"Yes, it was," the girl said with a lack of the enthusiasm which had marked her former grateful utterances. Her eyes were far away, and it was apparent that another matter held precedence in her mind. "You just got into Frisco last night, your partner said."

"Yes, ma'am."

"I could see that when you came in the restaurant. Your new

suit looks fairly nice." She scanned him frankly.

Hiram squirmed. "Tweet said I looked whittled out in it," he said truthfully.

"You don't any such thing! You don't mind my being so personal, do you? I've taken quite an interest in you since Mr. Tweet talked about you—especially as you are from Mendocino. You looked so forlorn and scared last night when you came in the restaurant. I could see that you didn't know what to order or how to order it, and that you were half starved. I remembered my first day in the city. Honestly, I was scared blue! But tell me—what part of the country are you from?"

"I'm from Bear Valley," Hiram told her.

"Bear Valley! Why, our old place is just on the other side of the range. I've been in Bear Valley lots of times. Our place is in Temple Valley."

"I know Temple Valley," Hiram put in quickly.

"Of course you do! Why did you come down here?"

"I was gettin' tired of the backwoods—been there all my life," said Hiram lamely.

Lucy's eyes grew dreamy. "I thought the same," she said pensively at last. "I was born there in Temple Valley. I was content, too, till I was about twenty; then I got to mixing with the summer boarders that came to the Mills place for the trout season. They'd have something on every night, and I got acquainted and was always invited. I got to wanting to go to the city, and I hated Temple Valley.

"Then my folks died. I didn't get along the best in the world with Emma—that's by [Transcribers' note: my?] brother's wife. So I pulled out the day after my twentieth birthday and came to Frisco—and I've been here ever since. But there was another reason why I left."

She sighed and leaned back.

"You've heard of Mrs. Cummings, the writer, haven't you? She was up at Mills' place one summer, and I got acquainted with her. I told her I'd always had the writing bug, and she encouraged me. I had no education but what I'd got in the Temple district school, but I'd read a lot.

"So I wanted to write, and finally I left and came to Frisco, and I had an awful time. Finally I got a job in a cheap restaurant and had to wait table, and when I got the cashier's job last night I got out of the rut for the first time in three years. I quit two or three times, thinking I could make a living writing scenarios, but I always had to go back to the beaneries.

"I'm going to hold down the restaurant job till things come my way. I've given up the idea that I'm a genius. My clothes cost a lot. Things will break for me some day. Maybe I'll get in the pictures. I want to go to Los Angeles and try, when I can save a little jack. I left the woods to win out, and I'm going to do it by fair means or foul. I'm ambitious. I'm determined to be rich some day."

Hiram drank in her chatter for two hours more, and when they returned to her rooming house he paid the driver of the car thirteen dollars and fifty cents, and now had only fifteen-fifty to his name. He was horrified at the prospects, but blissfully conscious that he had given Lucy Dalles an afternoon of pleasure.

"I want to show you my room," she said, as the car departed. "Come in. Don't make any noise going upstairs."

She led the way in, and he followed her softly. She opened a door on the second floor and stood back for him to look.

Arthur Preston Hankins

"I furnished my own room," she said proudly. "It's all mine, and paid for—pretty nearly."

Hiram stood aghast in the doorway. Never, except in the show windows, had his eye rested on such splendor.

There was a rug on the floor, soft and thick, which Lucy told him was a genuine Smyrna. There was a leopard skin, with stuffed head and red, gaping jaws. There were two handsome overstuffed leather chairs, and the bedroom set was Circassian walnut, so Lucy said.

She closed the door and hurried him below.

"You see, I've realized part of my ambition," she said, sinking into the squeaky rocker. "I'm not so clever or so cultured and all that, but I came from the backwoods to be somebody and have something, and I'll make good one way or another. What you saw is just a beginner. I might have bought a typewriter instead, but—well, I just didn't."'

"They're mighty nice," commented Hiram, as she paused.

"Yes, they made a fool out of me when I hit Frisco," she continued absently, "but my day's coming. I'm getting a toehold, as your Mr. Tweet says. I've rubbed off some of the Mendocino moss." She glanced a little vainly at her slim, well-garbed figure. "I'm after the money now—and I'll get it!

"But tell me about your partner," she continued. "Who is he, anyway?"

"I can't tell you."

"M'm-m!" She pursed her lips and frowned thoughtfully. "And he just wants you to go out with him, hit or miss?"

"That seems to be it, ma'am. And I don't think I'll go—now."

"Now? What do you mean, now?"

A wave of red ran over Hiram's face, and he began stammering.

The hint of a smile flickered across Lucy's lips as she hurried on without his answer. Hiram was a big man, ruggedly handsome. It pleased Lucy's vanity to have him gawk at her as he did.

"I think I can find out something about this gentleman," she said. "He came in the restaurant a few days ago, and I noticed two business men I know quite well talking about him. I'll find out something about this Tweet for you, and let you know. You don't want to let anybody play you for a sucker."

"Oh, I can take care of myself when it comes to that."

"*Yes*, you can!" She laughed. "You'll lose some of that confidence before you've been here many days. Now don't be offended. Shall I get this dope on him, if I can?"

"I'd thank you kindly, ma'am."

"Well, I will, then. Now let's forget it and talk about Mendocino. Go on—you talk so little."

CHAPTER IX

HIRAM WAKES UP

Hiram walked with an elastic step from Lucy Dalles' rooming house. It was hard to believe that all that was happening to him was true. In a sort of haze that floated before him as he walked along hung Lucy's face. He wished to go on forever thus. He found no fault in her—he refused to. Some imp whispered to him that his fifteen dollars and fifty cents would last forever. He did not actually believe this, but he refused to worry over the matter. Fate was kind. He was living a dream— and who needs money in Dreamland?

It was like the slap of a cold towel when Tweet's face suddenly displaced Lucy's in the haze. Up there in the lounging room Tweet had been waiting for him four hours! Tweet was doubtless hungry—he, Hiram, had been to a feast of love!

He felt like sneaking away to another lodging house till Tweet had disappeared. But he did not. Instead he sneaked up the dusty stairs and through the door of the lounging room.

Tweet was there, half hidden behind his paper. Hiram sidled into a seat, swallowed twice, and said "Hello."

Tweet at once lowered the paper and looked at him at if he did not quite recall his face.

"Why, hello there!" he returned carelessly. "Back, eh? Here's somethin' may int'rest you."

He got up, folding the paper, and carried it over to Hiram, pointing to an article headed:

"New Ditch Digger Makes Good."

Hiram stared at the heading in dire confusion. He had been half prepared for a rating; Tweet's complete disregard of his remissness was distressing.

"Mr. Tweet, I've got to apologize," he began.

"Bad practice," Tweet interrupted. "The better way is to never do anythin' that calls for an apology. Can't say that I live up to it, but I do my darnedest—and angels can do no more. After the first half hour I knew you wouldn't show up, so I went down and had lunch. More'n you've had, I'll bet. Just glance over that article and see what you think of it."

"I thought you were broke."

"Oh, they can't keep a good man down. The friend I went to see insisted that I take a dollar he had that wasn't workin'. Don't suppose I'll be with you for dinner, either, as I've got an engagement at about that hour. But read that article."

Hiram obeyed.

It told of a ditch digger that had recently been enlarged from the inventor's model, and which, at the first trial, was proving a decided success in moving earth more rapidly than any previously invented. With only his model to prove his claims, the inventor had managed to sell all the stock; and from the very beginning the operations would be carried out by a closed corporation. The question before the directors was whether to have machines manufactured and hire them out, or to construct a plant and manufacture them for the trade.

To Hiram it was dull and incomprehensible, and after finishing it he looked up at Tweet for an explanation.

"I got a sixth int'rest in her, Hooker," Tweet carelessly informed him. "My pay for sellin' the stock for 'em."

"Really! Is it worth anything to you?"

"I'm holdin' it' at eight thousand five hundred. It'll be worth double that in a year or two."

"Eight thousand five hundred!" Hiram stared unbelievingly at Tweet. "Why don't you sell it, then?"

"Didn't I say it would be worth double that amount in a year or two?"

"Yes, but you're broke and—"

"And I'll stay broke on a deal like that." Tweet's indignation caused him to grab his off-center nose and impatiently correct its obstinate trend, but to no avail. "But le's forget it and get back to that bugbear of our young lives. *When* are we *going* to southern California?"

Hiram sat framing a reply, which was rather a difficult process.

"Le's wait till to-morrow, anyway," he said at last.

"Had quite a little chat with Lucy to-day, eh?"

"Yes, I did. When you told—" Hiram bit his tongue. "The truth is, she's from Mendocino County, too, and we—we— that is, we found it out."

Not the faintest sign of suspicion or surprise showed in Tweet's face. "Well, suit yourself," he said nonchalantly. "It's a little late, or I'd go this afternoon. But to-morrow I go. My friend'll dig up the price, but I hate to hit him up any more.

Think it over a little longer, Hooker—I'm goin' down for a little stroll. But remember—before noon to-morrow I've gotta have a definite answer. I've found that Morgan & Stroud send their bunches out every day at one o'clock."

Tweet folded his precious paper, crammed it his pocket, and left the room.

A few minutes afterward Hiram followed. He ate lunch and dinner in one, then strolled about the city, dreaming of Lucy and fretfully counting the hours till he might expect to feast his material eyes on her again. At nine o'clock he returned to the lodging house, made sure that Tweet was not in the lounging room, and went to bed.

Next morning, close to nine o'clock, he was shifting from one foot to the other before the cashier's counter in the restaurant. From the little window inclosure came the clicking of typewriter keys, a little more spirited than before. Hiram had strategically chosen the slack business hour of the morning. He had eaten breakfast in a cheaper restaurant, two blocks down the street. He had not seen Tweet. He had been walking about the streets since six o'clock.

The keys kept clicking. Hiram cleared his throat several times, and at last, as before, tapped on the show case with a coin. The clicking stopped, a skirt swished, and the gates of heaven opened, it seemed to Hiram.

"Well, look who's here! Good morning."

"Ha-ha-ha! Good morning, ma'am."

"Then let's begin this good morning by dropping the 'ma'am.' They all say it up in Mendocino, I know. It's considered the *ne plus ultra* of good breeding up there. You see I'm trying to steer you straight, and I've got to be frank. I didn't have anybody kind enough to pick the moss off me."

"I'll stop sayin' it, if you say so."

"Sure, you want to. Now, I've had another visit from Mr. Tweet. He roasted me for not carrying out his orders. He's just the least bit too fresh, and I intimated as much. But he told me just about how much money you had, and I decided you'd better take his advice and go with him."

"But I've decided not to go at all now," said Hiram. "I'm goin' to begin lookin' for a job here in the city to-day."

"Aw, you can't get a job here that'll make you any money. Tweet told me something about where you're going down there in southern California. It's on the desert. A new railroad's building. Things will be lively. A friend of mine was in here at the time. He's got a lot of automobile trucks, and makes piles of money. Maybe you noticed him. Good-looking fellow in a brown suit. Drives a big drab car?"

"Ye-yes, I've seen him," admitted Hiram resentfully.

"Well, he was in here and talked with Tweet, and he said he thought he'd look into the freighting proposition down there. With his trucks, you know. There's a long haul over the desert and the mountains, it seems, and he says it ought to be good. Said maybe he'd take me down some time, if anything turned up."

"You wouldn't go!"

"Wouldn't I? Huh! You bet your life I would! I only hope he'll stick to what he says. Maybe I'd get to see you down there. Tweet said he'd heard that the place they freight to is a live one. Ragtown, he said they called it. That's the kind of a place to make money in. I'd go, if I were you. Go down and make a stake, and then come back to Frisco. Money talks here."

"With you?" Said Hiram, slowly drinking in dread suspicion.

"You betcha my life!" Lucy said lightly.

She broke off suddenly and turned toward the door with a smile of welcome on her lips. In came Hiram Hooker's hated rival, Al Drummond.

"Hello, Lucy!" he called breezily. Then he leaned over the counter, glanced hurriedly about the empty restaurant, and kissed the girl on the lips.

She slapped at him playfully. "You got a nerve, Al!" she exclaimed.

Hiram Hooker heard no more, for blindly he was stumbling out, crushed, heartbroken. Hiram Hooker suddenly had decided to go to southern California with Mr. Orr Tweet, and the sooner they could get away the better he would like it. He realized now that Lucy Dalles was not the adventure girl who had beckoned in his dreams. She was a cheap, scheming adventuress, and he hated the very thought of her now—and was plunged into the depths of despair and humiliation.

In the lounging room he found Tweet.

"Come on," he said huskily, "le's go to the employment office. I'm ready."

Orr Tweet arose, casting a curious look at Hiram's haggard face, but said nothing as he followed him out.

Fifteen minutes later they entered a large employment bureau on Clay Street, where were gathered perhaps a hundred workingmen reading the bulletins or lounging on benches.

Every now and then a brisk, leonine-headed man walked about among them, making announcements as a train caller does in a big union depot.

"Shippin' to Oregon—two o'clock to-morrow afternoon—I

want two hundred muckers—forty cents an hour—board one dollar a day. I want twenty skinners, same job, forty a month and found. Sign up, boys! Hit the trail and make yer stake. Two dollars is the bill!

"I want one hundred men to work in onions and potatoes. Three-twenty-five a day and board. Think of it, boys! Three-twenty-five a day and *board*! Like gettin' money from home! Get your blankets and line up for the chance of a lifetime.

"Then listen, boys! I want six rough carpenters—the rougher the better—mine work. Eight dollars a day, eight hours—*dollar an hour*! Fee two dollars. Think of that, huskies! Can ye swing a hammer or push a saw? You're on if you can—sign up! Ship ye out this evenin'. A snap! A cinch!"

"I want a sub-grade foreman at seven dollars—eight hours!"

"I want skinners, muckers, hard-rock men for Washington. I want lumberjacks for Washington—long job—good pay! I want hard-rock men for Alaska—the harder the better. And I want—"

Here Orr Tweet grasped the enthusiast's sleeve. "How about those jerkline skinners for southern California?" he asked. "Saw it in the paper."

"I'll see, old-timer—I'll look that up for you right away. Just step inside, please—you and your pal. Let you know all about it in two minutes. Line up for a good job, boys! Get out and make a stake! Just a minute, boss man. Step right inside."

Inside a railing, where many clerks were at work, the applicants were turned over to a sallow young man, who, being informed of what they wanted, consulted certain memoranda. Then he swiveled toward the two and gave them the particulars.

"Gold Belt Cut-off," he said. "Buildin' across the desert in southern California. Good camps—good pay—good grub—good water—"

"Cut all that," dryly interrupted Orr Tweet.

"All right, sir," replied the clerk cheerfully. "Main contractors, Demarest, Spruce & Tillou. Want fifty muckers and fifty skinners—two jerkline skinners—must be A-1. Fifty-five a month and found. Fee two dollars. Ship you out one o'clock to-morrow. On?"

Tweet nudged Hiram and nodded, and Hiram tendered four silver dollars.

"Just a minute," said the clerk—though accepting the money. "This office can't afford to get in bad with big contractors like Demarest, Spruce & Tillou. They've specified A-1 jerkline skinners, to skin eight, ten, and twelve over the desert and mountains. Are you there?"

"We are there," replied Orr Tweet.

The clerk looked doubtful. "Well, guess we'll have to take your word for it. Chances are you'll break away when you get to where you're makin' it, anyway. This is kind of a special job, though. Demarest himself wrote a personal letter about the two jerkline skinners. They're not for him, it seems—just to be shipped down with the other skinners and muckers and hard-rock men we're sendin' him. The jerkline skinners are for 'Jerkline Jo.' Ever heard that name? If you're jerkline skinners that have followed railroad work you ought to've heard o' Jerkline Jo. Usta be monakered 'Gypo Jo.'"

"We're not railroaders," said Mr. Tweet glibly. "We're from Mendocino County—the big woods you know. But we can skin 'em for Jerkline Jo or any other man."

"I'll take a chance," said the clerk briskly. "If you'd just wanted to get your railroad trip out o' Frisco you'd not thought to pick out the jerkline job, when only two were wanted. Jerkline Jo is a woman, though."

"Yeah?" returned Mr. Tweet, then said to the heartbroken Hiram: "You can't escape 'em, it seems, Hooker—you big mountain of a lady killer! This is gonta be good. Send us to Jerkline Jo, old hoss! She'll bless you with her last breath. Chances are you'll meet a regular woman, now, Hiram—not a doll with three years' wages on her back! A big outdoor picture like you fallin' for a bunch o' female French pastry like that!"

The employment agency clerk shrugged and took their names.

CHAPTER X

JERKLINE JO

About six months previous to Hiram Hooker's momentous debut into the world outside of the big trees of Mendocino County, a girl stood in her dormitory room at Kendrick Hall and read a telegram with tear-dimmed eyes.

This girl was Miss Josepha Modock. She was twenty-two, and Providence had been kind to her—nay, lavish. She was straight and sturdy and strong. Her hair was of a dark chestnut hue, and its beauty and luxuriant growth made it at once the envy and admiration of her fellow students of the Wisconsin boarding school. Her eyes were large and dark and luminous, her nose just far enough short of perfect, her lips full and distracting.

Josepha Modock had been two years at Kendrick Hall. She was older than most of the girls who were her classmates, for the desire and opportunity to acquire an education had come to her at a late day in her teens. She was ambitious, however, and was making fast progress with her college preparatory course. Then came the telegram which she now held, and over which she wept tears of grief.

Her name was not really Josepha Modock. Modock was the name of her foster father, and he and her foster mother, the latter dead now for ten years, had given the girl the name of Josepha, because, when they had found her a mere baby weeping and lost on the great desert of California, they had discovered a "J" embroidered on her underwear.

At that time Peter Modock—"Pickhandle" Modock—had been what is known in railroad-construction circles as a gypo man, or shanty man. A gypo man is an impecunious construction contractor whose light, haphazard outfit of teams and tools makes it necessary for him to subcontract in the lightest dirt work from a slightly better equipped subcontractor, who in turn has taken a subcontract from the main contractors in a big piece of railroad building. In the vernacular of the grade, a gypo man's daughter, if she follows the outfit, is known as a gypo queen.

Josepha Modock, then, had grown up in the camp of Pickhandle Modock, and in time had been known as a gypo queen, or shanty queen, and the prettiest one in the business at that.

It was when the Salt Lake Road was being built across the Mohave Desert that the baby girl had been found. Pickhandle Modock had taken a little piece of work from Grace Brothers, and was on his way across the sandy wastes to pitch camp and begin operations. His outfit was to be one of the first to arrive, and as yet no definite line of travel had been established to the work. A terrific sandstorm came up, and the outfit became lost on the desert, where men and teams wandered about without water for many perilous hours, some time in the midst of which the human atom afterward called Josepha was found.

She had been sole mistress of a tiny camp tucked away in a half-sheltered little arroyo, over which spiked yucca palms stood guard and helped to break the wind and check the drifting sands. There were provisioned pack bags there, and the blowing sand had not entirely covered the small hoof prints of several burros. A corral of corky yucca trunks held the child a prisoner, and more trunks had been laid on the walls to form a roof, which kept off coyotes. In here they found her sobbing, suffering for water, abandoned by her elders, while slowly but surely the sand was sifting in to bury her alive.

All trails leading to or from the spot had been wiped out. The child was cautiously given water and food, and the suffering contractor's party camped there, hoping for the return of the man or men who had left the baby to such dangers in the merciless desert. But no one came to claim her that day nor during the ensuing night; so next morning Pickhandle's outfit set out to search desperately to better their own alarming conditions, and took the child along. Modock left behind a note explaining their action and informing whoever was responsible how he might eventually be connected with, whereupon the child would be returned.

That day the sandstorm subsided, and the outfit stumbled upon the road to their destination. They found water before noon, and camped there to recuperate. Here also, when they took their leave, they left word of their appropriation of the baby girl. Later, when they had reached their camp site and settled down, Modock, having received no communication relative to the child, returned on horseback and sought for the spot where she had been found. At last it was discovered, and it was quite apparent that during the ten days' interval no one had been there. The pack bags with the supplies, and the few miners' tools that lay about, were all but buried in the sands. Modock's note was still there.

Deciding that the baby's guardians or parents had perished in the storm, Pickhandle Modock took the articles for the purpose of identification, if some one ever should claim the child, and returned with them to his camp, greatly to the joy of motherly Anna Modock, his wife. Anna Modock had no children, and now she loved the desert waif as if the child had been her own.

Slowly Pickhandle Modock prospered in the years that followed, for he was a thrifty, hard-working man. The child, whom they had named Josepha, grew to girlhood, and reached young womanhood as a sprite of the camps—a gypo queen.

　　　　　Arthur Preston Hankins

The Modocks were uneducated people, but knew it, and strove to make amends by educating the girl to the best of their ability. When the contractor had prospered to the point where he needed and could afford a bookkeeper, he employed a gray-haired derelict of the grade, half of whose duties were to educate Josepha.

The old man loved the child and did his best by her, guiding her successfully through the elementary branches and succeeding in implanting in her mind what is known as a common-school education. She learned rapidly, but showed no particular interest in her studies. With the work of the grade she was enraptured. At ten she was driving a slip team, loading and dumping without the help of any one. Later she drove wheeler teams, then snap teams, and even the six-horse plow teams. She became a wonderful horsewoman, and, when in the West, entered contests at rodeos in trick riding, riding buckers and so-called outlaws, and won many prizes. Horses and mules loved her. Her voice or her hand spoke to them in a language that they seemed to know. She could break a colt to steady work in half the time required by any man she had ever met. It was said that the only thing a horse or mule would not do for her was to talk, whereupon Josepha trained a colt to "talk," just to prove that her understanding of animals was virtually unlimited.

So Joshepha Modock grew to young womanhood, admired, loved, and spoiled by the thousands of nomad laborers who knew her. At eighteen she could truthfully boast of a hundred proposals of marriage, and some of them had been worth an ambitious girl's consideration. Gypo Jo they called her, and she was known all over the West, where her foster father's operations were confined, and stories of her beauty and horse-womanship had gone East and North and South, for railroad-construction laborers are a nomadic brood and repeat their tales and traditions from coast to coast.

Then Pickhandle Modock, whose wife had died some years before, made the move which finally brought his mounting prospects to the verge of ruin. Just when he was on the point of being recognized as a contractor of consequence, and owned a big, fine outfit of stock and tents and implements, he decided to change his activities to those of a freighter.

Numerous railroad projects were being launched in the West, and most of the lines were bound to extend through countries difficult to access. Contractors preferred to have their freight hauled to them by regular freighters, so that every team of their own could be put on the task of railroad building. Or so Pickhandle Modock reasoned.

Accordingly he sold his construction outfit, and with the proceeds bought heavy freight wagons and heavy young teams, and launched forth in his new career. For a year or more he followed railroad camps with his heavy freight outfit; then he suddenly decided that he was getting too old for camp life and to be eternally moving about. So when a new gold mine was opened up in the mountains that overlook southern California's desert, he moved into the little frontier town of Palada, forty miles from the new mines, and got the freighting contract from this railroad point up into the mountains.

He bought out the town's largest store, and set up a blacksmith and wagoner's shop to keep his great wagons in repair and his hard-working teams shod. Here for a year or more Josepha attended high school during the winter months, and drove eight and ten-horse teams with a jerkline to the mines in summer, and acquired her new title of Jerkline Jo because of her skill in training and handling the big teams. Here, too, she required [Transcriber's note: acquired?] her thirst for an education, and, torn between her new ambition and her love for the big outdoors and her devoted mules and horses, she at last set off for Wisconsin for her preparatory course at Kendrick Hall.

Pickhandle Modock, however, had reckoned without the automobile truck, which now was fast displacing heavy freight teams. While as yet the road into the mountains was not in the best shape for trucks, at least during winter months, still the noisy transporters of freight, of the lower tonnage capacity, were taking a great deal of business from him. Then the road on the other side of the mountains, connecting with the big coast-side cities, was paved; and this ended Pickhandle Modock's career as a jerkline freighter. The town of Palada, too, degenerated from an active little supply point to a stagnating desert village, with no visible means of support, and Pickhandle Modock found himself with a big stock of goods on hand with no one to buy, and with sixty or more heavy freight horses eating their heads off in their corrals.

His circumstances went from bad to worse, but he had carefully kept all this from his adopted daughter, in the preparatory school in the Middle West. Consequently the blithe and lovable Jerkline Jo knew nothing of the state of affairs when the telegram announcing her father's death reached her that fateful morning.

It stunned her at first. She could scarcely believe that lovable, hard-working, grizzled old Pickhandle Modock, the only father she had ever known had gone out of her life forever. The justice of the peace at Palada, who had handled Pickhandle's legal affairs, had sent the telegram, which advised her to return at once, as she was named as the sole heir to her foster father's estate. The telegram—a night letter and a long one—hinted of things of which she had not even dreamed, an prepared her for financial disappointments.

She at once realized that her school days at Kendrick Hall were ended, just when the future looked so bright. She would have entered college next year, and this, too, she must now forego, just when her ambition was at its height.

But she had been through many discouragements as a gypo queen, and she did not flinch. She had known poverty—even actual want—had fought mud and sandstorms and cold and heat and rain that hampered work for weeks and months. In her was the indomitable spirit of the pioneer. She bravely and silently packed her treasured belongings, bade a dry-eyed good-by to her tearful instructors and classmates, and set her face toward the Western desert to learn the worst, and meet it as hard-fighting old Pickhandle Modock would have wished her to meet it—as a girl called Jerkline Jo should meet life's threatening defeats.

CHAPTER XI

THE RETURN OF JERKLINE JO

When the long overland train contemptuously groaned to a reluctant stop in Palada the infrequent occurrence told the town that Jerkline Jo had returned for her foster father's funeral and the readjustment of his badly involved affairs. Old friends, old pals, old lovers crowded about her on the depot platform, wringing her strong hand in sympathy and offering help. The village hack was running no more now, so friends carried her baggage for her to the house on the hill, where lay the body of Pickhandle Modock.

Friends stayed with her that night. The funeral was solemnized next day. In all the world, now, Jerkline Jo had not the semblance of a relative, so far as she knew. She even did not know her name, and of Pickhandle Modock's family she had met not a single soul. But she had youth, courage, and ambition, and she went bravely at the many tasks before her.

With the old justice of the peace she took up her father's affairs, and it soon became evident that to attempt to continue the store under existing conditions would be the part of folly. The business was deeply in debt to jobbers in the cities on the coast side of the mountains, and such stock as they would accept must go back to them to cancel their claims. The store building was mortgaged; the residence property was mortgaged. The teams and wagons and the blacksmith shop seemed to be all that she could save from the wreckage, and these appeared to be more of an encumbrance than otherwise.

Still, she decided, against the advice of all well-meaning friends, to try to hold on to them and to be able to own them, clear of any claims against them. She knew the freighting business and construction teaming, and virtually nothing else; so with the idea that all of Pickhandle Modock's proud building must not have been for naught, she fought for final control of the freight outfit, and would not listen to those who claimed that the days of freighting with teams were over forever.

In a month everything was settled—all creditors satisfied. She had arranged to pay the store's debts with the acceptable stock on hand, having made great concessions. She had promised the store building and the residence property to the mortgagees, effective after the will had been probated. To her delight, she found that the teams, blacksmith's and wagoner's equipment, and the wagons would be hers intact. True, the teams were a great expense, and there was almost nothing left with which to buy hay and grain for them. But she was making inquiry here and there in an effort to put them to work again. Eventually she was successful in getting them on mountain pasture at a dollar and a half a head per month. There were sixty-one animals in all, and the pasturage fees amounted to quite a monthly sum, but it was far inferior to the monthly feed bills she had been paying.

For several months she hung on desperately, hoping against hope, with everything going out and nothing coming in, then one bright and long-to-be-remembered day came news of the new railroad which was to cross the desert a hundred miles from Palada.

Jerkline Jo made inquiry and found out the work was to begin at once, and that the project was a large one, involving difficult construction feats. By train she rode to the nearest railroad point, met the engineers of the preliminary survey, found an old friend in the party, and with him rode horseback on an old mining road over the range that stood between the railroad and that part of the desert which the new route would cross.

Close study of the engineers' maps and her general knowledge of construction conditions told her much. She decided on the logical place where the inevitable "rag town" would spring up. This, she reasoned, would be as close as possible to the biggest camp of the main contractors, Demarest, Spruce & Tillou.

There was water to be had at several widely separated places along the new right of way, but she knew that the water supply closest to the big camp would draw the tent city about it.

She knew, too, where the big camp would be, for the simple reason that the heaviest piece of work is eventually left to the main contractors; so she was able to figure to a dot just where Demarest, Spruce & Tillou's Camp Number One would locate. She had not the remotest idea, then, however, how this knowledge was to benefit her later.

To the tent town and to the camps of the many subcontractors who would come, thousands of tons of freight must be hauled. The railroad point nearest to the spot where the main contractor would camp was the town of Julia, from which the two had ridden horseback, and the mountain range lay between Julia and the right of way of the proposed, route. A forty-five mile trip through heavy desert sands, over the steep grades of an abandoned mountain road, and through heavy sands again would inevitable, and until the new steel rails had crept to a point opposite Julia, teams or automobile truck must supply the laborers and teams with the necessities of life.

Jo knew little about automobile trucks, but she did not fear them. They would give her keen competition, no doubt, at least during summer months but a study of the mountain soil convinced her that in winter there would be another story to tell. Anyway, she and her beautiful freight animals must take their chance against these modern machines. It would be a race between the tortoise and the hare; and every one knows that the hare has gained no little reputation from the outcome of that legendary contest.

From Julia, Jerkline Jo hurried by train to San Francisco, to the Western office of the big contracting firm of Demarest, Spruce & Tillou, whose headquarters were in Minneapolis. She knew Mr. Demarest personally, and was fortunate in finding him in San Francisco upon her arrival there.

"Well, well, well!" the big man cried jovially, as the girl was ushered into his private office. "Gypo Jo! Heavens to Betsy! Girl, I haven't seen you in five years. Put 'er there for old times' sake!"

"It's Jerkline Jo nowadays, Mr. Demarest," and she laughed.

Philip Demarest was a large, portly man, with a ruddy, red face, blue-veined and kindly. He had come up from the grade, and was eminently proud of his successful climb.

For thirty minutes he refused positively to talk business. He preferred to sit and dwell on bygone days with the one-time queen of Pickhandle Modock's gypo camp, to listen to the account of her father's rise and fall and his subsequent untimely death, and of the girl's ambitions and life in the Middle Western school. They told many a story, these old-timers of the nomadic camps, and had many a laugh over quaint remembrances. Then they got down to business.

Demarest listened carefully to Jo's ideas, and as she concluded he drummed thoughtfully on his desk.

"I think myself, Jo," he said presently, "that in winter you can grab off the money from any old automobile concern. But through the summer months they're gonta give you a nice little run for your money. And if they get freight there with less delay than you fail to avoid, and can do it for the same figure, they're gonta rampse you—that's all.

Arthur Preston Hankins

"Certain parties are lookin' into the matter already," he went on. "There's one fella here in Frisco that's got a fleet o' trucks—fella named Albert Drummond. Shrewd customer, too. He was tryin' to make a dicker with us. But we'll make no deals. We're not goin' to freight any ourselves if we can get out of it. But we'll sign no contracts in such a matter. Lowest bidder gets our business so long as he don't fail to keep us supplied with all we need. If you can underbid these truck men, you'll get the business; and from what I know about you, I have no doubt but that you'll deliver the goods."

"Gasoline is terribly high right now," Jo pointed out.

"So's hay, for that matter," said Demarest bluntly.

"I've heard, too, of a possible scarcity of gas," Jo told him.

"Yes, but the scarcity of hay is almost as threatenin', my girl; and those big horses certainly can eat the stuff. But tell me— what do you figure you can lay freight down for at the spot where you say we're bound to locate our biggest camp?"

"Two and a half cents a pound," was her prompt reply.

"It's an awful price, when you think it over," he said reflectively. "Just imagine, Jo; two and a half cents a pound bein' added onto the price of a sack o' flour—with flour at the unheard-of price it's already reached. And hay and grain! Jo, it's simply staggering."

"I admit that," she said. "But I suppose you took all that into account when you made your bid on the job."

"You bet your sweet life we did, girl! And I'll tell you what— we figured freight at three and a half cents a pound."

"You're fortunate. I'll get that, too, if I beat the trucks."

"Figurin' on gougin' us out of our profits already, eh?"

"Not at all, Mr. Demarest. Two and a half cents is my minimum. I'll freight for that only if forced to by the trucks. I doubt if I can make money at that figure. Only a trial over an extended period of time will tell. It all depends on the nature of the soil—on the condition that the roads develop after a period of heavy traffic over them, and the devastation of the winter rains. There'll be snow in those mountains, too. It's a gamble—a big gamble—but all that I can see against me is the fact that trucks don't eat hay when they're not at work."

"And how d'ye know where our Camp One is going to be located, girl?" he asked kindly. "I don't know myself yet."

"Of course you don't know positively," she replied. "But I'll bet you ten to one that you'll never sublet that piece of heavy-rock work through the buttes. I don't know a subcontractor—and I've not been out of touch with the grade so very long—who could tackle that stupendous task. So, if you can't sublet it—and I'm betting you can't—it will be up to you folks to do it yourselves. So that tells me where your largest camp will be, and at the nearest water to your largest camp the rag town will spring up. Isn't that all logical?"

"Sound as a dollar," he told her. "You weren't raised by Pickhandle Modock for nothing, were you?"

She rose from her chair. "Tell your subs to send me a wire at Julia when they're ready for any freight, at two and a half cents for a starter," she said. "I'll get it to 'em. But if no one meets my price, look for a raise to three cents for the second trip. Of course, if I don't hear from them, I'll know some one has beaten me out. Then I'll see what can be done. Your camp, of course, won't be in till last, I suppose. I'll go back to Palada now, take the stock off pasture, and begin hardening them up. Then I'll start for Julia, and will be there before your outfit moves in."

CHAPTER XII

SKINNERS FROM FRISCO

Back at Palada, Jerkline Jo began hunting up the expert skinners who had pulled the long sash-cord lines for her foster father, and who had drifted to parts unknown since the completion of the paved road that had virtually put Pickhandle Modock out of the running. The world has not an oversupply of expert jerkline skinners, and the plucky girl's chances for success depended in great part on obtaining good men to handle her teams. She was able to trace some of the men, and her offer to pay their expenses to Palada brought replies favorable to the project in each case. For jerkline jobs are scarce these days, and a jerkline skinner would rather follow his calling than do any other sort of work.

The blacksmith, horseshoer, and wagoner, Carter Potts, was still in Palada, and wished for nothing better than to serve the girl. They had decided to reopen the shop at Julia, and for his devotion Jo promised him a generous per cent of any profits which might accrue from work aside from the care of the immense wagons and shoeing the teams. This in addition to his monthly salary of a hundred dollars and board.

From Oregon now came "Blink" Keddie, who had driven teams for Pickhandle Modock since long before the old railroader had settled at Palada. Tom Gulick came from Utah, where he had been working on a cattle ranch. Heine Schultz and Jim McAllen came from remote regions in the northern lumber woods. But of Ed Hopkins, the prince of mule skinners, and Harry Powell the girl could get no trace.

With the dependable force that she had mustered, however, she took the stock from pasture, broke even on a job to a desert town to the west in order to put the teams in shape, and then made ready for the hundred-and-fifty-mile trip to Julia. She had written Mr. Demarest and asked him to advertise for two good jerkline skinners to be shipped with the first draft of laborers he would get from San Francisco. She had small hopes of obtaining good skinners by this method, but no other course presented itself.

Two days before the start for Julia came a wire from the San Francisco office of Demarest, Spruce & Tillou. It read:

Employment office notifies two jerkline skinners applied re advertisement in paper and have been forwarded Palada. Arrive day after to-morrow.

Jo showed the telegram to Heine Schultz when she went to the corrals this morning.

"I'll bet you get a couple o' peaches, Jo," he laughed. "Why, any tramp's likely to go to an employment office and say he's anything they want him to be, just to get on the job. And maybe, even, he'll ditch the train before he reaches the job. Just wanted the trip, you know."

Jo's broad, smooth brow puckered. "I do hope that will not prove the case," she said. "Jerkline skinners are so hard to get, particularly in this country. Every man who has ever driven a horse or mule seems to imagine he can drive jerkline, but you know and I know that it takes knack and years of practice. But I'm hoping that because these two applied for this particular job they're all right. If they merely wished to get free transportation out of San Francisco, it was not necessary for them to apply as jerkies. They could as easily have arranged to be shipped as plain skinners, or rock men, or muckers."

"I'll bet you draw a prize, all right," Heine chuckled disconcertingly.

Jerkline Jo postponed the start a day, and awaited the coming of the applicants.

As the local passenger train from Los Angeles whistled for Palada, Mr. Orr Tweet roused himself from his seat in the smoker and slapped the muscle-corded thigh of the disconsolate Hiram Hooker.

"She blows, Hiram, old boy!" cried Mr. Tweet. "Fame and fortune await us just ahead. She slows! She creeps! Palada opens her arms to us! Perk up, Hiram! The girl wasn't your kind, my boy. You'd have stepped all over her little feet, and she'd got a divorce and alimony on the grounds o' cruelty."

Hiram Hooker sighed and stretched his columnar arms. For a moment or two the new prospects that loomed kept his mind busy, then his thoughts reverted to Lucy Dalles, and gloom claimed him once more.

"Don't talk like that, Playmate," he said. "You don't understand. I loved the girl."

"Prune juice! She'd 'a' made a regular sucker outa you. Good thing I got you away. A big mountain o' blood and bone like you fallin' for a dash o' cake frosting like that little hasher. Hiram, you've got a man's body and a man's brains, and I like you better the more I see of you. If you're goin' to weep over a woman, weep over a regular woman, boy—a man's woman. There! Look out the window. See that straight, strong, black-headed desert girl in chaps and a Stetson? Look at the brown of her! Look at her stride! Queen o' the earth, hey? That's the kind of a woman for a man with the body of an elephant and the imagination of a poet, like you've got. There's a girl worth sighin' for, only she wears leather chaps! Well, out we go. Palada for a toehold on the ladder o' fame and fortune!"

The train had squeaked to a stop, and the effervescent Mr. Tweet and his huge companion descended the steps to the sunny platform. The businesslike Mr. Tweet buttonholed the first villager he met, and informed him:

"We're lookin' for a party called Jerkline Jo—a lady with a far-flung reputation. Can you steer us to her rendezvous, my friend?"

The man stared at him a moment, then jerked his thumb over his shoulder.

"There's Jo over there," he said. "She's lookin' for ye, I reckon. That pretty girl in the chaps."

"Her!" gasped Mr. Tweet. "Lordy! And I was just eulogizin' her through the window o' the coach. I saw her first—Hiram—I saw her first!"

Next second Mr. Tweet was before Jerkline Jo, lifting his hat and bowing politely. Behind him, Hiram Hooker stood awkwardly looking at the girl he had traveled six hundred miles to work for.

"Madam," said his companion, "if you are Jerkline Jo, permit me to introduce myself and my friend. I am Mr. Tweet—Playmate Tweet—Twitter-or-Tweet Orr Tweet. My friend and companion in arms is Hiram Hooker, from the virgin forests of Wild-cat Hill. I hope we find you well, and a look into your face tells me that I never hoped for a surer thing in my life. Madam, when you know me better, you will learn that I am not fresh, merely bubbling over with the joy of existence."

For a little Jerkline Jo gazed at him, then burst into ringing laughter. "Well, if you can drive jerkline," she said, "there's no doubt but that you will be a pleasant addition to our little family. I'm happy to meet you, Mr.—"

"Playmate Tweet—Twitter-or-Tweet Orr Tweet."

"*What?*"

"Orr Tweet—Twitter-or-Tweet Orr Tweet," patiently repeated Mr. Tweet.

"Are you trying to be funny?" The dark eyes narrowed dangerously.

"I am funny," corrected Mr. Tweet. "I can't help it. Allow me to explain: My last name, unfortunately, is Tweet. Tweet is the well-known conversational effort of a bird, and also 'Twitter,' if we are to believe the bird lovers. Therefore, I am ruthlessly called Twitter at times by my friends, and more often Twitter-or-Tweet. Orr is my first name. Orr Tweet. Suppose, for instance, my name happened to be Jim Brown, and I had been given the nickname of Blister. Then I would be called Blister Jim Brown, or Blister Brown. But my name is Orr Tweet, and my nickname is Twitter-or-Tweet. Therefore, I am Twitter-or-Tweet Orr Tweet, or Twitter-or-Tweet Tweet. You've heard the story of the lady who asked the ticket agent for 'Two to Duluth,' haven't you? He thought she was flirting with him, and came back with 'Tweedle-de-dee;' whereupon she slapped him. So far I have escaped such consequences when telling people my name. But if, when asked, I reply 'Orr Tweet,' they say 'What or Tweet?' Then if I reply 'Twitter-or-Tweet *Orr* Tweet,' they look at me as if they thought I was trying to kid 'em. So I begin my explanation by giving them my nickname, or monaker, 'Playmate,' and follow it with my second monaker, 'Twitter-or-Tweet,' as I am frequently called, or Twitter-or-Tweet Orr Tweet, or Twitter-or-Tweet Tweet. It's very simple."

Jerkline Jo laughed again at the end of this seemingly nonsensical harangue, and fixed her dark eyes on Hiram Hooker. The giant stood staring at her, and not a thought of Lucy Dalles was in his mind now. His blue eyes caught her dark ones, and his glance was lowered in confusion.

Womanlike, Jerkline Jo took him in at a glance, and something within her responded to the appeal that his handsome manhood made to femininity.

"What a godlike physique!" she thought.

Then impulsively she stepped forward and extended her hand.

"I'm glad you've come, Mr. Hooker," she said. "And I do hope you are really a jerkline skinner."

"And how 'bout me?" complained Mr. Tweet.

"I beg your pardon," said the girl, biting her lip. "What a stupid thing for me to say! But really—well, Mr. Hooker does look more like an outdoors man than you do, Mr. Tweet. I didn't mean to discriminate between you in my offer of welcome, though. Mr. Hooker, *are* you a jerkline skinner?"

For the first time Hiram's soft voice began to drawl. "Yes, ma'am," he told her earnestly. "I've driven jerkline since I was knee-high to a duck—eight and ten and twelve, and even sixteen, ma'am. I reckon I can make 'em pull, no matter how far out you hook 'em on."

"Where have you worked?"

"At home, ma'am—in the big timber o' Mendocino County— haulin' tanbark and ties and shakes and posts over the mountains to the lumber steamers on the coast."

"Do you love horses and mules?" she queried eagerly.

"I love everything that breathes, I reckon, ma'am," he told her softly. "I kill nothin' that lives, except rattlesnakes, unless I need the meat. Then sometimes I don't kill."

Jerkline Jo's dark eyes glowed. She turned to Mr. Tweet.

"And you?" she asked.

"Madam," he replied, "I came down here under false pretenses, but now I'll make a clean breast o' my treachery. I was broke; I had to get out o' Frisco and get a toehold somewhere. But after seein' you, I can't try to put one over on you. Couldn't if I wanted to try, I guess. I am not a jerkline skinner, but I love animals. I am one of those confident persons who will try anything once—even twice. The things I have done, and was told I could not do, are legion. If you will give me a trial for my inseparable friend's sake, I have no doubt at all but that in the course of a short time your mules will refuse to lift a foot unless I am behind 'em with my persuasive voice. In other words, Miss Jo, I am yours to command."

She smiled, a finger to her lips. "Well, come over to the corrals, both of you," she said, "and we'll see what we can do. I simply must have Mr. Hooker. So if you two are inseparable, why—" She paused.

"I understand," Tweet put in. "All women are that way, once they're subjected to Hooker's spell. I simply can't get it myself, but it's a fact."

Jerkline Jo blushed furiously. She who had withstood the ordeal of a hundred proposals, she who had been raised where men were continually twitting her about some man who was yearning to bestow his affections upon her, was blushing at Tweet's harmless suggestions.

CHAPTER XIII

THE START FOR JULIA

Jerkline Jo walked ahead of Hiram Hooker and Tweet to the stables and corrals, where her three-score horses and mules and her big wagons were awaiting the start.

"We're all ready to go," she told the pair. "I was only waiting for you. We'll start at once, whether you are jerkline skinners or not, of course; but if you're not, I'm afraid we'll go without you."

Mr. Tweet glanced at Hiram and whispered: "I'm 'fraid this is where we separate, Hooker. Still, I don't know. Maybe I'm a jerkline skinner, after all. I'll never know till I try."

In front of the stable Tweet came to an abrupt halt and studiously regarded one of the huge freight wagons.

"Just a moment," he began quaintly. "Was that wagon built to go, or is it just an advertisement to show what the wagonmaker could do?"

Jo's wagons weighed nearly six thousand pounds. Each separate wheel had cost her foster father seventy-five dollars, prewar price. The investment that a single complete wagon represented was in the neighborhood of six hundred dollars; and as there were seven of them, besides the lighter trailers, the total outlay was no mean sum. The spokes of the great wheels

         Arthur Preston Hankins

were as large as Mr. Tweet's thighs; the hubs were larger than his waist; the tires were ten inches in width; the entire running-gear looked as if a small forest of sturdy hardwood had been felled for its construction.

"It is built to go," the girl assured him.

"Stutterin' Demosthenes! I didn't think there were enough horses in the world to move the thing! Madam, I have swiftly reached the conclusion that I am not a jerkline skinner. Are you, Hooker?"

Hiram smiled and spoke to Jerkline Jo.

"That's a fine wagon, ma'am," he said. "I never saw any as good as that."

"We've six more just like it," she told him, "and some lighter trailers. The man who made them is dead. I doubt if the world will ever again see such wagons when these are gone. Now, I want you to hook up, Mr. Hooker, and show me what you can do."

"Hook up, Hooker!" laughed Tweet, always ready to embrace the slightest opportunity for a joke.

The girl led the way into the stable, and Heine Schultz, temporary wrangler, showed Hiram ten immense black horses, not one of them under sixteen hundred pounds.

"Get 'em out," ordered Jo.

Hiram went to work immediately, with a briskness that caused Heine to wink at Jo, he threw on the heavy harness and led forth the big-footed teams. He did not ask which were the leaders or the wheelers, for this was indicated by the nature of their respective harness and bridles. Heine noted this and winked again. Hiram was told, when he asked, the names of the ten, and pointers and swing teams were indicated. In a period of time utterly bewildering to Mr. Tweet the man from Wild-cat Hill had his ten black beauties strung out in twos before one of the wagons, and was speaking to Jerkline Jo.

"I see you ride in the wagons," he observed. "I always rode the nigh wheeler hoss, ma'am."

"You may do so if you choose. We've saddles."

"Your way suits me," Hiram returned. "It's easier work, I reckon."

The girl climbed into the wagon with Hiram. Heine Schultz did likewise. Mr. Tweet, being a gregarious person, did not like to be left alone, so followed the others' example.

"Which way, ma'am?" asked the new skinner.

Jo pointed. "Up that street, and turn the corner to your left," she directed.

The wagon was about half loaded with the blacksmith's outfit. To add to this the horse wrangler set the heavy brakes.

Hiram grasped the jerkline, but allowed it to hang slack in his hands. Now came his soft, caressing drawl, low and musical:

"Pete! Abe! Feel of it! Molly! Steve! Ben! Prince! Up ahead, there—Jane! Buck!"

As a team the great animals started the heavy wagon, and moved off with a jingle of chains and bells and the creak of harness.

Heine released the brake and looked at Jo, and this time he merely nodded.

A block up the street Hiram gave a single pull on his jerkline, and called: "Haw, Jane!" An instant later—"Gee, Steve! Gee,

Molly! *Gee*, Molly! Steady! Good enough!"

With the leaders and the swings pulling to the left and turning into the cross street, and the pointers heaving slightly to the right, the long string made the turn, and the wagon rolled around the corner in the middle of the street.

This street that they had entered was one of the oldest in Palada—built by Mexicans in the old Spanish style. There were no sidewalks—there was not room for them.

"Turn to your right at the next corner," commanded Jerkline Jo.

Hiram Hooker nodded.

As the leaders neared the corner Hiram cried: "Haw, Jane! Haw, Buck!" and tugged once on his jerkline. Obeying the command, the leaders, followed by the eight, brought the wagon close to the left-hand side of the street. Two quick jerks on the line, and the sharp cries, "Gee, Buck! Gee, Jane!" turned the well-trained leaders to the right and headed them toward the entrance to the cross street. "Haw, Steve! Haw, Molly! Over the chain, Molly! Haw, boys, haw!"

At Hiram's command, the off pointer, Molly, had stepped daintily over the heavy chain that ran between her and her mate, and now both of them were pulling the heavy tongue at right angles to the left, the wheelers helping. As neatly as most men might have made the corner with a single buggy, the string of ten and the heavy wagon swung into the intersecting street, as narrow as the other, and not a hub touched.

Jerkline Jo's dark eyes were sparkling. "You've got a job, Hiram," she said. "A jerkline driver who can make that corner without scraping a hub is a real jerkline driver."

"Thank you," replied Hiram, with a merry grin, thrilling at her use of his given name. "And I'll say that the man that trained this team was a jerkline driver, too."

"A man didn't train them," Jerkline Jo informed him proudly. "I trained them."

"Just the same," returned Hiram, "I stick by what I said."

"Now you take the line, Mr. Tweet," instructed Jerkline Jo.

"I don't care for it," said Tweet. "I'm a promoter and capitalist. I'll go to work and get a job here in this burg, Miss Jo, and pay you for my transportation down when I've earned the price. But I have a sneaking feeling that Molly wouldn't care for the cadence of my voice; and Pete he eyed me kinda suspiciously when Hiram led 'im out. No—there's a limit. I've reached it."

"Drive back to the stable, Hiram," Jo ordered. "We'll start for Julia at once."

She turned to Tweet. "I'm sorry," she said. "Why did you ship down here as a jerkline skinner, Mr. Tweet? You came over a rival railroad, of course, and your transportation will cost me full fare."

"Madam," he replied guiltily, "I was broke, and just had to get outa Frisco. And I couldn't leave Hiram. Why, that boy would 'a' been a suicide, if it hadn't been for me. He was in love, and wouldn't work, and in another day he'd been broke—a hick from Wild-cat Hill alone and friendless and in love in big, cruel San Francisco. If it wasn't for me, you'd never got 'im."

"That's right," spoke up Hiram. "He made me come."

"Madam," added Tweet, "I hope you'll forgive me. I'll pay you all I owe you with interest. I'm the original go-getter from Gogettersburg, on the Grabemoff River. I'm down and out right now, but any day I'm liable to turn into a skyrocket. Madam, you trust me. I've promised Hooker to lead him to fame and fortune, and to do that I gotta stick with 'im, ain't I? Well, then, can't you find somethin' for me to do for you, so's I c'n ride with you to this new railroad? That country sounds good to me. I'll maybe go to work and get a toehold over there. You'll never regret befriendin' me, Miss Jo."

The girl stood, thoughtful, her feet planted against the jolting of the wagon.

"Could you help about the cooking?" she asked.

"Madam, I could—and would."

"I like to be accommodating," she told him. "I know how it is. I was raised in the camps, and know all about being broke and knocking about the country. I'll take you along, and I'll take a chance on your paying me for the transportation."

"You'll never regret it, Miss Jo. Pile whatever you want done on me. I'm a good roustabout, willin' and cheerful, and always a kind, happy little playmate. Thank you."

An hour later ten heavy wagons, some of them trailing because of the lack of skinners, rumbled through Palada, with an eight or ten-horse team pulling, the remainder of the horses and mules and Jerkline Jo's black saddle mare following like devoted dogs. Palada was out in a body to wave good-by and good luck to Jerkline Jo. She drove the last team, ten magnificent whites, spotless as circus horses, with thirty tiny bells jingling over their proud necks. Ahead of her in the train Hiram Hooker drove his blacks. As long as she could see anybody at Palada, Jerkline Jo stood in the front of her wagon, facing rearward, and waved her hat. There were tears in her dark eyes as she turned to her team at last, and the desert opened its arms to their coming.

Slowly the teams forged ahead into the infinite sandy waste, where whispering yuccas and thorny cactus grew, and jack rabbits went looping away among bronze greasewood bushes.

A cloud of dust hung over the wagon trail. Ahead stretched seeming nothingness for mile after weary mile.

Jerkline Jo hoped to make twenty miles a day, loaded as the wagons were with only the blacksmith outfit. She might have made perhaps twenty-four miles under such conditions, had it not been for the counteracting softness of the teams. Loaded, they would make from ten to twelve miles daily, which seems intolerably slow in these days of speed and nerve-wracking restlessness. But with six of the teams working steadily the outfit would transport upward of thirty tons twelve miles a day, which represents an enormous amount of provisions for man and beast.

Twitter-or-Tweet Orr Tweet rode with Hiram. The train had been traveling perhaps two hours, and it was after eleven o'clock, when there came a "Who-hoo!" from Jerkline Jo. Hiram and Tweet looked back.

She beckoned with her hand. Both Hiram and Tweet placed fingers on their breasts inquisitively; then she cupped her hands about her mouth and called:

"*Hi*-ram!"

"'*Hi*-ram,' huh?" grunted Tweet. "For one hungering second I thought maybe she wanted me." He grasped his twisted nose and straightened it. "'Twon't stay," he observed gloomily. "Go on and ride with her, you big soft-voiced lady killer! I'll stick with Pete, and maybe he'll learn to love me. What'll I do if they begin to get rambunctious, Hiram?"

"Don't worry," Hiram returned. "They won't do anything they're not doing right now. Just let 'em drift right along."

He swung himself to the ground and waited until the girl's wagon came abreast, then climbed up over a brake-shoe and squeezed himself between the slats of the tall freight rack with which her wagon was equipped.

Arthur Preston Hankins

The girl stood in the front end of the rack, and such material as the wagon carried was piled behind her, leaving a little compartment free of encumbrance in which she might move about. There was no driver's seat, and therefore quite a little room was hers.

Hiram gazed in utter bewilderment at what he saw. A coal-oil stove was burning, and on it pots were steaming. There was a tiny oilcloth-covered table, and on it and under it were pots and pans and other utensils of the kitchen.

What surprised him more, though, was another lower table before which stood a collapsible stool. On it were books and papers and a portable typewriter, with a half-typed sheet on the platen. There were ink and pens and other articles necessary to an officer or a study. Against the front end of the wagon rack stood a chest, with its lid closed, and more cooking utensils were on top of it.

Jerkline Jo smiled at his bewilderment.

"I'm cooking our dinner, you see," she explained. "To keep good men, I figure that they must be well cared for. When my father ran this freight outfit our skinners cooked for themselves, and often were obliged to eat cold lunches. When they did cook, there was no time for anything better than fried steak, or fried ham, or fried bacon and eggs. One grows terribly tired of fried things, and, besides, they're not good for the digestion.

"I've resolved that on this job we're going to live like people who are permanently situated. That chest there is a fireless cooker. My own scheme. In it now vegetables and a beef roast are cooking, and they'll be ready by noon. I mean to make biscuits and bread and cakes and pies in my oil-stove oven, which is a dandy. I can arrange to do all that on the smoothest portions of the road. I'll roll my biscuit dough soon now, and when we camp there'll be fresh, hot biscuits, roast beef with brown gravy, and steamed vegetables all ready for us. What do you think of my scheme, Hiram?"

Hiram knew nothing of the advantages of a fireless cooker, but he did know that food such as she had spoken of was unheard of on a freighting trip, and told her so.

"Besides," she added, "I have bought some large thermos bottles, and no matter how hot the desert is we'll always have cold water to drink. Every night it will get almost ice cold in this country, you know; and if we bottle it early in the morning it will remain cold all day."

Hiram was looking at the typewriter. "This is my office and study," said the girl. "My foster father's recent death called me from a preparatory school back in the Middle West, just when I was getting along so well toward gaining an education. I decided not to give up. I am taking two correspondence courses, and mean to continue my studies here in my wagon. Also I am learning stenography and touch-typewriting.

"At first I thought I'd open an office at Julia or the rag town that will spring up soon, and not drive a team myself. Then it occurred to me that I could save money by driving a team, and could continue my studies and attend to my business affairs while on the road. With well-trained teams, like we have, a freight skinner has hours and hours on the road when he has nothing to do but loll on his seat and smoke. As I don't smoke, I mean to improve the time with study. Don't you think I'm a wonderful schemer, Hiram?"

Hiram nodded, and thoughts of pink-and-white little Lucy Dalles and her ambitions were far in the background of his mind. Jerkline Jo was a beautiful girl—as different in her beauty from Lucy Dalles as is day from night. Her hair was dark and heavy, and crowned a low, broad brow. Her skin was now tanned a rich mahogany, but was clear and flawless, and her bare arms were round and brown. Her confident poise, her sturdy shoulders, showed character and strength far above the ordinary. She was a man's woman, was Jerkline Jo Modock, and only a man among men might hope to become her mate. She wore a broad-brimmed Stetson with a horsehair band, a blue-flannel man's shirt, worn leather chaps for comfort, and riding boots. A holstered six-shooter hung close at hand, the ivory-handled butt of the big weapon ready to her grasp. Here was a wonderful woman, and Hiram Hooker knew it, and knew, too, that here at last was the adventure girl who, in his dreams up there on Wild-cat Hill in the big woods of the North had been beckoning him to come and work for her, to fight for her—to die for her if fate should so decree.

CHAPTER XIV

A WIRE TO JULIA

"I wanted you to tell me something about yourself, Hiram," said Jerkline Jo. "That's why I called you. What a giant of a man you are! Tell me about Wild-cat Hill and the big woods of Mendocino. I've never been so far north in California."

She seated herself on the stool, and Hiram sat cross-legged on the floor of the freight rack. Ahead the many silvery bells, hung on steel bows over the hames of each of Jo's white beauties, jingled merrily as the wagon rolled on into the illimitable desert.

Hiram began to talk, and gradually he grew eloquent, for at soul he was a poet. He told of the grandeur of the big, solemn redwoods, of the ice-cold creeks that plunged riotously through the mysterious fastnesses of great forests. He told of his dead father and mother, asleep forever between the big bull pines on Wild-cat Hill. He told of his cramped, starved life, of his hopes and vague ambitions and his dreams.

She listened silently, deeply interested, her dark eyes glowing upon him, her chin cupped by a strong brown hand. His simplicity was new and refreshing. Soon she realized that no ordinary mind lay dormant back of the well-formed forehead of this tender-hearted backwoodsman. His talk showed that he had read a great deal and had somehow grasped the significance of it all. Several times her eyes filled with tears as she listened; often she smiled understandingly at his quaint confessions. Presently she asked:

"Hiram, have you any ambition for an education?"

"Yes," he told her. "I've always wanted that, I guess. That's why I read so much, I s'pose. But there wasn't much chance up there. I learned all they could teach me at school—learned it easy. But there wasn't any chance to go farther."

"You've that chance now," she told him softly.

"Do you mean—" He stopped, his lips parted as he gazed into her eyes.

"Just that," she said. "I'll help you. We'll study together. Right here in my wagon. Your blacks will jog along without you over many stretches in the road from Julia to the camps. Through the mountains, of course, we shall have to be at the jerklines constantly. We'll be four days traveling between Julia and the camps, loaded, and between two and three days returning empty. Only one day of the trip going will be over a mountain road. The rest of the time you may ride with me and fight for your education. I'll help you."

"Miss Jo—" There was a lump in Hiram's throat.

"Just Jo, please. No one ever troubles to call me miss, and I don't want them to."

"I'll do it, then, Jo," said Hiram huskily. "I never dreamed I'd ever have such a chance. And I'll work, too—I'll study night and day. But why—why are you doin' this for me?"

Slowly the rich color mounted to the cheeks Jerkline Jo. "I—I know how it is," she said. "I was raised in a gypo camp, and had no chance until late in my teens. Knew nothing but mules and horses until I was eighteen or over—cared for nothing else. And I love them still; but I've grown ambitious to get all that I can from life. I like you, Hiram Hooker. You're a big, clean-minded, simple-souled man. I'll help you all I can."

Hiram's experience with Lucy Dalles, and now with this splendid girl called Jerkline Jo, might have turned the head of a more sophisticated male. But the big woods of the North teach a man his insignificance in the scheme of life, teach him honesty and simplicity of heart and sincerity. So now Hiram Hooker's ego was not inflamed. He had no idea of his appeal to the other sex. Few women could help admiring such a handsome young giant as was Hiram, strong as a bull, symmetrical as some sturdy plant; and his drawling, soft voice was a caress that bespoke the kindly heart of a child and the tenderness of a woman. Withal he had a poet's soul, and all women love poetry in a man.

"Tell me about Twitter-or-Tweet, and so forth," she begged finally. "I can't understand that man. Is he a pure fake?"

"I don't know," Hiram replied. "He was mighty good to me in a way. He's been about a heap."

"Hiram, if you'll pardon me, we'll begin your lesson right now. I wouldn't say a 'heap.' You must try to overcome such colloquialisms."

"I'll try never to say it again," Hiram promised unblushingly.

"But listen," she added. "Don't take me to task if you hear me saying things in the vernacular of the railroad grade. I have to. As Gypo Jo, I know thousands of the old-timers, and they expect certain things of me for old times' sake. As Jerkline Jo, the situation will be much the same. I am obliged to be a mixer. Men whose friendship I could not afford to dispense with even if I wished to—which, I assure you, I do not—won't stand for a high-and-mighty attitude in me. I am of the railroad grade, and proud of it, and I must continue to be a part of the rough-and-ready frontier life. Hiram, I suppose your ideas of womanhood are very hallowed. Will you be greatly shocked when you see me go into a tent saloon and drink a glass of beer with the rabble of the big camps?"

"Do you do that?"

"I simply have to, Hiram. Ever since I was knee-high to you, until a very few years ago, I lived with one or more tent saloons within a stone's throw of our camp. Morals are, after all, a local conception, Hiram. What is thought to be wrong in one country will be the accepted practice just over the border line. It's all in the viewpoint. I not only go into saloons with men friends of mine, but sometimes I play poker or roulette or faro just to please them. And listen: Never in all my rough-and-ready life in railroad camps have I been insulted by regular stiffs, as the laborers are called. Certain outsiders have misunderstood my freedom from conventionality on several occasions, but always to their sorrow. Understand, I don't care the snap of my finger for beer, or to gamble; but these things will be expected of me now as in the old days when I knew no better, and I dare not assume a superior attitude toward people who have known me since I was found, a mere baby, half buried by the desert sands."

She told Hiram about her childhood then, and that she knew nothing of her parents, not even her own true name. Hiram gave ear eagerly to her story, and thought he understood her situation.

"I couldn't think anything wrong of you, ma'am,' he told her gently as she finished.

"And don't call me 'ma'am,' please," she corrected with a friendly smile. "And that reminds me that I made us wander from the subject of Twitter-or-Tweet. You were telling me about him when I interrupted. What is he? He's not a common tramp—a stiff."

"He says he's a promoter and capitalist," Hiram repeated.

"Of course he's talking nonsense."

Hiram then told of Mr. Tweet's card, which promulgated his operations as a salesman of banana lands, and of the stock he claimed to own in the new ditch digger.

"I thought perhaps he was some sort of a book agent," said the girl, laughing.

"I don't know much about people," Hiram confessed with naive simplicity. "I can't judge folks very well—some folks, anyway."

"I'm afraid he's a wind bag," decided Jo. "Well, we'll befriend him to the grade, anyway, and I guess that then he'll be obliged to shift for himself. If freight were moving freely, and every day, I might manage to use him—but that won't be the case at first. So we'll have to bid him good-by at the camps. I have an idea he can take care of himself."

Jerkline Jo glanced at her leather-protected wrist watch.

"It's eight minutes of twelve, Hiram," she announced. "I'll roll out my biscuit dough. Can you yell? If so, shout ahead to Blink Keddie and call a halt for noon."

Hiram rose to his six feet one and cupped his great hands about his mouth. The mellow call that he sent out had rung through miles of Mendocino forest, and now caused every skinner in the line to turn and look back. A wave of Jo's hand and they understood the noon had come.

When they were in camp, and the teams had been fed and watered from the great tank wagon, and Jerkline Jo, with the able help of Twitter-or-Tweet, had made ready the steaming meal, there arose loud praise of the girl's idea concerning the fireless cooker.

"By golly, Jo, this here's grub!" applauded Jim McAllen.

"Some scheme, ol'-timer!"

"I thought it was a kind of a nutty idea when you sprung it, Jo," confessed Tom Gulick, "but I'm strong for the cooker now. Long may she wave! Pass the gravy, Blink."

Jerkline Jo glowed with pleasure over her success.

Mr. Tweet made himself very useful by acting as waiter, and hopped about with pots and pans, leading the steaming food on the skinners' plates. Jo watched him with interest, but still was unable to consider him anything but an imaginative failure—a man who perhaps had seen better days.

When they had finished eating, he collected the dishes, and, as water was heating on the oil stove, had everything washed up and in its place before the resumption of their travel.

"He's clean and neat and thoughtful," Jerkline Jo reflected. "Perhaps I'll be able to use him after all. We could use an extra man as roustabout, if business gets good. I'll see. He seems so fond of Hiram, and, really, if it weren't for him, I'd never heard of Hiram."

She grew thoughtful then, and a trace of red showed under her brown skin. Why had she become so interested in this big countryman from the very start, she wondered.

It was a long, tiresome trip, and days before they reached their temporary destination Hiram Hooker was riding in Jo's wagon, deep in history and algebra and grammar, for Jo had with her all of her schoolbooks.

The days seemed short to both of them. As the magnificent whites plodded steadily on, there was added to the music of the nickeled bells the rapid clicking of Jo at the portable typewriter, or the slower, hesitating peck of Hiram Hooker. They were a silent pair, for they were deep in their studies.

Strange indeed was the picture they presented as they were moved slowly along under the hot desert sky. But for Hiram, at least, this was the beginning of everything. Some magic touch had set him on the road that for years he had longed to travel—the road to knowledge and a better life. Beside him rode the adventure girl who had been beckoning him out of the woods of doubt and ignorance, the girl who had colored his dreams up on lonely Wild-cat Hill.

Hiram quickly became a favorite with Jo's skinners, too; for anybody or anything that the girl approved of was sure to make an appeal to the loyal little crew who swore by Jerkline Jo. Besides, Hiram was irresistible in his quaint geniality and his musical drawl. They called him "Wild Cat" at first, but when they considered his hugeness and uniform good nature the name seemed a misnomer; so they amended it and called him "The Gentle Wild Cat." This moniker clung to Hiram Hooker through all of his subsequent life in the desert.

The seventh day after their start, at evening, they rolled into Julia and set the populace agog with speculation.

As the whites passed the depot the station master came out.

"Does a fella named Jerkline Jo belong to this outfit?" he asked, walking along beside Jo's wagon.

"I'm Jerkline Jo," she told him.

"You! Huh! Well, there's a wire for you. I'll run and get it."

Jo called to her ten whites to halt, and the wagon came to a rest. A minute later the yellow paper was in her hands. She read:

Twenty tons awaiting you at Mulligan Supply Company, Julia. Get it over the mountains at once to Breece Brothers, Hunter & Stevenson, and Washburn-Stokes. Drummond's trucks are coming. You are in for a stiff fight. Good luck. DEMAREST.

CHAPTER XV

MR. TWEET NEGOTIATES A LOAN

Oblivious to the staring eyes of the little desert town of Julia, Jerkline Jo, after pitching camp near water on the edge of the village, began hurrying about on her business.

She was directed to the man who owned the land on which the teams and men were now resting, and found that she could make a deal to lease the property at a reasonable figure. She made a freckle-faced boy happy with a bright new dime, and sent him back to her men with instructions for them to pitch the tents permanently and proceed to make the spot the Julia headquarters of the outfit.

She wired her thanks to Demarest and assured him that the order would go forward next day, if the dealers had it ready. Next she hunted up the Mulligan Supply Company and found that it was a new concern in Julia, having just moved in with a large stock of goods from Los Angeles. It was a branch of a big Los Angeles jobbing firm, and the new railroad across the mountains had brought it here.

The manager greeted her warmly, and told her that he had heard of her through Mr. Demarest. The entire order was ready for immediate shipment, he said, so Jo hurried back to camp and had her men hook two horses on each of six wagons, now empty, and drive to the store, where they were backed in to the loading platform.

They ate their supper then, and afterward worked far into the night loading case goods, baled hay, grain, new tools, and innumerable like commodities. When the wagons were loaded and the great tarpaulins hauled down over everything but the hay and grain, it was necessary for Jo to appoint a watchman for the night. She had no more than broached the subject when Playmate Tweet, who had helped manfully with the loading, offered his services.

"I been just ridin' all day," he said, "and tryin' to convince Pete that I'm a reg'lar fella. I'll squat on the goods till mornin', come what may."

In truth Jo did not just like to trust him. The goods, amounting in value far up into the thousands, were now under her complete control, and she was accountable for every penny to the purchasers of them. But she had not the heart to refuse Tweet's offer, and she wanted her skinners to rest for the remainder of the night, in view of the hard work that lay before them. So she accepted, and Mr. Tweet took his post.

He was there like the boy on the burning deck when they came with the teams early next morning, walking about briskly to keep warm through the cold desert dawn, whistling merrily. Jo had brought his breakfast on a plate, and hot coffee in a bottle.

Carter Potts, the blacksmith, was left behind to set up his shop and care for the extra mules and horses.

Quickly the teams were hooked on, and with complaining groans and heavy wagons, each now weighing with its load upward of six and a third tons, moved through the sleepy town toward the distant mountains.

"Hooker," said Tweet, as he sat beside his friend behind the laboring blacks, "this is a man's life. This is doin' somethin'! This is gettin' somewhere! This is livin'! I envy you, Hiram. I envy you that big body of yours and the way you can handle ten big horses as if you were drivin' a trick donkey hitched to a clown's cart. Wild Cat, you're a lucky man. And what a glorious woman, Hooker, to throw the magic over it all! You're the man for her, my boy—the only man I ever met that oughta have the nerve to try to win her. And she fell for you, you big buffalo with the voice of a turtle-dove! Play her carefully, boy, and you can win. Don't go at it like you did with Cream Puffs, up there in Frisco. But you'll win her, Hiram—it's in you to do it. Now, Hooker, can you slip me a five-spot when we get to the camps?"

"I haven't much more than that, Playmate," Hiram averred.

"Well, you got a job, ain't you? I haven't. Money didn't seem to worry you much when you were puttin' on your Follies o' Nineteen-twenty with Lucy, up there where the white lights gleam."

"What are you going to do with it?" asked Hiram.

"This is your foolish day, ain't it? I'll tell you what I'm *not* goin' to do with it. I'm not goin' to hire an automobile at four dollars an hour and take a lassie out for a ride over the desert."

"I'll try and let you have it."

"Just how much jack you got on you yet, Hooker, old friend from Wild Cat?"

"Seven dollars."

"That's a mint, man! Say, try to slip me all of it, will you, Hiram? I got a scheme. You won't need it—you got a job. And remember who was the means o' gettin' it, Hiram. Why, it's worth seven bucks for the privilege of just lookin' once into those eyes o' Jerkline Jo."

"Can't you go to work over at the camps and earn some money?" Hiram wanted to know.

"I *could*—yes. But I don't earn my jack that way, Hiram. I'm a promoter."

"Jo told me she thought she might be able to give you something to do, after all."

"Don't want it. Tender her my heartfelt thanks just the same, Hiram. All I wanted in the first place was to get down here and look things over, then go to work and get a toehold and start the fireworks. If things are like I think—say, I'll be givin' you people jobs in a week or so. B'lieve it, Hiram?"

"No," replied Hiram bluntly. "Buck, step up a little! Molly! Pete!"

Playmate Tweet sighed heavily. "Hardest folks to convince I ever struck," he complained. "Listen, Hooker: last night while I was guardin' the loads the night watchman at Julia strolled around, and we had a little talk. He's an old-timer in this country, and he told me all about it from there to Ellangone. I got some dope from him about this country we're makin' for; and puttin' what I heard from him with what Jerkline Jo has told me, I gets a grand scheme. It'll put me in on the ground floor, if things break right and then—' Oh, boy! Richard will be himself again!"

"Tell me about it!"

"Too deep for you, my son. You'd never savvy the ins and outs. Besides, when Twitter-or-Tweet Tweet gets his nose to a trail, he's one old hound that don't bark his head off—see? There'll be other bright young promoters lookin' for the secret, and I've learned to keep my mouth shut.

"Now," he went on, "when I get over there and have a little look-see, I may decide to beat it out pronto and start the clockworks. If I do, I'll need your seven dollars to get me back into the land o' the livin', where I can start the performance. If I give you the word, Hooker, slip me that jack. If I don't tell you to, I'll go to work at some o' the camps and make a stake and beat it for more promisin' pastures. You'll never regret it, Hooker. It'll be bread cast on the waters, and she'll come back chocolate cake."

"I'll think about it," Hiram promised.

"Do that! And in the event that I say things look extra good, you'd better slip Jerkline Jo a little sob story, and get her to let you drag down what you got comin' on your wages—and slip that to me, too. By golly, Hooker, once I get a toehold, Millions is my middle name."

Hiram smiled wryly.

On through the day the teams plodded toward the mountain pass. Hiram rode with Jerkline Jo in their movable school-room, and left Tweet to his own thoughts behind the blacks. They camped on the desert that night, at a ranch conveniently situated between Julia and the mountains, where was an abundance of artesian water. Next day at one o'clock they left the flat, hot sweeps and ascended steadily into firs and pines on the old mines road.

They were obliged to stop frequently and make repairs in the road and to clear away brush that for years had been over-growing the course of their steep climb.

Often as they ascended laboriously they followed shelves hacked in mountainsides, with the desert they had left thousands of feet below them. There were places where a solid wall of rock upreared itself on one side of the narrow road, while on the other side a precipice dropped straight down, and tall pines at its base looked like toothpicks. There were hair-pin curves which taxed the skinners' ingenuity, where the one or the other of their pointers would cross the chain to pull the wagons away from the banks, and often both pointers were obliged to leave the road entirely and pull along the sides of precipices.

However, they topped the highest point in the pass before darkness had overtaken them completely. They camped for the night beside a picturesque and cold mountain lake, at an altitude of six thousand five hundred feet.

Morning showed them the desert, sweeping away again on the other side of the range. There still remained twenty-five miles to be traveled, eight of them comprising the descent through the pass.

Once down on the level again, Hiram turned his team over to the care of Tweet, and boarded Jo's wagon for the continuation of his education.

So they crawled on persistently, and eventually, ahead of them over the desert, white tents glowed pink in the sunlight like toadstools in a great timberless pasture, and their first trip was nearing its end.

When they reached the first cluster of tents Jerkline Jo discovered that they represented the largest of the subcontractors to whom her freight had been consigned. The next one was situated five miles farther up the line, and the third six miles beyond that. None of them had been there when she made her horseback trip. Close to the first camp that they reached, that of the Washburn-Stokes Construction Company's, the inevitable rag town had sprung up.

Already there were a dozen or more tents, most of them housing saloons, dance halls, and gamblers' layouts, and here and there a board or corrugated iron structure was under process of building. Only the three construction camps, as yet, had arrived on this portion of the work; the next camp beyond this group was fifty miles to the north.

Jerkline Jo knew, however, that before many days had passed camps large and small would be dotted along the right of way, and that all must be supplied by some one.

She stood talking to Mr. Washburn, the head of the firm, while his freight was being stacked before the huge commissary tent, when Mr. Tweet approached her.

"I'd like a word with you, Miss Modock, when you're at liberty," he said politely.

"Why, I'm just loafing with Mr. Washburn now," she said lightly, and turned away with him.

"Will you please tell me again what you did a few days back about the camp at Demarest, Spruce & Tillou?" he asked. "Explain it all, please—just why you think the tent town will eventually be located in a different place than it is now."

"Why, it's simple," she told him. "It's this way: Demarest, Spruce & Tillou have the main contract here—a hundred miles, I've heard. When a big company like that contracts to build a hundred miles of grade, they at once begin to sublet portions to smaller contractors. Some take a mile; some two miles, some five—according to the nature of the work and the respective capacities of their outfits. Understand?"

"Yes—I got that."

"Well, it's natural, then, that the most difficult pieces—the biggest work—will be the most difficult to sublet. Consequently when the main contractors can sublet no more, they move in and get at the difficult pieces that remain on their hands.

"Now, I've seen a good bit of this line, and I've talked with the engineers. Also I know the names of most of the subcontractors who have figured on the job. I know that none of them have adequate equipment to tackle the big rock cut that will be necessary through that chain of buttes, twelve miles to the south of here."

She pointed to the buttes, blue and hazy in the evening light of the desert.

"So, my friend, it follows as the night the day that Demarest, Spruce & Tillou will eventually move in with their heaviest-hitting outfit to run that cut, which certainly will be left on their hands. It follows as the night the day, again, that the leeches who always drift in to get the stiff's pay day away from them will settle near the biggest camp, if there's sufficient water.

"Down near those buttes, where the big camp is bound to be, there's plenty of water, and before many days have passed Ragtown in all its glory will be erected right there.

"These supplies that we're hauling now are charged to the account of Demarest, Spruce & Tillou," she further explained. "You see, they furnish their subs with everything they need. Now when Demarest, Spruce & Tillou move in there will be little or no freighting for us to any camp but theirs. All goods will be concentrated in their commissary then, and the subs will buy direct from them and do their own hauling to the various camps. Of course, Ragtown will have to be supplied— but Ragtown and Demarest, Spruce & Tillou's Camp Number One will be virtually the same as regards our freight terminus."

"And how long before the main contractors will get here?" he asked, working his twisted nose from side to side as if in the hope of eventually persuading it to point dead ahead.

"That all depends on whether they have given up trying to sublet any more work or not. If they think they won't be able to load any one else up with a job, they'll be in directly— almost any day. But if they still think there's a chance to get rid of the hard pieces, they'll hold off until the matter is settled, of course."

"Thank you," said Mr. Tweet abruptly, and was turning briskly away when she remarked:

"I've decided that perhaps I can use you after all, if—"

"Sorry," he interrupted, "but I can't accept your offer, even though I appreciate it and thank you from the bottom of my heart. Truth is, I gotta get busy. I've heard there's a stage goin' out to the north to-night, and I gotta make it. By the way, did Hiram speak to you about advancin' him what pay was comin' to him?"

Jo's eyes narrowed. "No," she said coldly, "he didn't mention such a matter."

Twitter-or-Tweet came back to her. "Listen," he said, "you owe him about twenty bucks. I want it. I'll need it. You slip it to Hiram, and I'll borrow it off o' him. You see—"

"Why, I'll do nothing of the sort!" she cried vehemently. "Do I look like a sucker to you, Mr. Tweet?"

"Oh, dear, dear, dear!" he cried. "You don't understand. I'm gonta swing somethin' big. I need that and what Hiram's already got to float me along till I can hit the ball. For Heaven's sake, put a little confidence in me, ma'am, can't you? I'm gonta send the Gentle Wild Cat to you. He'll tell you. He trusts me."

"He trusts everybody," she remarked evenly. "Besides," she added, "you seem to forget, too, that you owe me for your railroad fare down here."

"Oh, that! Why, I'll pay you that in no time now. But wait— I'll unload freight in Hiram's place, and send him to you."

Sure enough, Hiram came presently and asked her, as a special favor to him, to let him have what money was owing to him.

"Hiram," she said, "you're going to lend it to Tweet, and he's going out in the auto stage to-night."

"I know it," said Hiram. "I got to help him. He's been a pretty good friend to me, Jo, and—and—I just like him. Why, if it hadn't been for him I'd never met you."

Jo colored and looked away. "You big, simple-hearted boy!" she cried. "Do you know what he is going to do?"

"No—he won't talk."

She was thoughtful a little, then took out a purse and handed him a twenty-dollar bill.

"Kiss it good-by," she said; "but I suppose the experience will be worth something to you."

"Thank you," said Hiram, very red of face. "I'm sorry for what I said about you meetin' me through Tweet, Jo. I meant to say, o' course, that if it hadn't been for Tweet I'd never got the job."

"Oh," said Jo, straight-lipped, "I understand."

Tweet was not with the outfit when it pitched camp close by for the night. He sat in the automobile stage instead, and waved a friendly good-by to them. "Bread on the water, Hiram, comes back chocolate cake!" he cried. "That is, Tweet bread does. Ha-ha, Hiram! You been mighty good to me, folks. So long for a time!"

CHAPTER XVI

TEHACHAPI HANK

Toward the middle of the following afternoon Jerkline Jo's freight outfit, minus the diverting Mr. Tweet of the twisted nose, was wending its way empty back toward the distant mountains, hauling the necessary water in the tank wagon.

They were still ten miles from the mouth of the mountain pass when they went into camp on the desert for the night. When they started next morning the tank wagon was taken on a way and left, for, with the lake at the highest point of the pass, and the artesian water at the desert ranch on the other side, they would be well supplied for the remainder of the trip.

Before noon they were entering the pass and moving up the steep ascent into cooler atmosphere, and light, invigorating air, scented with the breath of pines and junipers.

Hiram Hooker was lazing on his high seat, dreaming and watching his leaders, when from behind came the familiar call:

"Who-hoo!"

He turned his face back toward the mistress of the ten gigantic whites.

"Who repaired the road back there?" she shouted.

"I don't know," Hiram called back. "I can't remember that we stopped there."

"We didn't. Some one else has done that. Keep your eyes open, Gentle Wild Cat."

Hiram did this, and presently began to see ruts had been filled in repeatedly and the marks left by boulders that had been snaked to the edge of the precipice and allowed to thunder down a canon.

This continued all the way to the summit, where they camped for a late nooning beside the mountain lake.

When they took up the journey again, and had reached a point half a mile beyond the lake, came upon a lone touring car and a little camp. Frequently now Hiram looked back, to see perplexity and worry on the usually placid brow of Jerkline Jo. A half mile beyond the camp they found seven men working with ax and pick and shovel, repairing the road.

Jo set the heavy brake and called to her ten to stop. Hearing her command, Hiram also halted his blacks. The rest of the skinners moved on slowly down the mountain, looking back for Jo's signal for them to stop. She gave none, however, so they continued on.

"Who is repairing this road, please?" Jo called from her wagon to a group of men.

One of them approached her a few steps. "Fella called Drummond," he replied.

"Isn't he the automobile-truck man from San Francisco?"

"Yeah."

"Is he here?"

"No, ma'am. He come to Julia and got us to come over here in a machine and go to work, and he went back to Los Angeles, I think. Said he'd be out in a day or two."

"Thank you," said Jo, and threw off her brake.

There was no good opportunity for Hiram to talk over this matter with her until they had left the mountains and were in camp at the desert ranch. "I don't quite like it," Jo said then. "It seems that Mr. Drummond should have come to me in this matter, and if the road needed repairing to the extent that he is doing it we should share the expense between us."

"Drummond?" queried Hiram. "I think I know that man. I've seen him, anyway."

"You! Where?"

"In San Francisco. It seems that Tweet was in a restaurant there talking to a—a waitress about coming down here. This Drummond he—he knew that waitress, and came in to see her while Tweet was there. They got to talking it over, I guess, and Tweet told him all about the new railroad. The waitress told me—"

"You mean Lucy?"

Hiram's face reddened. "That was her name," he admitted. "I—I suppose Tweet told you about her."

"A little. But I interrupted."

"Well, Lucy said Drummond had been interested in what Tweet had to say, and he said he might look into the freighting possibilities of the new road. He's got a string of trucks, I was told."

"What sort of a man is he, Hiram?"

"Big fellow—always seems to be having fun. He's as big as I am, but not so awkward, I guess. He wears fine clothes. But I don't know anything about him at all. I never spoke to him."

The outfit reached Julia in the course of time, and found that "Blacky" Potts had set up his shop in a large circular tent, and was hammering away briskly on his anvil. Also he had made the camp snug and comfortable under whispering cottonwood, and had fenced off a corral with barbed wire.

Jo at once went to the Mulligan Supply Company to learn that a message had come to her, in their care, from Demarest. It stated that their big construction outfit was then on its way from northern California, and would cross to the new railroad from a point seventy-five miles to the north. In view of the long trip, they wished to travel as light as possible. Consequently there was another big order for Jo to freight in ahead of them at once. What interested Jo more, though, was the fact that Demarest ordered it delivered at the buttes, asking that a watchman be camped there to guard the supplies, provided they arrived ahead of the outfit.

Immediately they went to work at the loading, and in the end six wagons were carrying capacity. The seventh lead wagon was an extra, which Jo had decided to use only in case of a breakdown. With thirty tons of hay, grain, case goods, and barreled provisions they started back early the following morning. Jo's heart was light, for this was exceedingly good business, and it was coming faster than she had dared to hope, with so few camps established. Still, she was puzzled over the repairing of the mountain road.

"Fellow called Drummond has a big order to haul in trucks," the manager of the supply company had told her. "It's for a store that's going to open up at Ragtown, I understand. Guess he'll get it out tomorrow or next day."

All went well with the wagon train during the first lap of the desert trip. Hiram rode with his employer, and their migratory institution of learning was in full swing. Then when they reached the beginning of the mountain pass they found a shock in store for them.

The head skinner, Blink Keddie, had no more than entered the pass with his eight bay mules when a man stepped into the road and held up a hand for him to stop. He was a Western-looking individual, a seamed-faced son of the deserts, and an immense Colt revolver dragged at his hips. He had come from a tiny tent set back from the road a way, half hidden by junipers and close to a trickling spring.

Keddie clamped his brake and stopped his eight, eying the stranger curiously. Keddie, like Heine Schultz and Tom Gulick, had been on the railroad grade with Pickhandle Modock when Jo was a little girl. He was devoted to her and her interests, and anything that threatened her prosperity he was wont to look upon as his personal affair.

"Mornin'," he drawled as the following teams came to a stop, and skinners cupped hands behind their ears to listen.

"Quite a jag you got there," observed the man in the road.

Blink was entirely sober. "Jag" referred to the enormity of the load of freight.

"Little matter o' sixty thousand, altogether. I wasn't aimin' to let 'em blow right here, though, I pardner. Was there any particular reason ye had for stoppin' me?"

"Well, maybe there was, stranger. How many teams ye got pullin'."

Blink counted rapidly. "Four tens and two eights," he made reply.

"Uh-huh—but I mean how many span, pardner?"

Once more Blink struggled with arithmetic. "That'd make twenty-eight pair, wouldn't it?"

"Just about—just about, pardner. And two times twenty-eight is fifty-six, ain't it?"

Blink Keddie promptly agreed.

"Agreed, eh? Then I'll ask ye kindly for fifty-six dollars, stranger."

Keddie thoughtfully began rolling a cigarette. "If I had fifty-six dollars, ol'-timer," he said, "I wouldn't converse with the likes o' you."

The gunman grinned. "Does take some time to save that amount skinnin' jerkline or bein' toll master on a mountain road," he admitted. "Are you the boss?"

"If I was the boss," slowly returned Blink, "I wouldn't live in the same county with you."

By this time Jerkline Jo, who had been hurrying forward along the wagon train to find out what had occurred, arrived on the scene of their airy persiflage.

"What's wrong here, Blink?" she wanted to know.

"This fella has been insultin' me," claimed Blink. "He insinuated I belonged to the idle-rich class. I guess he's institutin' some sort of a drive or other. You talk to 'im, Jo."

"Well?" The girl wheeled and faced the man, hands on hips.

The Westerner swept off his hat. "Ye see, ma'am," he said to her, "this here's a toll road now—from here clean acrost the mountains to the desert on t'other side. I'm toll master. I'm to collect two dollars a loaded team for the trip through the pass. The price includes the return trip, empty."

Jerkline Jo paled. Up behind her crowded Tom Gulick, Hiram Hooker, Heine Schultz, and Jim McAllen, and, if looks could have killed, the man with the gun would have been ripe for the undertaker's care.

"Two dollars! You mean—"

"A dollar a head, then, ma'am. You got fifty-six animals. That 'u'd be fifty-six dollars, wouldn't it?" He smiled persuasively.

Jo gasped, and turned and glanced helplessly over her little army of loyal men.

"By whose authority are you demanding this?" She spun back to the toll master, her dark eyes now aflame.

"Mr. Al Drummond he's the boss, ma'am. He's from Friscotown. He's gotta keep up the road, so o' course he's gonta charge other folks to travel on it. It's jest like as if it was his private prop'ty, as I savvy the deal, ma'am. I got papers to show ye, if ye wanta see 'em. Course I got nothin' to do with it—nothin' atall. Mr. Drummond he jest hired me to collect the fees and keep folks off that refused to pay. I might add, though, ma'am, that I've always been considered a pretty good keeper-off when I'm hired for that purpose. I'm from the Kitchen Rancho, over toward the Tehachapi. They call me Tehachapi Hank. At yer service, ma'am."

Jerkline Jo's red lips were straight. She was indignant. A sense of defeat almost overwhelmed her. Such a situation had not even remotely occurred to her. In a wave of despair the realization swept over her that she had attempted something of which she knew nothing. There had been no one to advise her, and in the unbounded confidence of youth she had not sought counsel. On the railroad grade few men could have put anything over on her. But this was another matter.

Fifty-six dollars for the eighteen-mile trip through the pass! It would be ruinous. She would be obliged to advance her rate to meet this additional expense, and then the truckman holding the franchise would be able to haul freight cheaper than she could.

Back of her the men were muttering useless threats among themselves. Jo found her voice at last. There was no need to ask to see a copy of the franchise, because there was not the slightest doubt in her mind that everything was aboveboard in that respect. She simply had been outgeneraled. There was nothing to do but to pay—for the present, at least—as the freight on her wagons must be delivered at any cost, now that she had contracted to deliver it. What she said was:

"Will you accept my check?"

"Certainly, ma'am—most certain," was the ready reply.

"I'll go back to my wagon and write one for you then," she said, trying to keep her voice steady. "Let the wagons go on, please. When mine reaches you I'll hand out the check."

Tehachapi Hank touched his broad-brimmed hat again. "All right and proper, ma'am," he assured her.

He was waiting by the roadside when her stanch whites marched past him, and she reached the check out through the slats of the rack. He touched his hat brim again and smiled then with true Western politeness, pocketed the slip of paper without so much as glancing at it.

Dully she watched the broad straining backs of her beloved animals as they planted their great fetlocked feet and heaved their burden ever upward. Ahead of them she could hear her skinners shouting back and forth from wagon to wagon above the jingling of the bells, their tones high-pitched and angry. Why had she not consulted with Demarest and asked him to lay before her details of every angle that might present itself in such an undertaking as hers?

Demarest knew all the twists and turns of modern business ruthlessness. He might have been able to foresee a situation like this and to put weapons into her hands with which she might have combated it.

She shrugged her sturdy shoulders finally, and as noon was close at hand gave attention to her cooking. For the present she would drive the matter from her thoughts. There was work to be accomplished, which was a part of the present delivery of freight. When this task was completed she would see what could be done.

CHAPTER XVII

IN LETTERS OF BLACK

There was a general outburst of indignation on the part of Jerkline Jo's devoted retainers when the outfit went into camp at noon, quarterway through the mountain pass.

"We'll fix 'im, Jo!" Heine Schultz exclaimed angrily. "All we gotta do is make out to get ahead o' his old cough wagons and not let 'em pass. We can hold 'im back clear through the pass, if we string out. Le's figger it out fer the rest o' the trip, Jo. There's not over six places where one vehicle can pass another. Now what we gotta do is string out our outfit so's none o' us'll hit one o' those places when the machines are comin'. Say, we can hold 'em up till—"

"Heine," said Jerkline Jo quietly, "is that your idea of business."

"Course it is. Stick it to the Al Drummond, Jo! He's started somethin' that he'll have a hard time finishin', that's all. Say, we can slip it to him till he'll be sick o' that dirty deal he handed you. Leave it to Blink and me. We got it all schemed out."

"Heine," Jo remarked, "we'll travel right along as we have always traveled. If one of Mr. Drummond's trucks comes up behind us and wants to pass we will let it pass when it is convenient to do so."

"Not here, Jo! My team don't put one foot outa the road to let a truck pass."

"No, I don't expect you to do that. But it will depend on conditions. If you are loaded and he is empty, of course he must look out for himself. Again, if you are climbing and he is coming down, he must get out of the difficulty as best he can. But when you, loaded, reach a place where a truck can pass you, and you know one is coming up behind you and wishes to pass, you will stop your team in the road and let it circle around you."

"I won't, Jo! I—"

"Yes, you will. You will do as I say, as you always do." She smiled at him sweetly and patted his shoulder. "Loyal old Heinrich!" she said. "Just the same old-timer, we must observe the courtesy of the road always. Think it over—you'll see I'm right."

"Jo, you can't afford a jolt like that," said Jim McAllen.

"I can't," Jo told him frankly. "Right now I don't know what to do. I must keep on, by some hook or crook, till I can get advice from some one who's onto such tricks—Demarest, perhaps."

"It's a rotten deal!"

"I have an idea it's perfectly legitimate, Jim."

"They ain't gonta do anything to the road to make it worth a tenth o' what they ask to travel on it. You saw the little putterin' jobs they did, Jo."

"I have an idea," replied the girl, "that when winter comes they'll be quite busy. And it also occurs to me that, now that they've agreed to maintain the road if given the franchise, we can make them do it down to the letter, or render their

Arthur Preston Hankins

franchise void."

"By golly, I bet you can at that, Jo!" put in Tom Gulick. "I've heard, though, there's a rotten bunch of grafters runnin' this county. They'd probably beat you out some way, so long as Drummond was puttin' up cigar money for them."

Up until now Hiram Hooker had said nothing. Now came his soothing drawl, and the others listened.

"I don't know much about automobiles and what they can do," he said. "But I do know mountains and mountain roads, and somethin' about mountain soil. And I've this to say: If Jo can hang on till winter there'll be no trucks runnin' against her. Then if they still collect for crossin' through the pass, all she's got to do is raise the freight rate to meet the extra expense. There's exactly ten places on the road where we're goin' to hook maybe thirty horses on every wagon to get across next winter. And I'll bet my month's wages against a dollar of Mr. Drummond's money that he'll be begging for teams to haul him out. Then, of course, the price ought to be about fifty-six dollars a haul, regardless of distance, hadn't it?"

"Good boy!" cried Keddie. "Listen to our Gentle Wild Cat pur! He's right, too, I'll say. If we can hang on till winter, Jo can collect back all she's paid out for tolls—and I'll say a little profit on the deal wouldn't make me weep."'

"But winter's a long way off," Jim McAllen gloomily pointed out.

After this there was thoughtful silence.

To add to the misfortunes of the second trip to the camps, Jim McAllen broke a reach when the train neared the foot of the grade. There were spare reaches in the outfit, of course, but they had to unload the wagon to substitute one, and it all took a great deal of time. Then a horse became sick, and Jerkline Jo positively refused to work a sick horse. The animal was taken out of harness and allowed to tag along behind with his mate, who automatically became useless, too. A ton of supplies was taken from the wagon to which the sick horse belonged, and distributed among the other loads. This took more time, and night overtook the outfit with several miles between them and the tank wagon that awaited their coming on the desert.

Hour after hour they plodded along, not daring to camp until they had water. There was no moon, and as the desert road was little more than a trail Heine Schultz let his team tag Keddie's and walked ahead with a lantern to guide the lead skinner. Thirsty and hungry and weary, they reached the tank about nine o'clock. Then came a hearty curse from the man with the lantern, followed by:

"Lord, be merciful unto me, a skinner! The tank's empty, Jo!"

The party descended hurriedly and crowded about him. It was a steel tank, and a careful search failed to show that any of its plates had sprung a leak. Then the light was held under the spigot, and, though the hot desert sun had evaporated every drop of water, there was a hole worn in the sand where it had fallen in a stream. The spigot was open.

"How 'bout it now, Jo?" Heine queried. "Is this what you call legitimate business—huh? I guess now you'll let me hold 'em back when I can."

Without replying Jo stooped and made an examination.

"Some one has turned the water out," she said, rising wearily. "Will we be obliged to hire a watchman to camp by our water tank? This is serious, boys. The unwritten law of the desert would condemn whoever did this to a lariat and a yucca palm. Still, we don't know who did it. It's too dark to find tracks or to learn anything about it. It's seventeen miles to the Washburn-Stokes outfit—the nearest water ahead. Or it's eight miles back to the lake in the mountains. What's best to do?"

They turned the problem over and over, and finally decided unanimously that to send the tank with six horses back to the lake, to be refilled, was the wiser plan. Hiram volunteered for the trip, and Schultz volunteered to go with him. At once the two set off behind six of Hiram's lamenting animals for the long night trip, eating a hasty lunch as they traveled.

Dawn was breaking when they returned with a full tank, and were greeted by the braying of the mules and the expectant nickering of the horses, who smelled the water from afar.

Jo ordered a rest until ten o'clock, to counteract the suffering that the thirsty animals had undergone and to rest Hiram's six after the performance of their double task.

These setbacks made them late in their arrival at the scene of coming toil, but gradually the distant buttes grew plainer as they moved on steadily toward them over the crunching sands, so hot and barren.

Hiram Hooker was riding with Jerkline Jo as they approached the buttes. She was hammering away on her typewriter, while Hiram was deep in a mathematical problem, his tongue out and gripped by his teeth. The clicking of the typewriter ceased suddenly, and Jo asked:

"Isn't that a tent over there near the buttes, Wild Cat?"

Hiram looked up and shielded his eyes, straining his vision over the rolling white backs of Jo's team into the yellow vastness beyond.

"Looks like it," he said.

"We'll not have to arrange for a watchman then. Demarest has sent a man, I guess. Get out my binoculars, please, and see what you can make out."

Hiram took the strong glasses from their case, and, steadying himself against a side of the freight rack, trained them on the distant speck of white that represented a lonely tent.

At once the tent seemed to jump across the desert to a point a short distance ahead of them. Hiram's lips parted and a snort of surprise escaped him.

Before the front of the tent, on a pole planted there, was a big sign composed of black letters against a white background. And this is what Hiram Hooker read:

The Homesteader's Promised Land of Milk and Honey

OFFICE OF THE PALOMA RANCHO INVEST-MENT COMPANY

Orr Tweet, President. Walk In

CHAPTER XVIII

GREATER RAGTOWN

Indeed he was an important-looking individual who greeted the freight outfit of Jerkline Jo when it came to a weary halt at the foot of the desert buttes. He wore a new olive-drab suit, composed of Norfolk jacket and bellows breeches, an imposing Columbia-shape Stetson, and shiny new russet-leather puttees. From one corner of his mouth, aligned with his twisted nose, protruded long, expensive-looking cigar. This was Twitter-or-Tweet Orr Tweet.

Hat removed, bowing like a Japanese, he approached the astonished skinners and offered his hand to Jerkline Jo.

"Madam," he said, "permit me to extend to you Ragtown's most cordial welcome. And you, gentlemen, are included, of course. When you have the time, Miss Modock, I should like the pleasure of your presence in the office of the Paloma Rancho Investment Company. If I may offer a suggestion, too, it might be well to deposit Mr. Demarest's freight close to my office, so that I can look out for it until the arrival of the outfit. Hooker, come with your employer if you can conveniently do so."

So saying, Mr. Tweet recrowned himself with his new Stetson, turned, and strolled impressively toward his tent, disappearing between its lazily flapping portals.

With the exception of Hiram Hooker, Jo's skinners shouted with laughter. Jo and Hiram merely exchanged bewildered looks.

"We'll go over now, Wild Cat," she said. "There's lots of time to unload. We can't make it out of here to-day, anyway."

Side by side they walked toward the lonesome little tent with the big sign on a pole in front of it—a mere atom of white in the vast desert.

Orr Tweet sat at an oaken desk in one corner of the tent. In another corner was his bunk, a new suit case, and a new trunk, both in keeping with Tweet's expensive outdoor clothes. There were several chairs. Tweet arose briskly and held one for the girl with all the ceremony of a head waiter in a restaurant of repute.

"Jo," he began, "I hope you'll pardon the familiarity; there is a matter of sixteen or seventeen dollars due you, I believe, for my transportation from Frisco to Palada. And, Hiram, I believe I owe you somewhere in the neighborhood of thirty dollars— the exact amount escapes me temporarily. Now, both of you, the question is this: Do you prefer cash, or stock in the Paloma Rancho Investment Company, or land? The choice is yours."

"Tweet," ordered Hiram, "get down off your high horse and talk sense. What on earth is all this, anyway?"

Tweet laughed and winked and became himself again.

"Hiram, old boy," he confided, "I'm on the road to fortune. This is gonta be the biggest deal I ever tried to swing. And, by golly! I'm the little boy that c'n swing 'er!"

"Tell us about it," pleaded Jerkline Jo.

"Well, sir, Jo, I owe everything to you, and I'll prove I'm not the man to be slow in showin' my gratitude. I'm a go-getter, and no mistake. I couldn't make you folks believe it, so I had to go to work and show you. But I bear you no ill will. You didn't know anything about me.

"Well, dear little playmates, here's the dope:

"That night watchman over there at Julia told me who owned all the land about here, and said they were in tight financial circumstances—badly in need o' ready money. They're big land owners—land poor. I drank that all down, and she listened good to me. For the rest, I banked on the accurate judgment of a party known as Jerkline Jo. I says to myself: 'Jo's been on the grade all her life and savvies conditions. If she says Ragtown is goin' to be located at the buttes, that part o' the country's the part to get toehold on. Anyway, Playmate,' I says, 'we'll take a chance on Jerkline Jo.' And that's what me and Playmate did.

"I hunted up the owners o' the land when I gets to Los Angeles, and makes 'em an offer on twelve thousan' acres—comprisin' the entire tract known as Paloma Rancho, an ancient Spanish grant. Good for nothin', I'd been told, but to run cows on in winter, when the filaree and bunch grass are green. Just the same, there are other parts o' this ole desert that are comin' out with a bang here lately. Lookit up in Lucerne Valley and around Victorville! Good pear land, once she's cleared o' the desert growth and a little humus-bearin' fertilizer added to the soil. Produces good alfalfa, too. Anyway, I says I'll take a chance, so I made 'em an offer.

"They pretended like they thought the railroad was gonta do 'em a lot o' good in a few years; that they didn't care whether they disposed o' the property or not. But that bunk's old stuff to me, so I shut 'em up and made 'em talk turkey. I made 'em an offer o' ten dollars an acre for Paloma Rancho, payment to be made in quarterly installments of six thousan' dollars, each, contract to run for five years, with interest at seven per cent on deferred payments—first payment o' six thousan' dollars to be made in advance.

"They refused, and I picked up my hat and started out. They called me back, and for ten minutes we puttered around between ten dollars an acre and fifteen, and at last they fell into my arms. We had the papers drawn up, and I slips 'em a certified check for six thousan' buckerinos."

"You gave them six thousand dollars!" cried Hiram.

"Sure," Tweet replied easily. "I'd already wired to Frisco and disposed o' my ditch-digger holdin's for over eight thousan'; I got over a thousan' left, five hundred paid on an automobile that's now asleep back o' this office, and a toehold on Paloma Rancho, twelve thousan' acres o' perfectly beautiful sand.

"And now that you folks have dumped a cargo o' freight here marked D., S. & T., No. 1, I know we win. We're goin' to make this one o' the liveliest propositions in the West. Ragtown will move down here as soon as the big outfit lands at the buttes. City lots in Ragtown—which later probably will be known as Tweet—will be worth from a hundred dollars to two hundred and fifty, accordin' to location. My engineers will be here soon, and we'll lay off the town site. I've made application for a post office, and by the time the papers come from the department there'll be plenty o' signers here. Concessions will be granted at reasonable figures. Farming lands will be sold at from fifty dollars an acre up to a hundred and fifty, accordin' to location, depth to water, et cetera. This will include stock in the company's water right. Water will be developed up in the mountains, on a site that goes with the ranch, at an approximate expense of one hundred and seventy-five thousand dollars. I am organizing my water company now, and will let all old friends in on the ground floor, of course. Water at Butte Springs, by the way, Ragtown's present supply, will cost twenty-five cents a head for stock, and five cents a drink for human beings who are recognized citizens of Ragtown, the Tweet-to-be. Old friends, however, are hereby extended the privilege of watering free of charge while life shall last.

"So folks, we're off in a bunch. Keep your eye on Ragtown,

metropolis of the Homesteader's Promised Land of Milk and Honey."

"But how about your next payment?" asked Jerkline Jo. "If I'm not too impertinent, can you meet it?"

"Right this moment," replied Tweet, "I couldn't even look like I wanted to meet it. But why worry for nearly three months more? Ragtown will pay it for me. I'll meet her when she's due—never fear. I always get out some way. My middle name is Millions. Gogettersburg is my birthplace. You folks and Pete are my first failure in convincin' others of my shrewdness, honesty, and unbounded ability."

For an hour Mr. Tweet told of his glowing plans, but he found it difficult to convince either Jo or Hiram that he had success within his grasp. Not until the conversation worked around to the mountain-road franchise did Jerkline Jo realize that, in befriending Orr Tweet, she had enlisted an ally who would and could help her.

"Why, we've got 'em by the tail, girl!" he cried. "Just keep on payin' what they ask till Ragtown moves down here, which will happen as soon as Demarest gets settled. Then it'll cost this Drummond to travel across Paloma Rancho exactly what it has cost you to come through the pass. And I'll get me a roughneck with a gun, too, and see that he pays. And if he eventually falls down and quits, you make him live up to that franchise and keep that road in perfect repair, or sue him, by golly! Leave it to me, Jo. I'll fix his timepiece. Every spare dollar you get, you slip it to me to help me meet those payments. It'll let you in on the ground floor, by golly! We'll make a million out of it, Jo—you and me and the Gentle Wild Cat. And I'll show 'em how to try and take advantage of a girl like you! Folks, the future looks mighty bright for all of us!"

While they were conversing Blink Keddie's voice Came from outside the tent:

"Jo! The trucks are comin' in."

The three went out and joined the head skinner, who pointed far over the shimmering desert at three dots moving along from the mountains toward the Washburn-Stokes camp.

"Poor fish!" Tweet said disgustedly. "They don't know what's in store for 'em. Next trip they make, probably, Ragtown and the big camp will be on Paloma Rancho, and then they're blocked."

Mr. Tweet ate supper with Jo and her skinners, and afterward the outfit spent a pleasant evening listening to the promoter's rosy plannings. Even the most skeptical among them gradually became convinced that, if he could hold on and meet his payments, he might make a go of it. Early next morning they started back, passed the polite Mr. Tehachapi Hank in the course of time, and arrived in Julia without further mishap.

Now came a period of inactivity. There were orders for goods to be hauled, but a great portion of what was demanded had not yet arrived by train from the coast side of the mountain range.

Such delays were expensive. Jerkline Jo could have made a profit running into four figures every month, allowing for deterioration and a reasonable per cent on the investment represented, could she have kept her teams moving steadily, with the wagons loaded to capacity every trip. As yet, though, with so few camps established, this could not reasonably be hoped for, and she had made due allowance for such setbacks when deciding upon her freight rate. She had charged Demarest, Spruce & Tillou three cents a pound for the last consignment.

The three trucks that they had seen returned. They were of two-ton capacity. More came in from the coast, which carried five tons, and there was a fleet of five-ton trailers. Jo learned that Drummond had made a price of two and three-quarter cents, so she promptly met it and, by wire, notified Demarest to that effect.

She was anxious to see the five-tonners in operation. She believed that machines carrying a large tonnage would meet with serious difficulties in the pass, and also in the desert sand, in places. But they would make the trip so quickly that she began to have grave doubts. They might worm their way out of many difficulties, and still make the camps while her teams were on the first lap of the journey. So far, she had seen nothing of her competitor, Al Drummond.

There reached the Mulligan Supply Company a telegram from Demarest instituting a standing order for baled alfalfa, and instructing that all freight be hauled by Jo so long as she could keep ahead of the congestion and haul as cheaply as others. Promptly, then, Jo loaded to capacity with hay, and they were off again.

Four light trucks had preceded her with case goods, for Ragtown's store, she supposed. But the remainder of the fleet remained idle at Julia, and seemed to have no business. Jo was reasonably sure that, for old friendship's sake, Philip Demarest would see to it that she got all of his hauling, providing she could make deliveries to his satisfaction. She thought that until new camps settled on the grade—camps of bigger contractors who would buy their supplies direct and not depend on Demarest, Spruce & Tillou—Mr. Drummond would have many idle days. Then, of course, he might cut to the bone on the freight rate, and Jo feared that, with the trucks eating nothing while they rested, Drummond might be better able to withstand a rate war.

They were held up by the genial but exacting Tehachapi Hank at the foot of the grade, as on their last trip. Jo paid cash this time, and demanded a receipt, as ordered to do by Tweet.

As the wagon train neared the highest point in the pass she noticed that her whites and Hiram's blacks seemed to be lagging behind. Still, both teams seemed to be moving briskly enough and steadily. But the other teams were far in the lead.

Then Hiram's wagon entered upon a system of hairpin curves, and for nearly fifteen minutes none of her skinners was in sight.

She continued to wonder at the unwonted speed of the skinners ahead of Hiram.

Just as she reached the outmost point of a bow in the second hairpin curve, she heard a dull rumble behind her. Looking back, she saw nothing unusual, for in this place the road wound about U's and S's in the mountainside, and one could not see far along it, either ahead or behind. Deciding that a tree had fallen, she dismissed the matter from her thoughts, and gave her attention to manipulating the jerkline over an exacting piece of road.

She worked out of the curves eventually, to see the other teams moving placidly along ahead of her, but now she and Hiram had caught up again.

She spoke about it when they camped for the midday rest. It was Hiram who made reply.

"I was wondering at their speed, too, Jo," he said. "The rest of 'em were all way ahead of me and out o' sight for twenty minutes, maybe."

There followed a bantering conversation on the relative merits of the various teams, with minute explanation by the foremost skinners as to just why it was impossible for such miserable animals as the whites and the blacks to keep in sight of the rest. And for the time being, this ended the incident.

They left the delicately scented mountain country in due course and took up the long, weary journey over the desert. When they were near enough to the buttes to make out objects at their feet it became plain to all that the big outfit of Demarest, Spruce & Tillou had arrived and pitched its camp.

Shortly after they became aware of this a machine was discovered coming toward them from the distant tents. Then another put in an appearance, following the first. Jo now heard the cough of motors behind her, and, looking back, saw two trucks.

The first machine coming from the camps swung from the road when it neared Blink Keddie and waited, panting, until the outfit had passed it. Only the driver was in it, a man Jerkline Jo had never before seen. He lifted his hat politely as her whites rolled past, and she thanked him for his patience. Then he moved his car into the road and continued on toward the trucks. Looking back, Jo saw that all three stopped when they came together.

Now, from ahead, came the second car, and at the wheel sat Twitter-or-Tweet. He signaled Keddie to stop, and the outfit came to a halt.

"Hello, Jo, and fellas!" cried the beaming Mr. Tweet, descending from his car. "The man who just passed you in the touring car is Mr. Richard Huber, one of our first citizens. He's Ragtown's first merchant. He's gone to direct the trucks to come to Greater Ragtown with their loads. For, folks, Ragtown is moving in a body, with its traps on burros' and men's backs and in wagons and flivvers to the Tweet-to-be. Talked Huber out o' leasing, and sold him fifteen town lots, by golly! Half down, balance in three years—seven and a half per cent interest on deferred payments. Man of discernment. I'll proclaim to the high, green mountains! I'm on my way to collect our fee for allowin' the trucks to cross Paloma Rancho. How much you been held up for, Jo?"

"One hundred and twelve dollars," she told him.

"Just a minute. I'll hand it to you. Move on now, and I'll get back in the road and collect."

CHAPTER XIX

WHAT MADE THE WILD CAT

Jerkline Jo's wagon train snailed on over the desert toward the tents of Demarest's big camp. The tires of Mr. Tweet's shiny new car plunked down into the road, and that gentleman continued on toward the trucks and the machine of Ragtown's first merchant, Mr. Huber.

Hiram Hooker was riding with Jerkline Jo, and the two had been deep in their studies when the appearance of the various automobiles had distracted their attention. Hiram now climbed to the top of Jo's immense load of baled alfalfa, and, looking back, made reports to her.

"They're all together now," he said, "and having quite an argument. Tweet's swinging his arms about as if he wanted to fight.

"Now he's getting into his car. He and the storekeeper are turning in ahead of the trucks. Here they all come, Tweet in the lead!"

A little later Tweet shouted to Hiram to stop, and Hiram relayed the command to Jo, who called to her ten whites and brought them to a standstill. A little later five angry men hurried on foot alongside the wagon.

"Here's your hundred and twelve dollars, Jo," Tweet said

exultantly, passing the girl a sheaf of bills, "And that settles that. Now, Mr. Drummond, step over here and be introduced to Jerkline Jo Modock and my friend Hiram Hooker, from Wild-cat Hill. We'll see if you folks can't get together and conduct your affairs amicably."

Al Drummond, Hiram Hooker's one-time rival, was indeed there, dressed after the fashion of Mr. Tweet, and looking big and important and business-like. There was a dark scowl on his brow though as he came forward and nodded to Jo, but did not offer his hand.

"Well, I've been held up," he muttered, "and I'm going to see about it, but—"

"See about it all you want to, my friend," put in Tweet smoothly. "I have complete control of this land, and have the sole right to say who shall cross it and who shall not, and under what conditions. The ranch is posted, and everything is in order. This road is a new one, and you can't make the claim that it has been used so long that it must be considered in the nature of a public highway. You've not a leg to stand on; so every time you turn a wheel on this property it's goin' to cost you just what the last trip through the pass cost Jerkline Jo. You started something, my friend, and you can't finish it— that's all. Take your medicine like a sport."

"I'm going to keep up that mountain road, and I'm going to charge to move vehicles and teams over it," replied Drummond angrily. "My operations are legitimate. Yours are a holdup."

"Suit yourself." Tweet shrugged indifferently. "But, as I pointed out, you'll pay back every cent you collect from Jo. And, besides, you'll be out the expenses of your toll master."

"Others besides this lady will be crossing—lots of them later on," said Drummond. "I'm not going to keep that road in condition for the general public free of charge."

"Then the best thing you can do is make a dicker with Jo to share her part of the maintenance expenses, and you two divide the spoils that you collect from others."

"I can't agree to that," Jo put in hastily. "The road will serve very well as it is for our purposes, with a few repairs now and then which my boys can attend to themselves. We don't have to have a road in as good condition as the trucks will demand. We are entirely satisfied as matters stand."

Tweet slapped his thigh. "Spoken like a man!" he cried. "Now it's your move, Mr. Drummond. Fix your road all you want to and gouge travelers for the last cent you can, but this outfit travels through the mountains free, any way you can figure it out. Better write out a permanent permit for Jo, and do away with this collectin' back and forth and only breakin' even."

The truck man was so angry he scarcely could contain himself.

"It's a dirty, rotten deal!" he said between gritted teeth. "And this is only part of it. This bunch of roughnecks rolled a big boulder in the road after they'd passed yesterday, or some time, and it took us three hours to get it out. Had to hook on the trucks, and unload, and cut poles—and I don't know what all we didn't have to do to get the thing out so we could pass it. That's dirty, low-down business, and anybody who would do such a thing is a dirty piker—I don't care if she is a woman! If I've got to come out here and buck a wild woman with no principle I'll—"

Al Drummond paused abruptly. A mountain of bone and muscle had swooped down from the top of the load of baled hay and loomed large before him.

"Mr. Drummond," said a caressing voice with what seemed a totally disinterested drawl, "you're a liar!"

For a few seconds there was not a sound as Hiram Hooker stood before Drummond and eyed him placidly. The truck man's face had gone chalk-white. They were big men, both of them, and for all that Drummond's life had not been a rugged one, he was physically pretty much a man. Jo's skinners had come running back, and, with Tweet and Huber, looked on expectantly, sensing that a crisis between the two big huskies was imminent. Then came the voice of Jerkline Jo.

"Hiram," she said, "don't be hasty." Jerkline Jo had seen many a fight between big men of the outdoor life. It was no new experience, and there was not a quaver in her tones. She had been brought up where men settled matters with fists or guns or pick handles. "Listen, Hiram," she continued, "Mr. Drummond is telling the truth, I think, up to a certain point. When you boys were way ahead of me yesterday I heard a rumble behind me. Evidently a big boulder rolled down in the road after we had passed. Just the same I'll thank you, Hiram, to ask Mr. Drummond to apologize for accusing me of being responsible."

"Yes, ma'am," drawled Hiram, reverting to his old speech of the redwood forests. "Ye heard, Mr. Drummond. We didn't roll down any stone. I'd apologize now if I was you. That's best."

"Listen to the Gentle Wild Cat pur," said Heine Schultz, looking abstractedly up at the clouds.

"Well, you ain't me, you gangling hick!" said Drummond. "I saw footprints up above the rock wall that the stone fell from. It was pushed down. There are six of you. You could roll down a rock that we three couldn't budge. You even could hook on teams and drag it in the road behind you. Then when you came back, if it was still there, you could easily snake it out of your own way with these big horses."

"I reckon you're right," admitted Hiram. "But we didn't do that, so you oughta apologize to Jo." There was a deceptively soothing note in Hiram's tones. He seemed to be patiently pointing out the better course for Mr. Drummond to pursue, with no suggestion of what might be the penalty for guessing wrong.

"Well, I'll not apologize! I'm not a fool! That rock was rolled down. It—"

"You're a liar, Mr. Drummond," repeated Hiram.

Then they came together with a thud of big bodies and a shower of hooflike fists.

"Hi-yi!" yelled Blink Keddie. "What made our Gentle Wild Cat wild? Come on, boys! Back up ol' Wild Cat! Eat 'im, Hiram! Eat 'im alive! Le's send this outfit to the cleaners!"

"Blink!" called Jerkline Jo shrilly as the pugnacious skinner charged threateningly at Drummond's truck drivers. He came to a stop. "Don't make it general unless it becomes necessary," Jo added smoothly.

Meantime the two huge belligerents were hammering stunning blows at each other. About them now stood silent men in a circle, with the vast, hot desert stretching away on every side.

It developed shortly that Drummond was an athlete. He was quicker on his feet than Hiram and knew more tricks of offense and defense. Hiram, on the other hand, was a bull for strength and endurance, and in the big-woods country had maintained a reputation as a rough-and-tumble fighter and wrestler, though most of his encounters had been friendly bouts. Furthermore, he was cool as one of his Mendocino trout streams, and he fought in a businesslike way and never allowed himself to lose his temper.

He was therefore the more deadly, for his endurance was unbounded, and the punishment that Drummond was able to inflict seemed to have no effect whatever. And when one of his big fists found its mark a groan went up from Huber and Tweet. But Jerkline Jo and her rough-and-ready skinners, the latter all old fighters of the camps and used to unseemly sights, and the sickening sound of a big fist landing on giving bone, only watched and waited for the result.

In no time at all, it seemed, the face of the truck man was raw, while Hiram's showed only bruises. They clinched repeatedly, and soon it became apparent that Drummond was forcing these clinches.

"You've got 'im goin', Gentle Wild Cat!" yelled Tom Gulick. "Keep after his mush, ol'-timer! Pretty soon he won't be able to see you; then clean house with 'im!"

Drummond played for Hiram's wind now, but there was not an ounce of fat over the stomach that he hammered so repeatedly, and it seemed as if he were battering hard rubber. He was fast losing his own wind, for his life had not been so healthy as had that of the man from the Northern forests. Hiram's punishing fists were finding their target more frequently now, for the truck man's defense was failing him. He was slowing up—breathing hard—gulping.

"Guess it's time to stop it, Gentle Wild Cat," complacently observed Jim McAllen.

Then Hiram finished it. He crowded his big antagonist and beat him to his knees with blows that seemed to be skull crushing. Drummond's nose and mouth were badly damaged. Both eyes were mere slits, blazing between coloring puffs. One crushing, blow straight into his face as he came up defiantly sent him reeling about, head down, groping blindly.

"One more in the same place, Wild Cat!" called Gulick.

But Hiram desisted, though continuing to trail the groping man as he reeled through the sand, stumbling frequently.

"Lock the door, Hiram!" begged Heine Schultz. "It's all over but closin' up."

Hiram shook his head, and then Drummond wilted and sank in the sand.

Water was quickly provided, and the pulse of Jerkline Jo leaped as she saw that Hiram himself was taking the most prominent part in the whipped man's revival. It was fully five minutes before Drummond was conscious again; then Hiram helped to bear him to one of the trucks.

"Thank you, Hiram," Jo said softly as he returned.

He looked up into her eyes, which were moist round the rims. He had fought and won for his girl of romance, and he knew now that it had been she who through all the years had been beckoning him to come.

With a damp cloth she tenderly touched his bruised face here and there as the wagon train moved on again.

"Don't think any the worse of me, Hiram," she pleaded. "Perhaps I'm a roughneck, after all, as Drummond intimated. But I can't faint and carry on at the sight of blood and the sound of battering fists as most women do. I like a fight—a fair fight—a good fight—a manly fight. Life for me has been always a fight. I've learned not to shrink. Am I brutal—for a woman?"

"No," said Hiram. "I think I want you that way. Nobody could look into your eyes, Jo, and think you weren't tender and compassionate. I'd want my woman to be a fighter, I guess, when it was the time and place to fight."

Jerkline Jo's face was radiant with color, but she said softly:

"And I want my man to be a fighter. It's in my blood, it seems."

They said nothing more about it then, but each knew that love had spoken, and the unfriendly desert seemed a delectable land.

In camp that night Blink Keddie made a confession.

"Jo," he said, twisting and squirming, "me and Heine and Jim and Tom did ease that boulder into the road. We done it to get even for the empty water tank."

"Why, Blink!" Jo cried, aghast.

"We made it up to do it, and not even let Wild Cat in on the deal, 'cause he seemed to think like you did. So we rampsed our teams and got way ahead o' you folks, then stopped 'em when they was outa you folks' sight around the curves, and ran back through the trees with bars. We had our rock all picked out, and it didn't take the four o' us no time to ease her to the edge and let 'er plunk down in the road behind you. Then we run ahead through the woods and got on our wagons before you caught up. Now you know—what're you goin' to do about it?"

"Shall I have Wild Cat take you out, one at a time," Jo asked mischievously, after a thoughtful pause.

Keddie shrugged. "I ain't achin' for my portion o' that," he confessed, "but ol' Timberline will know he's been in a fight."

"It was despicable of you boys," Jo said sternly. "We'll not fight that way."

"But the empty water tank, Jo!" cried Heine. "My goat ain't through gettin' got about that deal yet. You gotta fight the devil with fire, as they say."

"I'm terribly sorry," Jo continued, her brow clouding. "That act is responsible for to-day's trouble, and we haven't yet heard the last of that, I'm afraid. And now *I'll* have to apologize to Mr. Drummond and explain."

Arthur Preston Hankins

"No, no, Jo! Let Hi-*ram* do it. He knows how to apologize. Think o' the water tank, Jo!"

"We have no proof that Drummond or his men were responsible for the empty tank, boys. I'm terribly sorry. I must think over what's best to be done now. We mustn't stoop to such methods. Even though we are subjected to underhand competition, we ourselves must fight fair and not descend to our enemy's level."

"You're aimin' to go to heaven, Jo," Gulick accused. "Drummond started the dirty work. We can show him a dozen tricks to offset emptyin' our tank. Better tell him not to do anythin' more. We'll stop his clock if he does."

"You'll do it fairly, then, or you'll not drive teams for me," Jo emphatically told them.

Their silence disturbed her. They knew that she could not do without them. Even as matters stood, she could have used one more jerkline skinner could she have found one good enough to handle her much-loved animals. They were loyal to her, a stanch little army, hard to defeat if their crude but forceful methods of fighting could be brought into play. All of them looked upon the girl as their especial charge in life, and whenever they fought for her they would, with only her well-being in mind, fight as they saw fit. Still, she could control them if forewarned of their plans. She always had controlled them—not by condemning and issuing orders and threatening, but by the exercise of her sweet womanly personality; for there was not a man of them but loved her and fairly worshiped at her shrine.

CHAPTER XX

DRUMMOND'S PASSENGER

The summer progressed, and great changes were wrought on the desert. To the last soul Ragtown moved from its first location into the hospitable arms of Mr. Tweet—but Tweet's hospitality demanded its price. Outfit after outfit came crawling across the desert to pitch camp somewhere along the line and begin its portion of the big work in band. There was a post office at Ragtown, twenty or more saloons, dance halls and gambling dens combined, restaurants, tent hotels, stores, and even a bank and a motion-picture show. Thousands of rough, hard-drinking, hard-fighting men thronged the mushroom town, and it resembled a mining town of California's early days. Miners and cattlemen, too, made the town headquarters, and there were frequent fights and an occasional shooting scrape. The cost of everything was high. Money flowed freely, as did bootleg jackass brandy. It seemed that the prohibition enforcement officers had been unable to locate the infant town. The rough, unrestrained life of the frontier was rife at Ragtown, and Twitter-or-Tweet Orr Tweet gleaned shekels right and left.

Jerkline Jo had not seen Al Drummond to speak with him after the fight. He had been laid up for a week from the terrible battering that Hiram had given him, and when he was about again he left the country in his touring car.

His drivers continued to transport freight to the new Ragtown and to certain independent contractors who had reached the work. In truth, it developed that there was plenty of hauling to keep both outfits busy, and Jerkline Jo was making money hand over fist, as was every one who had services to offer or something to sell.

Tehachapi Hank no longer stood like an ogre guarding the portals to the mountain pass. Drummond had been beaten on that deal, and the gunman's removal was an admission of defeat. Consequently, Tweet exacted no charge for the trucks to cross his ranch. Things were running smoothly between the two freighting enterprises, and Jerkline Jo hoped against hope that there would be no more trouble. But she had not liked the baleful look in Drummond's eye when she caught it on the street in Ragtown one evening. It was plain that he considered great humiliation had been heaped upon him, and that he was waiting and watching for an opportunity for revenge.

Then one day she met him face to face in Julia, and stepped to him to tell him about the boulder in the road. His glance was like a knife thrust as he turned on his heel and stalked away before she could speak. After that, of course, she made no further effort to enlighten him.

As the weeks passed it developed that Orr Tweet was not the slowest salesman in California, where salesmen—especially land salesmen—achieve their greatest triumphs. Not only did he sell lots and building sites in Ragtown, but he disposed of the surrounding acreage to would-be ranchers and speculators, and had been able with ease, he informed his old friends, to meet his second payment on the ranch. He urged Jo to invest her earnings in the company, and after consideration she resolved to take a chance with him; for here and there, where wells had been sunk and pumping apparatus installed, the once barren land was turning green and showing evidences of rich and productive soil.

So things stood, or refused to stand, in Ragtown and the vicinity when Drummond drove in one day with no less a passenger than a pretty girl, all pink and white, named Lucy Dalles. Hiram Hooker came face to face with her in Ragtown's boisterous business street an hour after her arrival, for Jo's freight outfit was at rest there for the night.

Lucy was as pretty in her petite, doll-like way as when she had so fascinated him in the city, but now he could not help comparing her hothouse beauty with the brown-skinned, outdoor desirability of Jerkline Jo. Jo could have picked up this frail, silk-garbed creature and thrown her overhead; yet in pure womanliness and tenderness Lucy was not her equal. Jerkline Jo was a queen—a ruler—a fearless woman with a purpose in life, big of body and soul and brain. Lucy Dalles was merely a pretty girl, with an ambition for money and life's frivolous pleasures. Hiram understood this now.

She greeted him glowingly, and called him by his first name.

"I told you I was coming," she cried, giggling. "And isn't this rich? If only I were writing scenarios now!"

"Aren't you?" asked Hiram.

"No, I gave it up. They got too exacting for me, and began buying the picture rights of books and magazine stories by established authors in preference to original scripts for the screen. I was a piker, anyway—nothing in me, I guess. So I threw up the sponge."

"You're still a waitress, then?"

She looked at him archly. "Not on your sweet young life!" and she laughed. "I didn't throw ambition overboard when I quit writing scenarios. Writing in any form is usually a slow road to success, I've learned. I never wanted to be a writer just for the sake o' the work. I want jack, and lots of it, and what it'll buy."

Hiram felt a sudden disgust for her and her sordid aims in life. But to appear polite he asked:

"What are you doing, then?"

"Everybody I can," she retorted. "I worked in a beauty parlor for a little as a hairdresser and manicure. I'm out for the money, Hiram. I'm not a pickpocket yet, but that's because I don't know how to be one. But if you've got any loose change in your pockets watch out. I'm out for the coin. But here comes Al. He brought me down. He's going to set me up in business."

"Drummond?" he asked. "He and I don't speak. We had a little trouble."

Again she arched her penciled brows. "He didn't tell me," she said. "He'll be sore at me talkin' to you then. See him over there by that saloon? He's stopped and is scowling at us. Well, I'll just stick with you to show him his place. Take me somewhere, Hiram; I want to see the life."

Hiram did not know what to say. He would have preferred to terminate the conversation. Lucy Dalles held no fascination for him now. Hiram had met and loved a woman without parallel in his brief experience of life. But he could not be impolite, so he sauntered down the street with the girl, trying to make conversation and hoping that Drummond would not be offended all over again.

In all the resorts men and women were crowding before the bar, gambling with abandon or dancing.

"Buy me a drink, Hiram," Lucy pleaded. "I just want to go into one of these places. Women do it here, I understand."

Hiram shrugged and led her into the Palace Dance Hall, conducted by a notorious character, who followed big construction camps, called "Ghost" Falcott because of his chalk-white skin.

It was pay day at Demarest, Spruce & Tillou's, and the Palace was crowded. They found a place at the bar, however, and the girl stood looking over the half-drunken throng with eager eyes, now and then casting a glance through the door to see if Drummond was following her.

Their drinks had just been served when into the dive, with a grinning construction stiff on each arm, marched Jerkline Jo, laughing gayly.

This was no new sight. Frequently Hiram had seen his adventure girl in such places, laughing and chatting with old friends of the grade. Always, it seemed, they respected her and took her actions for granted.

"Hello, Gentle Wild Cat!" Jo called, catching sight of him. Then she noticed that he was with the girl, and a quick look of puzzlement came in her dark eyes.

Hiram made haste to call her.

"I want to introduce you," he said quickly.

Jo turned, still holding to the arms of the stiffs, and Hiram made the introduction. Jo responded pleasantly, and the look that came in her eyes told Hiram that she remembered the name and knew who Lucy was.

"Sorry I can't join you, Hiram," said Jo. "These plugs have got me dead to rights, and I've promised to set 'em up to the house."

She released the arms of the stiffs, and, cupping her hands about her mouth, shouted above the general din:

"Drinks for the house on Jerkline Jo! Le's go!"

Some one nudged Hiram on the other side, and he turned to find Orr Tweet.

"Did you ever see the likes o' that Jerkline Jo?" he said admiringly. "What a woman, Hiram! She can get away with anything, and there ain't a stiff on the grade that would think any the worse of her for it. She's pure-hearted and clean-minded, and everybody knows it and treats her like the lady she is. But say—For Heaven's sake! Look who's here!"

His steel-blue eyes had taken in Lucy, who stood studying Jerkline Jo, the center of a crowd of rough, appreciative men who wrung her hands right and left.

Lucy turned and flashed Tweet a bright smile. "I remember you, o' course," she said, shaking hands. "They tell me you hit the ball an awful bang down here in Ragtown. I always knew you were there when you talked to me up in Frisco."

For several minutes, while bartenders worked frantically to supply Jo's big order, Tweet and Lucy talked, and Hiram watched Jo. Then Tweet excused himself and hurried away after some man—a prospective citizen of Ragtown, no doubt —and Lucy turned to Hiram.

"So that's Jerkline Jo, is it?" she said half scornfully. "What is she, Hiram?"

"A lady," said Hiram with a dangerous note of warning in his tones.

Lucy sensed it and shrugged. "Maybe she is," she said lightly. "I don't know anything about her beyond what I've heard, of course—except that she's a heart-breaker—a man-killer. But what's she doing here?" she could not help tacking on.

"I might come back and ask you what you're doing here," Hiram retorted coldly.

Lucy shrugged. "Oh, I don't make any pretenses of piety— now," she said significantly. Then, casting a defiant glance at him, she produced a silver cigarette case, took a cigarette from it, and begged for the end of his cigar at which to light it. "They say Jerkline Jo is grabbing off big jack. How 'bout it?" She puffed indolently, greatly to her companion's disgust.

"She works hard and earns money," Jo's supporter defended. "She raised the wages of all of us, too, as soon as business began to look up. We skinners get ninety dollars a month and board now."

"Ninety dollars a month!" Lucy said jeeringly. "D'ye call that money! I didn't think you'd continue to be such a fish as long as this, Hiram."

"Well, I'm investin' it," said Hiram. "It may be more some day."

Luck looked suddenly into Hiram's eyes, then let her lashes cover her own.

"I guess this pious Jerkline Jo has got you goin'," she observed.

"I work for her," said Hiram awkwardly.

"Any man would, I guess. Men are all suckers."

Hiram said nothing to this, and presently, stating that he would be obliged to return to camp, asked Lucy if she was ready to go.

Rather petulantly she gave in, and just outside the door they encountered the glowering Al Drummond.

"Lucy," he said sharply, "come here!"

"I'll have to go," Lucy said to Hiram. "See you later, honey boy from the woods. Good night!"

Hiram saw Drummond take a step and roughly grab Lucy's arm as she tripped up to him. They walked away, plainly indulging in a heated argument.

"'Honey boy,' huh!" and Hiram snorted. "Men are suckers—till they meet a regular woman!"

He hurried back to camp and rolled himself in his blankets without further thought of the girl who had caused him to make such a fool of himself in San Francisco. Had he but known it the advent of Lucy Dalles in Ragtown was to have a great deal to do with the future fortunes of both Jerkline Jo and himself.

CHAPTER XXI

LUCY SEES A PROSPECT

There was so much freighting that summer that the combined outfits of Jerkline Jo Modock and Al Drummond were taxed to capacity. The new settlers made constant demands upon them, and, though their wants were puny in comparison with those of the camps, Jo accommodated them whenever she could. Water had been struck at the surprisingly shallow depth of forty-five feet in some places, and many pumping plants were transported over the mountains. Things looked as if Twitter-or-Tweet was about due to make his fortune, and Jo kept investing more and more of her surplus earnings, and he was meeting his payments promptly. There was talk of Ragtown eventually being made a division point. If this transpired, the railroad shops would be erected there, and the permanent success of the town would be assured. Already a few venturesome souls were building permanent structures whenever they were fortunate enough to get building materials hauled in.

Drummond's five-ton trucks seemed to be meeting all requirements, and he had added to his fleet. Jo, however, remained conservative. She had seen rag towns spring up on railroad grades before—many of them—only to disappear forever with the laying of the steel. Still, she had confidence in the farming possibilities of Paloma Rancho—but she bought no more equipment, principally, perhaps, because she could not get desirable jerkline skinners, and because extra equipment would mean more work for her, more time taken from her studies. She was content with a good thing so far as financial success was concerned—her great ambition was for an education.

Drummond, of course, was also making money; but he fell a prey to the lure of the free-and-easy life of the frontier town, and gambled and drank perpetually. There were stories of big losses at faro, under which Drummond did not always bear up as a good sport should.

As for Lucy Dalles, that ambitious young woman entered with gusto into the feverish life of Ragtown. Drummond had leased a shooting-gallery concession from the accommodating Tweet, and had ensconced the girl behind the rifles—or in front of them—to run the gallery.

So she confided to Hiram Hooker, when he passed along Ragtown's main thoroughfare one night, and for the first time saw her on exhibition in the gallery. She had partitioned off one corner of the gallery and set up a manicure and hair-dressing parlor. Of mornings, when business in the gallery was dull, she made many an extra dollar by beautifying the women of Ragtown.

"Yes, there's money in it," she said. "Al had the gallery stunt in mind when he brought me down, so I quit the beauty parlor where I was working in Frisco and got a job in a shooting gallery and learned how to run one and to keep my noodle from getting in front of a gun. My face is my fortune, after all, Hiram boy. One look at my smile, and the hicks come right in and pick up a rifle. I'm coinin' money, and I'm having the time of my young life. Last night a miner bet me five dollars against a kiss he could knock over ten ducks in ten shots. He did it, and I paid up like a sport. It got the gang started at the game, and in the end I grabbed off thirty bucks, and only kissed twice. Pretty soft—what? I guess you're horrified, Hiram?" She glanced at him with coquettish defiance.

"Disgusted," Hiram could truthfully have said, but he only grinned and thanked his stars for his escape.

Lucy's dark eyes flashed daggers at the broad back of Hiram Hooker as he left her and swung along indifferently up the street. With a woman's intuition she had known in San Francisco that the big, handsome countryman with the soft, drawling voice had fallen a victim to her charms. Now, because of Jerkline Jo, he was utterly indifferent to her. Lucy was piqued, angry at him, angrier at Jerkline Jo. She did not love Hiram, but she wanted him to love her, and though she did not want him she wanted no other woman to own him.

"I'll fix you one o' these days, you big hick!" she threatened between clenched teeth.

Summer passed all too quickly for those who labored incessantly, and the winter rains set in. They at once grew harder and more frequent, and then it poured as it does only in the West. Snow fell in the mountains. Then the activities of Al Drummond ceased abruptly.

No wonder, for often as high as twenty teams were hooked on to the enormous wagons of Jerkline Jo, and every animal was obliged to pull to the limit of his strength to move the terrific weight, hub-deep in the clinging mud. This did not tend to improve the road, of course, and all of Drummond's efforts to corduroy it and otherwise preserve a firm path for his machines were unavailing. The tortoise had won the race!

Drummond had gambled away his profits, and now it was whispered about that he still owed money on his trucks. Before the last of November he gave up in despair, allowed his trucks to be taken by the mortgagees, and settled down to a life of gambling on the proceeds of his shooting-gallery concession.

One day there trudged into Ragtown a strange figure, marked by the desert, bent and old, in the wake of six lamenting burros laden with mining supplies and tools. He gave the name of Basil Filer, and said that he was seeking gold. Ragtown promptly wrote him down as a crazy prospector. His eye caught the eye of Lucy Dalles, leaning over her carpeted counter between her rifles, and when he had made camp he limped along and accosted her.

"Come in and try a string, Uncle," she begged with the little pout she had found so effective in coercing male humanity into her lair. "An old desert rat like you oughta hit the bull's-eye every shot."

Filer grinned and stepped up to the counter, eying the girl from under heavy, fierce eyebrows that looked as if the dust of a thousand trails had settled in them. Lucy lowered her dark lashes and looked demure.

"B'long on the desert, girlie?" rumbled the deep voice of the old prospector.

"Sure, Uncle."

"Uh-huh. And how old might ye be, now?"

"Nearly twenty-two."

"Uh-huh—pretty near twenty-two. That's nice. Where's yer paw and maw?"

"They're both dead," Lucy told him, trying to appear innocent and unsophisticated as she lifted her glance to his face.

"Maybe now yer paw was a desert prospector," he suggested.

"Uh-huh." Lucy nodded her fluffy head vigorously up and down. This was another childlike action which she had found pleasing to men—especially the older men. Of course she was lying like a little sailor; but "Uncle" seemed interested in her, and business was dull just then. She would pretend to be all that he seemed to wish her to be as long as she could successfully follow his conversational leads.

"What do they call you, girlie?" he asked next.

"Lucy."

"Lucy, eh? Lucy what, now?"

"Lucy Dalles."

"Dalles, huh? Dalles!" His weird old eyes, peculiarly tinted from years of looking into the mirage-draped distances of the desert, were strangely reminiscent.

"Maybe that ain't your right name, though," he kept on feelingly.

"Maybe not," replied Lucy quite truthfully. After all, she had only her father's and her mother's word for it. For all she knew she might be the reincarnation of the Queen of Sheba. "Let's try a shot, Uncle," she added, sensing deep water ahead.

Indolently he picked up a .22 rifle, and rang the bell of her most difficult bull's-eye target eight shots out of ten. He paid her and seemed in nowise elated over her fulsome praise, designed to keep him shooting.

He took up his long cane again. "I'll drift up the drag a ways," he said, "and see what's goin' on. Nothin' but desert owls lived here when I traveled through last—two years ago. I'll be back. Maybe I'll want to ast ye a few p'inted questions. Will ye answer, eh?"

"Sure," she told him lightly, whacking her gum for emphasis. "Come and pour your heart out to me, Uncle—I'll listen."

Lucy had taken more of the well-filled buckskin poke that the old man had pulled from the neck of his greasy shirt to pay her for the pastime.

She leaned out and craned her neck to watch him moving up the street, glancing through doors and openly investigating on every side.

Her intuition told her that the gray old rat had something on his mind. Lonely old soul that he was, she reasoned, he was bashful and at a loss how to conduct himself in the unfamiliar presence of a woman. "When he's all gowed up he'll talk my head off," she decided. "He's going to fortify himself now. Guess I'll have to look into this."

When the bent, plodding figure had disappeared through the entrance to Ghost Falcott's Palace Dance Hall, Lucy called across the street to a boy sitting on the edge of the new board sidewalk. The boy crossed to her and she handed him a dime.

"Find Al Drummond and tell him I want to see him at once," she directed.

A little later Al Drummond presented himself. His face showed the effects of a sleepless night, but he was already refortified with jackass brandy for the ordeals of the day, and was in nowise stupid.

They leaned on the carpeted counter, heads close together, and talked in lowered voices.

"What this old bird has got on his chest I can't tell," Lucy explained. "But I played up to him, and if he gets all gowed up he'll spill it. He's crazy as they make 'em, Al. It may not amount to anything at all, but I'm for always lookin' into such little things. You never can tell, Al. Maybe this'll be good. Anyway, he's got a leather bag that's heavy with jack, and he won't need that when he hits the trail again. Warm up to him and get 'im started, then steer him to me."

"Wise little kid," Al Drummond commented. "Leave it to me."

The male plotter experienced no difficulty in finding the grizzled desert rat. He was evidently a self-starter, having brought his own, and, all alone at Ghost Falcott's bar, he was pouring raw jackass brandy down a throat that seemed urgently in need of it. Seeing that he was satisfactorily working out his own destruction, Drummond shot craps to divert himself until the prospector should become mellowed to a point where it was safe to approach him.

It seemed though that the old man had an enormous capacity. An hour passed, and, though he drank repeatedly on his high-lonesome, he seemed little the worse for it. Drummond patiently watched and waited. He knew that with some newly distilled brandy does not take immediate effect, but that drunkenness comes on suddenly when the victim least expects it.

CHAPTER XXII

JERKLINE JO'S SURPRISE

Meantime events were happening out in the street which were to have a distinct bearing on Lucy and Al's plot to separate Basil Filer from the contents of his buckskin poke.

These events, however, were quite commonplace on the face of them. The first was the arrival of Jerkline Jo's wagon train, loaded to the gunwales with case goods, general merchandise, and food for stock.

The arrival of Jerkline Jo and her proud huskies always was an event of importance at Ragtown. They made a picture as the heavy eight and ten-horse teams with the hundreds of bells a-jingle rolled the immense wagons down the street, while Jo's skinners, quite aware of the furor they were creating, called "Gee" and "Haw" and manipulated their jerklines unnecessarily, for the sole purpose of awing the spectators. One wagon was stopped at Huber's store; the rest continued on through to Demarest, Spruce & Tillou's Camp Number One, a half mile beyond the town.

It was Jo's whites that had been brought to a halt before Huber's. The proprietor came out and asked that the load be discharged in the rear, as he had just completed a new freight platform at the back entrance.

"Right!" called Jo. Then, "Annie! Ned! Feel of it, white folks!

Bert! Snip! All together. Let's go!"

Like a well-trained company of infantry, the ten whites leaned to the collars, and the eight tons behind them moved off as easily as a baby buggy. The hub of all eyes, the attractive girl with cries of "Gee" and "Haw" and picturesque manipulation of the jerkline, swung her team around the corner and into the alley. Men with whom she had a standing agreement to unload freight for her when their services were needed already had come through the store, and were waiting for her on the new platform. Dexterously she guided the team with the jerkline and by word of mouth, so that the load crept along not two inches from the edge of the platform and came to a stop.

She left her team standing, for Hiram Hooker was to ride back on her black saddle pony for them as soon as the remainder of the outfit had reached the camp. Whistling, with her leather chaps swishing, she walked through the store, smiling right and left at the clerks.

"Well, Jo, how was the trip?" asked Huber as she leaned on the edge of the window to the proprietor's office and handed him her bills of lading.

"Oh, much the same as usual," she replied. "The whirlwinds gave us some trouble. They're prevalent this time of year on the desert, and are sometimes fearfully annoying—especially so if it's been dry for a few days and the top of the sand isn't moist."

"What do they do to you, Jo?" asked Huber interestedly.

"Drive you crazy sometimes," she laughed. "They're just like little cyclones, you know. You'll be moving along serenely, when one of them will steal up behind you, and before you know it you're the center of a maelstrom of sand and dust, unable to see, your hat gone, your mouth and nose filled with—well, about everything that the desert boasts of. I was feeding hay to a pair of my horses this noon, when a whirlwind slipped up on me. I threw myself flat on the ground, as one must do or be swept off his feet, and when it had passed there was not one scrap of that dry alfalfa hay where I'd thrown it. I found my hat a mile distant. My nostrils and ears and eyes and mouth were literally loaded with dirt and fine hay chaff. And my hair! Heavens!" She put her hands to it. "I usually wear it in braids, you know, but to-day I thought I'd be smart and perk up a bit. Now I'll have to 'go to the cleaners,' as Heine says."

Huber laughed. "Say, Jo," he said, "that reminds me. There's a girl here that'll give you a shampoo. She runs a shooting gallery, and has a little beauty parlor on the side. Oh, we're getting quite urban at Ragtown. We'll have Turkish baths next. Go to see her—she'll fix you up."

"I'll just do that," said Jo, and went out on the street.

Then for the first time she became aware that Lucy Dalles was the proprietress of Ragtown's beauty parlor, and even then she did not find it out until she was inside the parlor and Lucy entered by a side door that connected with the gallery. It was too late to back out gracefully, even had Jo been inclined to do so.

"Why, hello!" she said. "I didn't know you ran this place. Miss Dalles, isn't it? We met in the Palace Dance Hall one night, didn't we?"

Lucy smiled professionally. She did not like this strong, rugged, beautiful girl who strode along the street with such a firm, conquering tread and left men gaping after her. Still, she could not afford to show her dislike.

"Oh, yes—I remember you perfectly well," she said. "Who wouldn't remember the famous Jerkline Jo! Is there something I can do for you?"

"Mercy, yes!" laughed Jo. "One look at me ought to show you

that." She told about the whirlwind, and Lucy smiled thinly, and indicated the chair.

Jo climbed into it, and was bundled with clean, perfumed towels that caused her to grow reminiscent of school days and dainty dresses and all the things that as Jerkline Jo she had been obliged to put aside.

"Do you know," she said as Lucy began her delicate ministrations, "I've never before in my life been in a beauty parlor."

"You are one of the few women who do not need one," said Lucy, forced to a sincere compliment by the undeniable, fresh beauty of her patron.

"Oh, thank you!" said Jo with a laugh. "It's not just that, though. I expect, if the truth were told, I've needed the services of a beauty artist for years. But I was raised in a construction camp, you know, until I was pretty much of a young lady, and such things were entirely out of my ken. Then at Palada, where my foster father eventually settled and went into the freighting business and running a store, we were not so progressive as Ragtown even. So when I went to boarding school in the Middle West I was virtually immune from many of the new fads. You, then, are the first person that ever washed my hair— except myself, of course. I remember even that my dear old foster mother always made me wash it when I was a kid—once a year perhaps," she ended with a laugh. "Poor ma! She had little enough time to fuss with a child's hair, cooking for big, hungry men all the time as she was, and driving a slip team while she was resting."

Jo was merely trying to make conversation, for she could think of little to say that she thought might touch a responsive cord in the fluffy girl from the city. Jerkline Jo was a man's woman. She could talk about almost anything that other women could not bring into their conversation.

"You've had an interesting life, haven't you?" observed Lucy, manipulating Jo's scalp till the skin tingled pleasantly. "I wish I could have met you when I was writing moving-picture scenarios. What a character you would have made for the heroine of a Western thriller!"

"Oh, you've written scenarios! How interesting! And—and—if this isn't trespassing on delicate ground—sold them?"

Lucy tittered. "Yes, I sold some of them," she replied.

This gave them a basis for conversation, and they progressed famously until the grinning face of a railroad-construction stiff appeared suddenly at the door.

"Hey!" he called to other stiffs behind him. "Look wot's goin' on!"

"Hello, there, 'Squinty' Malley!" and Jo laughed. "Get your face out of that door. This is sacred ground, you roughneck!"

"Look at Jo!" derided Squinty, an old friend of the girl's in many a half-remembered camp. "Hey, youse plugs, gadder 'round here and lamp Jerkline Jo dollin' up! Good night!"

"Beat it now!" Jo reiterated.

"Say, dis here's good!" retorted Squinty. "I to't youse was a reg'lar woman, Jo! Youse know more 'bout cuffin' ole Jack an' Ned dan youse do 'bout fixin' yer hair. Say, lady," he addressed Lucy, "fix 'er up—hey? Doll 'er up proper, an' le's see wot de ol'-timer looks like."

"You'll oblige me by getting out of the door," said Lucy indignantly.

"Oh, don't scold the poor eel!" pleaded Jerkline Jo. "He doesn't know any better. So you want to see me dolled up, do you, Squint? By George, you're on, old-timer! I've got some glad rags here in this burg. Go on now! I'll be the queen of the ball to-night!"

"Lucy," Jo laughed familiarly when the tramps had vanished, "fix up my hair the best you possibly can. Give me the latest, will you? I'm going to have some fun to-night."

An hour later, when darkness had settled over Ragtown and the night's revel was on, there entered the Palace Dance Hall a figure that brought gamblers from their absorbing games, stopped the dizzying whirl of the dancers, and caused glasses that were halfway to eager lips to pause in mid-air.

Jerkline Jo's almost black hair was piled on top of her head in bewildering fashion, and set off with flashing rhinestone ornaments, furnished by Lucy Dalles. Jo wore a semievening dress of pale-blue silk, and Lucy had powdered her face and neck until little contrast could be noted between skin that had braved the desert winds and that which had been protected. Jo wore fashionable slippers with great shell buckles and high French heels. She cast a dazzling smile over the silent assemblage, then threw back her glorious head and let her laughter ring.

That laugh revealed her identity.

"Jerkline Jo!" came a chorus of yells, and men stared at her, while women drew together in groups, their comments expressed in lowered voices.

As they crowded around her Lucy Dalles peered in at the door, a contemptuous sneer on her lips.

"Have a good time, old girl!" she muttered, grinding her little white teeth. "But I learned something to-day that'll set *you* back a step or two. Get me to doll you up, will you, you impossible roughneck? You'll pay for that!"

CHAPTER XXIII

DRUMMOND WEAVES A DREAM

Shortly after Jerkline Jo left the beauty parlor of Lucy Dalles, mischievously bent on giving Ragtown a harmless little shock, Al Drummond sidled up to the old prospector at the bar in the Palace Dance Hall.

"Hello, old-timer," he said with a cheerful smile. "How's prospecting these days?"

The old desert rat fixed a filmy eye on him. "Have a shot," he invited with the suggestion of a thickening tongue.

"Thanks, old hoss. Don't care if I do. That is, if you'll have one with me."

They drank, and Drummond promptly ordered another. A lowering of his left eyelid gave the bartender his instructions, and a sprinkling of powder found its way into the glass that was thumped before Basil Filer.

Not long after this he became agreeable to anything that Al Drummond might suggest. Al took him from place to place, always standing his share of the exorbitant prices demanded in Ragtown, and finally suggested that they try their marksmanship as a diversion.

"Good!" agreed Filer gutturally. "Little girl, eh? Pretty!" He winked knowingly at Drummond. "I wanta have talk with her. I know who she is. B'en trailin' her fer years. Le's go, pardner. You're goo' scout. So'm I—hey?"

"You bet your sweet life you're a good scout! Come on—we'll have a time to-night."

Drummond had previously sent a boy to Lucy with a note informing her that the come-on was about ripe for plucking, and telling her to put some one else in charge of the gallery and be in readiness. Lucy had sent out and found the man who at times relieved her, and when Drummond and the old gold-seeker lurched up she was free to act as the circumstances might demand.

The two men fired at the targets for a little, Filer failing to display the same wonderful marksmanship which he had done earlier in the evening. Eventually Lucy invited the two to go back into the little cabin in the rear of the gallery where she carried on her trifling domestic activities. Filer readily agreed to this, and presently the three were seated around a table in Lucy's cabin, with a coal-oil lamp on it, a deck of cards suggestively in evidence, and a bottle of precious brandy and glasses. Lucy had brought from San Francisco her leopard-skin rug, the overstuffed chairs, and her other extravagances in house furnishings. Their contrast with the new pine walls of the cabin produced an effect quite startling and bizarre. Basil Filer saw none of it, however. He became very drowsy when he was seated. Al Drummond winked at Lucy.

The girl shook her head, and presently, seeing that the prospector was almost asleep, leaned toward her fellow conspirator and whispered:

"Don't hurry about getting his roll. Try to liven him up and get him to talking. I'm curious. He's got something on his mind that may make that buckskin bag look like thirty cents."

"Get the jack," ordered Al. "To-morrow he won't even

remember he ever saw us. You're letting your story-telling instinct warp your judgment, Lucy. You're looking for mysteries. I'll get that roll right now."

"No, leave it, Al, please! You can get it later, if I'm wrong. But I just feel that this old fella's got something locked up in his breast. Rouse him and leave him to me. I'll make him talk. I'm sorry you doped him. You may have spoiled everything."

At this instant she looked up to see the bleary old eyes fixed on her intently.

"Feeling better, Uncle?" she asked lightly. "I've got some bromo-seltzer. I'll give you a shot; it will liven you up. Don't want to go down and out so early in the evening, old sport!"

"Desert girl, huh?" thickly muttered Basil Filer. "Huh—I know somethin' 'bout you. You was found on the desert, wasn't ye—when you's li'l' girl—baby girl? I know. Can't fool o' Filer. B'en huntin' you f'r years." He closed his eyes again, and his head sank forward on his breast.

Lucy shook him awake and prepared a dose of bromo-seltzer, which he readily drank at her command.

"How did you know about me, Uncle?" she asked. "What you said is the truth. I was found on the desert here when I was a baby girl. But how did you know? Tell me all about it. Do you know my father's name?"

"Sure! Sure! Name was Len-Len-Len-Leonard Prince. You're Jean Prince. Len Prince was m' ol' pardner. I'm lookin'—lookin' for the claim Len Prince and me and The Chink found—and lost ag'in. Rich! Yellow with gol'. You're Jean Prince—I know. I c'n prove it by your head. Tha's what I wanta see—yer head—down under the hair. That'll tell me you're Baby Jean Prince. Then I c'n find the gold."

Lucy clutched Al Drummond's arm. "Listen to him! Listen to

him!" she breathed.

Hiram Hooker stood aghast in the entrance of the Palace Dance Hall. All eyes within were focused on a couple waltzing in the center of the floor to low music. The man was a Mr. Dalworth, Ragtown's new banker, in charge of the branch of a Los Angeles banking institution that had been opened in the frontier camp. The girl, smiling and radiant and glistening with pale-blue silk and gems, was his adventure girl, Jerkline Jo.

Never had Hiram seen Jo in anything but a flannel shirt, Stetson hat, and chaps or divided riding skirt. Despite the fact that she was making money fast and that he was working for her at ninety dollars a month, Hiram had not before looked upon her as entirely out of his reach. He was learning fast, and had lost much of his backwoods uncouthness. He loved Jerkline Jo as only a big-hearted, simple-souled man can love a woman. Some day, he had told himself, he would do some-thing to make himself worthy of her, for he never would ask her to marry him while he was in her employ. He was too proud to ask an independent girl to marry him when he had nothing to offer.

That rare feminine creature gliding so gracefully over the floor with the dapper, well-dressed banker, however, plunged Hiram into the depths of despair. Financially, mentally, and now socially, he felt her altogether out of his world. He had forgotten until now her days at school and in polite society.

It did not make him think the worse of her to see her dancing in a saloon, with rough men from the cities standing about and looking on admirably. Ragtown was Ragtown, and people did things here which would have ostracized them from decent society elsewhere. It was not this that hurt; he knew that the girl was pure-minded and that her morals were flawless, despite what prudish persons—of which there were none in Ragtown—might have thought of her choice of the place which she chose to satisfy her whim of the evening. Jo was one of those rare souls who can pass among evil men and women and not only not be contaminated, but preserve an unsullied reputation, too. It was the dress and the glittering tones and the wonderful coiffure, and her gentlemanly, well-groomed partner of the dance, that caused him to turn away, bitter and broken in spirit.

"Well, how do you like her to-night?" came a taunting voice.

Lucy Dalles had stepped beside him and peering in at the revel.

"Some class, eh? Some lady, I'll say! Oh, sure!"

Hiram could have choked her, but without a remark he sped away from her into the night.

It was then that Lucy Dallas clenched her teeth and hurled invective at the radiant girl within.

She left the scene and hurried back to her little cabin, where the crazy prospector, Basil Filer, lay in a heap on the floor, snoring loudly.

A moment after her entry Al Drummond came in again with another man following him.

"How much jack did you leave him?" he whispered to the girl.

"I left it all. It's safest. What I copied from the paper will be worth a thousand times what's in that money bag."

"Just the same, I want money now—to-night," Drummond said, and, stooping, pulled the poke from the shirt front of the unconscious miner.

"Take only half of it, then," Lucy pleaded. "Then he'll think he spent that much. Don't be a piker, Al. You've got something big to work for, and you try to spoil it by rolling a stiff for a few dollars."

Drummond grunted, slipped a wad of bills into his trousers pocket, and replaced the poke in the desert rat's shirt.

"All right, Stool," he said to the other man. "You take his head; I'll take his feet."

A little later a train of pack burros moved away from Ragtown into the desert night.

A mile from town the man Stool halted them and waited, and presently heard the chug of a motor. Soon Al Drummond drove up in the last of his five-ton trucks, in the bottom of which, tossed about, lay the still unconscious form of the old prospector.

The two men worked swiftly, and slanted two twelve-inch planks two inches thick from the rear end of the truck to the ground. With ropes about the necks of the desert rat's six burros, they hauled and hammered and coaxed them one by one aboard the truck. Then on into the night they drove, over the vast, black desert.

Seventy-five miles from Ragtown they stopped the car, and unloaded the burros and their snoring master. They rolled the man in his blankets, then set the burros' packs about in orderly array and loosed the little animals to crop the bunch grass that was green and succulent in winter. From one pack bag they took cooking utensils and other articles, and ranged them about on the ground as the old man himself might have done upon making camp.

"He'll wake up to-morrow and think he dreamed about Ragtown," chuckled Drummond.

"He sure will know he's nutty then," said Stool.

They climbed once more into the truck, and before dawn were back in the city of tents and new pine shacks.

CHAPTER XXIV

WHAT HAPPENED AT THE LAKE

Shortly before dusk on the night following Jerkline Jo's revel in Ragtown, the empty wagons of her train rumbled to the highest point in the mountain pass and were drawn up side by side, like an artillery organization in "battery-front" formation, on the shores of the mountain lake.

Jo's fireless cooker had been working for her throughout the trip, and while her bantering skinners cared for the teams and greased the great axles in preparation for the morrow's journey, the girl made ready the evening meal.

At last supper was over, and, as was their custom, the men helped her wash the dishes. Thus the task became a short one. The men settled down to their smoking about the crackling camp fire, and as light still remained at this high altitude, Jo decided on a stroll along the lake shore.

All about stood the tall peaks, their crests snow-mantled. Over the level lowlands about the lake the silent forests of pine and fir swept away on all sides. The lake, some two miles in length, lay like an opal in the palm of the mountains, flashing fiery colors that it stole from the sunset clouds above it.

The air was chill and quiet. Not a ripple disturbed the surface of the tranquil lake, so cold and remote. Jo buttoned her coat for warmth and trudged on away from the camp, watching

Arthur Preston Hankins

flocks of chattering mudhens and mallards that fed on a long spaghettilike growth which grew on the lake bottom and floated to the surface.

She walked for a mile before she turned. She was thinking of the previous night, and of the banker's unexpected proposal of marriage when she had accepted his invitation for supper after the dance. She had known Dalworth only a short time, and his ardent wooing had come as a distinct surprise.

Now she had turned back toward the winking eye of the camp fire, which threw a brilliant dagger of light across the now dark lake. In the stream of fiery color, water fowl bobbed about grotesquely. Close at hand was a grove of pines, a few trees extending down to the shore, though for the most part the land immediately about the lake was an open, grassy meadow. She heard a slight rustling in among the pines as she passed them.

She had not strapped on her cartridge belt and six-shooter when leaving camp. In fact, she seldom carried the weapon, but always kept it hanging close to her hand in the wagon. Now and then she strapped it on when in Ragtown, for of late an element had been sifting in with which she was not familiar. It represented the riffraff from the cities—men who knew nothing of construction camps and were unaware of the fact that she, because of old associations and a thorough understanding of frontier men and frontier life, could enter a dance hall and still be respected and absolutely safe from harm. One of these had put an arm about her one night, and promptly had been rewarded with a blow on the nose; for Jo did not slap when she administered rebuke, but punched expertly and powerfully, as does a man. Next moment the offender had been pitched bodily into the street by as many rough hands as could lay hold of him. Only Jo's intervention had saved the man from being kicked into insensibility.

Once again she heard the rustling, and wished that she had her gun. It was only some animals, she told herself—a coon or a skunk, or perhaps a wild cat or coyote prowling about to spring upon an unsuspecting mudhen that had swam too far inshore. Still, a strange dread seized her, and she quickened her step.

Again she heard the rustle and the sound of a soft footfall. No animal would have produced that single, rather heavy tread. She glanced apprehensively toward the dark trees, and it seemed to her that she saw a black upright bulk move stealthily from one trunk to another.

Then two things happened at once. From the pines stealthily emerged the figure of a man—there was no mistaking it. But in the same instant there came a call from close at hand:

"Jo! Jo! Where are you?"

A feeling of vast relief came over the girl as she recognized the caressing voice of the man from Wild-cat Hill. Instantly the figure on her left faded; the blur of it became one with the shadows of the trees.

"Hiram!" she called gladly. "Here I am! Hurry!"

The sound of running feet answered her, and in a little while the big form of Hiram Hooker reached her side.

Jo was breathing weakly. She could not remember of ever before having been so near a panic or fright. What had caused the unfamiliar feeling now was a mystery to her—unless the suggested menace in the sight of the dark, skulking figure had been augmented by the ghostly quietude of the black forest and the unfriendly solitude of the cold mountain lake.

"Oh, Hiram!" she cried. "I'm so glad you're here! Hiram—I—I believe I'm sc-scared."

How it happened neither of them knew, for all at once his powerful arms were about her, and she had crept into them as less courageous women instinctively seek the protection of the stronger sex. His arms tightened and she pressed closer to him as if she were cold and seeking warmth. Hiram was ablaze with love for her and exultation. He lifted her bodily from the ground, and her lips quivered against his.

"Oh, Hiram! Hiram!" she cried then as if in terror. "What am I doing? What is the matter with me? You kissed me, Hiram, and—and I let you! I must have been terribly frightened. I—I seem to have lost my reason."

"No! No! Don't say that!" begged Hiram huskily. "Jo, I love you! You love me, Jo. Say you love me."

She hid her face against his breast and said nothing, but her shoulders shook.

"Jo, say it!" he pleaded. "Don't torment me! You must love me. You came to my arms when trouble threatened. Tell me that you love me, Jo!"

She only trembled and shivered as if cold.

"Tell me, Jo! Don't torture me. Tell me that you love me!"

There was a stifled sob; then, in muffled tones:

"You big, blind country jake! If you don't know that I'm telling you that with every nerve and fiber of my being, you deserve torture!"

The forest and the lake came together in Hiram's vision, then vanished. There was no lake, no trees, no sentinel peaks about them.

"But, Jo," said Hiram as they walked back slowly toward the camp, his arm about her waist, "I can't marry you. I've got nothing—I'm only your skinner. You—why, your profits every month run up into four figures. Oh, I wish you hadn't a cent! I wish Drummond had beaten us out!"

"What foolish talk!" she said scornfully. "What is money? I care so little for money, Hiram. It was only to try and preserve from total collapse all my hard-working, indomitable, old foster father had built up so patiently that I undertook the freighting job. I've made money—lots of it—and if you think you and the rest of the boys haven't had a big share in my success you're all wrong. We'll keep on skinning them to Ragtown till the steel is laid; then I mean to do something handsome by the men who have been so loyal to me, and sell the outfit. Then"—she sighed—"then something else," she finished.

"But that's neither here nor there," Hiram pointed out. "I'm penniless compared with you. I couldn't marry a girl who had money while I have nothing to offer her. I'm too much of a man for that. Why, everything that I have I owe to you—even the education I am so slowly acquiring."

"Oh, I won't listen to such talk, Hiram! Most of my money is invested in Tweet's project, anyway. We'll let him handle it, and you and I will continue to study and improve ourselves. Then when Tweet begins to pay us dividends we'll travel, and—"

"On your money! Not in a thousand years!"

"You're bull-headed about a trifle, Hiram," she accused.

"Jo," he said after a thoughtful pause, "don't wear that blue silk dress and those diamonds and have your hair fixed that way any more. It—it makes me feel hollowlike."

They had almost forgotten the man in the pines, there was so much else to think about now. Jo was almost ready to confess that she had imagined the entire incident—that she had heard only a prowling animal and had seen the shadow of a shrub. Hiram, on his part, was too triumphant over the thought that he, only a few months from the backwoods of Mendocino County, had captured the heart of this splendid girl, whom men praised and admired and swore by throughout all the desert region.

Still the man was stubborn. In him was a knight-errantry which forbade him to marry a girl and profit by the rewards of her pluck, energy, and business courage. If he could not make money to offer her, he must do something big for her, must win for her some conflict that threatened her fortunes, must make himself worthy of her by some great service.

Hiram still kept his boyish dreams of the adventure girl who had beckoned him from the forests to deeds of emprise. He had found his adventure girl, but he would not consider that he had won her yet. He little knew that night that his opportunity was close at hand, and that the shadow which the coming event had cast before it had lurked there in the lakeside pines.

CHAPTER XXV

JO LOSES HER SUPPORT

Eight days later Jerkline Jo leaned on the ledge of the office window in Huber's store at Ragtown and handed him the various papers which accompanied a consignment of freight from Julia.

"There's no hay, Jo," he cried, looking up in perplexity and worriment.

"The Mulligan Supply Company was short of hay when we left," Jo explained. "They hoped to have a trainload in by the time I got back."

"There's the dickens to pay!" he grumbled. "They know I have to have hay right along. I've a standing order for at least half a load of hay every trip. These settlers are buying it fast. I have only ten bales on hand. Next fellow that comes along will probably want all ten of them. A nice mess! What's the matter with those Ikes over there at Julia? Are they asleep?"

"It seems they've had some difficulty in getting alfalfa here lately," the girl explained. "I'm sorry, Mr. Huber. The best I can do for you is to promise to bring every bale I can next trip."

"Rush it," ordered the merchant. "If you can make it, let somebody else's order ride, Jo, and bring me every pound you can."

Arthur Preston Hankins

"I'll see what can be done," was her promise as she left and went to the little cabin that she had had built for her at the edge of town.

Here she cleansed herself of the stains of the trip, and substituted for chaps and flannel shirt a new tailor-made suit which had just come from Los Angeles. As she was about to go out again Twitter-or-Tweet Orr Tweet knocked on her door.

"Jo," he said with his whimsical smile, "I'm showing a couple o' men some property, and thought you might like to take a ride. You've never seen much of the cultivated land, have you—except from a distance? Come 'n' see what chances your money's got in Paloma Rancho, the Homesteader's Promised Land of Milk and Honey. Won't be gone over an hour."

His car was waiting, with his two prospective land purchasers in the tonneau. Jo readily agreed, for she had nothing to occupy her, and Tweet helped her in beside the driver's seat, after introducing the men to her.

Tweet drove slowly and talked a great deal, steering the car with one hand and directing his conversation at all three of his listeners. He dwelt at length to the strangers on Jerkline Jo's great success in her freighting enterprise, not neglecting to mention that she was investing a great portion of her profits in Paloma Rancho. The men were impressed.

Jo, too, was impressed with Tweet's abilities as a salesman. He emanated confidence, and his enthusiasm seemed well-founded and sincere. In fact, the new alfalfa ranches and the orchards of young pear trees looked promising indeed, and the projects showed evidences of thrift and capability on the part of the ranchers and near-ranchers who had bought land on contract from the discoverer of Paloma Rancho's dormant possibilities.

Tweet told of his idea of eventually tapping the mountain lake near which Jo was wont to camp and bringing the water down to irrigate such portions of desert land as might require it; for there were places where three hundred feet of boring had not developed a drop of the precious fluid. The promoter had an engineer's estimate of the cost of the entire water system, and said that his original figures had been pretty close.

It all seemed feasible, and things looked generally prosperous. Jo enjoyed her ride and the opportunity to see what had been accomplished. Returning, however, the complete enjoyment of the trip was marred by tire trouble, and, with one thing and another, it was nine o'clock at night before the party, reached Ragtown.

They were ravenously hungry, and Tweet invited the three to dinner in the town's closest approach to a satisfactory restaurant. It was after ten o'clock when they left the table. Tweet gallantly asked to accompany Jo to her cabin, and both were laughing at the absurdity of a girl like Jerkline Jo needing an escort, when Hiram Hooker hurried up to them.

"Well, I c'n see who's cut out," said Tweet, assuming a mournful expression. "So, if you don't mind, Jo, I'll get over to the hotel and keep after those two suckers. Take care of her, Wild Cat, and do whatever she tells you to do, or answer to me with your life. There's only one Jerkline Jo, you know, and the world needs her all the time. So long, playmates!"

"Jo," said Hiram when Tweet had bustled away up the dimly lighted street, "there's an awful mess. Heine and Jim and Tom and Blink are all drunk as fiddlers!"

"What!" Jo stopped in her tracks and held him by the arm. "Oh, dear!" she cried. "How could they do such a thing! I've watched them so carefully, and they've been so good. But the moment I'm out of their sight for a few hours—Oh, dear! I didn't think that they'd treat me that way!"

"I can't get it straight myself, Jo," Hiram told her. "They always hoist a few when we get in, and sometimes I join them.

I've never before seen any of them when he wasn't at least able to ramble safely back to camp. But to-night they're all four dead to the world. I can't even shake a word out of them. Heine just sits there in the Dugout, with his head on his breast, and is like a dead man."

"Where were you?"

"In camp—studying. About half past nine I thought I'd stroll into town and get a cigar and see what the boys were doing. I couldn't find them in the Palace, and went from place to place till I stumbled on them in the Dugout, every last one of them down and out. I was looking for Tweet, to have him take the bunch of them to camp in his car, when I saw you folks come out of the restaurant."

"The Dugout," puzzled Jo. "Do they go there often?"

"Hardly ever. It's the worst dump in town, as you know. They're all crooked enough, but I've heard strange whisperings about certain shady happenings in the Dugout."

"Was anybody with them?"

"Not when I found them."

"Hiram," said Jo, "it sounds like dope to me. They're loyal to me, I tell you. No, they're not to blame—they'd never treat me that way. They've been doped."

"But why? And by whom?"

"Those are questions. None of them have any money on them to speak of, I know. I've got the bank pass books of every one of them in my chest. Again, who'd have the nerve to dope and try to roll a skinner of Jerkline Jo's? He'd be playing with fire. These dive keepers know all about me; they know my power. I could mobilize an army of two hundred stiffs in an hour's time, and if I asked it they'd lay every dump in Ragtown flat.

You bet these parasites know better than to trifle with Jerkline Jo."

Her dark eyes flashed angrily in the light of a store window.

"Well, let's not stand here bewailing our fate like children lost in the woods. We've simply got to *get* out to-morrow. Mr. Huber is wild about the shortness of his stock of hay, and I promised to rush him all I could. Get Tweet and dump my boys into his car and take 'em to camp. We'll see what we can do to bring them out of it and make them fit for the trip by morning."

Far into the morning hours, in the outfit's camp on the edge of town, Jo and Hiram strove to revive the stupefied men, but nothing beyond groans could they get from them.

"They're doped, Hiram—pitilessly doped!" Jo cried in despair at last. "Go for Doctor Dennison. Carry him on your shoulders if he won't come."

The medical man came readily at Hiram's request, and after a brief examination of the sluggish men remarked that Jo's surmise had been correct. He then ordered her to go to her cabin and get some badly needed sleep, and at once went to work on the unconscious quartet, with Hiram aiding all he could.

"Whoever did this cursed thing, Wild Cat," said the physician, "was an amateur. He might have killed them. They've taken aboard terrible doses, and I can tell you right now that not one of them will start for Julia to-day. You may as well tell Jo to make other arrangements."

His prophecy proved correct. Heine Schultz had regained consciousness when dawn came, but was unable to tell a coherent story of what had occurred, and was deathly sick. The other three still remained unresponsive to the doctor's treatment.

"Well," said Jo, when she answered Hiram's knock on her cabin door at five-thirty, "what must be must. Huber has to have hay. I promised it, and Jerkline Jo never, never breaks a promise. So hook up the blacks and whites, Hiram, and lead six of Heine's team to be added to yours and six of Jim's for me. Hook on two trailers. You and I will make it to Julia and drive sixteen each back here with Huber's hay. That's the very best we can do, but we'll do that the best we know how. I'll be out by the time you get 'em hooked up. We'll nibble our breakfast as we travel. Shoot the piece, Hiram boy, my knight from Wild-cat Hill!"

That night in a pelting hail storm Jerkline Jo and Hiram went into camp beside the mountain lake, and the stage was set for the second act in the plot cooked up by the two who had lost all principle under Ragtown's subtle influence—Al Drummond and Lucy Dalles.

CHAPTER XXVI

AT THE HAIRPIN CURVE

The storm in the mountains continued all night, the downpour shifting from hail to sleet and from sleet to a cold, drenching rain. Jo in her remote little tent kept dry and comfortable. Hiram kept the same, rolled in his blankets under a wagon, the ground about it ditched to run the water off. There was shelter for the mules and horses, too, for at the approach of winter Jo had freighted to the mountain camping site sufficient lumber for a roof, which was supported by poles cut from the forest.

It was still dark and raining when the two beleaguered freighters continued their journey next morning. Hiram, with eight of his own black horses hitched to the wagon, and four span of mules and horses leading, went ahead, as usual. They left the level mountain valley that swaddled the lake and started down the steep grades toward the Julia side of the desert.

"We'll have a pull coming back if this keeps up!" Jo shouted through the rain, just as Hiram's teams began negotiating the system of hairpin curves upon which Jo's skinners had rolled the boulder in retaliation for the drained water tank.

Hiram did not hear her, for the wagons were rumbling, thirty-two sets of big hoofs were sloshing in mud, the bells a-jingle, the rain a roar.

Arthur Preston Hankins

Jo wore a yellow oilskin slicker and a sou'wester of the same material, and rubber knee boots. Only her pretty face, smiling from the concealing garments, showed that she was a woman.

The animals that trailed behind Hiram's wagon went out of sight around the first curve. The last of these mules were not a hundred feet ahead of the noses of Jo's white leaders. As her leaders reached the curve Jo called shrilly to her off-pointer to cross the chain and pull the wagon away from the rock wall on the right-hand side. Obediently the mare stepped over the chain, and she and her mate began pulling the pole at an angle of forty-five degrees from the direction in which the leaders and swings were traveling. The wagon and its trailer made the sharp curve, and the mare was stepping back into place at Jo's command, when suddenly the girl's breathing was shut off, and she was whipped from her feet as if a cyclone had struck her.

Several pairs of arms were about her; a heavy cloth was over her mouth and nose and eyes. Fighting frantically against she knew not what, she was borne rapidly toward the tail-end of the wagon. Some one's arms were about her middle; another pair circled her shoulders; still another held her booted legs at the knees.

She tried to scream, but only a vague b-b-r-r sounded through the cloth that covered her face. She kicked and clawed and twisted and jerked and squirmed with surprising suddenness. Nevertheless, a rope was bound about her slicker, round and round from her shoulders to her ankles, swathing her like the bandages of a mummy, until she was almost as stiff as one. She heard the roar of the rain, but no sound of her moving team. She was whipped from the ground as if she weighed no more than ten pounds; and in a horizontal position the three pairs of arms bore her along rapidly in the direction that she had come, much as if she were a roll of canvas bound about with marline hitches.

Presently she felt herself ascending; then wet foliage brushed her face. Not a word had been spoken—almost she had heard not a sound, because of the noise of the rain and the slushy hoofbeats and the bells. Whoever her captors were, they had lain in wait until the elbow of the curve separated Hiram's outfit and hers, and then had climbed in her wagon at the rear and stolen stealthily upon her from behind. Their work had been distressingly thorough.

She was not greatly frightened, merely stunned and bewildered. What on earth could be the meaning of such an act, was the question that kept uppermost in her thoughts as she felt herself borne swiftly along through the dripping forest.

Meantime, Hiram Hooker had looked back to watch Jerkline Jo's whites round the curve. There were not many opportunities for looking back at the girl that Hiram did not improve. He loved to watch Jo's expert handling of the team in tight places. It made a picture to delight the heart of any man. He saw the leaders come around, then the swings. Next he saw the off pointer mare recrossing the chain and returning to place. Then came the butt team and—an empty wagon.

For an instant or two Hiram gazed unbelievingly, then turned and set his brake, calling to his team to whoa. Next moment he was running back.

He sprang into Jo's empty wagon, set the brake, and stopped her team. Then he was out by the tail end, running back along the road, calling frantically.

On the left-hand side of the road yawned a chasm, five hundred feet in depth. Had something happened? Had Jo fallen down this precipice?

As he ran he skirted the edge, shouting down. Only the pelting rain and the swish of forest trees made a mocking answer. If for any reason the girl had been obliged to leave the wagon, she would have stopped her team. This was no place to allow a team to travel alone.

He was thunderstruck—scarce able to believe his senses. Back in the road he trotted along, his blue eyes searching expertly in the mud for signs of what had happened. But it seemed that the trampling of the animals that were following Jo's wagon had obliterated every trace, provided the girl had been afoot in the road. And she must have been afoot there, or flown up into the sky!

Ah! He came to an abrupt halt. In the mud at the roadside was a single footprint—the print of a man's shoe. Then on the rock wall on the right-hand side of the road, and close to the footprint, was fresh mud. On hands and knees Hiram climbed up the rocky slope, and at the top found mud again. Buckthorn bushes grew close by. Some one had brushed against them recently, for the raindrops had been shaken from the leaves. In all the big-timber country of Mendocino County there had been no surer trailer than Hiram Hooker. For days he had followed panther and bear, eventually to track them to their lairs. No big animal hunt ever had been considered complete without Hiram Hooker to go along.

He remembered the incident of the man in the pines by the lake shore and groaned: "Fools!" he muttered. "They thought the rain would help cover their trail, where it only makes it plainer. Men can't travel through wet bushes without leaving a trail that looks like it had been made with whitewash and a broom. What has happened? Oh, Jo! Jo!"

He was off at a lope, his eyes darting glances hither and thither, following the trail as accurately as a hound follows a scent. Here leaves glistened with raindrops—there they looked dull. The trail was plain.

What has happened? The footprint of a man, and no sight of tracks made by the girl! Hiram was unarmed. He had left his wagon too surprised to think of grabbing up the Colt that he carried. Should he go back now and get Jo's six-shooter? No, the rain was falling too fast. Soon the bushes that the kidnapers had brushed in their escape would be covered with drops of water again, and the tail would vanish, since the land was rocky and showed no footprints. He must keep as close to the fleeing men as possible. He knew there must be more than one to manhandle Jerkline Jo!

Thus raced his thoughts as he sped on, never for an instant faltering on the trail.

"If it only doesn't rain harder!" came his groan. He prayed with childlike simplicity against this calamity, for more rain would wipe out the trail altogether.

He saw a large pine knot as he ran along, and paused to grasp it up. It was heavy with pitch and shaped like the warclub of an Indian. It was, in fact, too heavy, and few men would have considered it in the light of a weapon. Fifty yards farther Hiram found a mate to it, and picked it up too. Then he sped on and on into the forest of pines and firs, praying that the brush would not give out and make his trailing slower.

If these men ahead of him were trusting to their own legs to get away with Jerkline Jo, their legs would have to be better than any Hiram Hooker ever before had matched his own against. Why, he could keep up this pace for hours and hours! He knew more about surmounting the difficulties of a forest wilderness than any man in the south, he proudly told himself. These woods were as nothing compared with the majestic, seemingly endless sweep of the vast forests which he had roamed since childhood! If they did not take to horses, he'd make them sick of their bargains before they had gone many miles!

CHAPTER XXVII

UNDER THE DRIPPING TREES

Vaguely Hiram Hooker sensed a diabolical plot as he pounded on through the rain, tireless, determined, remorseless, on the trail of the abductors of Jerkline Jo.

The doping of his four fellow skinners at Ragtown had a part in the plan. It had been done deliberately to force the girl and Hiram into the wilderness alone. Some one had known of Huber's shortage of hay, and had schemed accordingly, aware of Jerkline Jo's eternal willingness to do her best by her patrons, regardless of the strain upon herself. The plotters had not been able to get at Hiram. Perhaps they had not tried. Jerkline Jo would hardly essay a trip to Julia and back alone. Too many difficulties might arise on the road that a lone skinner—even a man skinner—could not cope with. So they perhaps had not molested Hiram, hoping, if he were on his feet, that the girl would attempt the trip with him. They had waited at the first U curve, and the moment he was out of sight had pounced upon her. Suppose he had not chanced to look back? The many curves ahead would have hidden her from him for nearly an hour after that first one had been passed. That would have given them a start, the disadvantage of which he could not have overcome. As it was, though, he knew that he was hot on their trail, and burdened as they were, was gaining on them at every leap. Was Drummond back of this? Hiram could think of no one else who would be even remotely at enmity with the lovable Jerkline Jo.

He brought up suddenly and squatted behind a bush of southern manzanita. Just ahead, in an open portion of the forest, was a group of three men, standing in a circle about a stiff, immovable figure on the ground. Three saddled horses stood close by, their tails turned toward the rain, their heads lowered disconsolately.

The men had just stopped and laid down their burden, which was nothing else than the tightly bound body of Jerkline Jo. All three men wore masks over their faces and new bright-blue overalls to further aid in hiding their identities. Hiram saw the rope about the girl, running in a spiral from her shoulders to her ankles. He saw the cloth over her face, knotted behind her head.

What should he do? There were three men standing about the girl, rubbing their arms, which probably ached from the strain of carrying her. Beyond a doubt they were armed. He tried to think, to plan; but in the midst of it all half-formulated schemes deserted him because of the sudden action of one of them.

He had taken something from his pocket, and now he and another stooped over the prostrate figure of the girl. One man grasped her head in both hands; the next instant Hiram realized with horror that a blade was gleaming dully through the rain in the right hand of the other man. The third stooped and squatted on Jo's ankles.

Hiram Hooker had at least one more accomplishment than has been mentioned. As a boy he had used it to terrify his elders on dark nights in the forest. He could imitate the piercing, blood-chilling scream of the prowling panther until women in lonely forest cabins clutched their breasts in fear, and men's faces blanched. Sprinting from his place of concealment like a football player, crouching low as he ran, he bore down upon the three men, and had almost reached them before he loosed that terrorizing cry. Before it had died out in the lonely, dripping wilderness, he was flailing right and left with a huge pine knot in either hand, amazing and invincible as Sampson with his jawbone of an ass.

With yells of terror, the trio rocked back on their haunches and struggled frantically to gain their feet. There was a sickening crack, and the man who had held Jo's head pitched backward, a victim of one of Hiram's warclubs. Swinging about, he aimed a blow with his left-hand club, but its intended target ducked, and the club descended on the man's shoulder, wringing a cry of pain from lips that whitened suddenly.

The third man was up now, and sprang upon Hiram's back. The other charged him from in front. Hiram hurled his left-hand club straight into this man's face, and with his free hand reached down and grasped the left leg of the man who had climbed him in the rear. Carrying this man, who all the time was raining blows on his head, Hiram ran with all his might for a close-by pine. As he neared it he whirled about and threw himself at it backward with every atom of his force.

There followed a terrible impact, and in his ear exploded the breath of the man on his back, as he came in violent contact with the trunk of the tree. The shock pitched Hiram forward on his face, and the man who had climbed upon him fell limply to the earth, the wind entirely crushed out of him.

Hiram bounded to his feet and confronted the man into whose face he had thrown the pine knot, and who now was rushing him, brandishing a revolver. Hiram's blow had knocked the mask from this man's face, but it was a face that Hiram had never seen before.

A shot barked dully in the heavy atmosphere of the forest, and the smoke hung in a little ball. Hiram felt the impact of the bullet, and was whirled half around with the force of it. He knew he had been hit some place—in the breast or shoulder perhaps—but as yet felt not the slightest pain. Fire flashed in his very face, now, and this time he smelled the acrid powder;

but he had been in motion when the trigger was pressed and the bullet whined away fretfully through the trees. On the heels of the second report came that sickening crack once more, and the face of the man that glared through the smoke at Hiram went red with a smear of blood.

He sank to his knees, and Hiram spun about just in time to aim another crashing blow at the skull of the man whom he had catapulted into the tree. His mask still held in place, but his hat was off and Hiram saw that his hair was brown and wavy. There had not been time to aim, and the blow fell on his assailant's neck.

They clinched, went down together, rolling over and over, clawing at each other like fighting lynxes.

"Gi' me the paper! Gi' me the paper!" yelled a voice, as Hiram climbed uppermost on his man and fought to free his entangled arms.

At the same instant other arms were thrown about him from behind. The man he had hit first had reentered the fight, it seemed.

With a herculean heave the man from Wild-cat Hill lurched backward, carrying his lighter assailant with him. Hiram had lost his club. He grasped the man on his back by the under part of his thighs, as he had the other, and lifted his feet from the ground. Then, so quickly that the man was taken off his guard, Hiram leaped into the air and fell backward, falling with all the weight of his huge body on the man who clung to him like an abalone to a rock.

"*Wuff!*" he heard again, as the fellow's breath forsook him in a spasm of pain. He lost his hold on Hiram, and Hiram flopped over.

"Run! Get a horse! Get away with the paper!" this fellow choked; and as Hiram sprang upon him he saw the other rise and totter toward a horse.

Crashing a blow to the face of the man under him, Hiram sprang to his feet and lunged at the one who was fleeing. Whatever "the paper" meant, it was the nucleus of the plot, it appeared, and Hiram purposed to have it.

But, grasping frantically for a stirrup, then sprawling along the neck of the nearest horse, the man yelled to the animal, and it leaped away with him through the trees.

Hiram whirled back, beaten in that direction, and made for the other, who was on his feet and also running toward the two remaining mounts. The third man still lay inert.

Hiram started running for the second escaping man, but suddenly his knees refused to hold his legs to their accustomed task. Blindness was coming upon him, but he continued to grope toward the horses. Then again came the sounds of rapidly thundering hoofs. Hiram Hooker sighed weakly and placed both hands to his breast, which seemed weighted with some heavy object, or bound about tightly with a rope. His hands came away red and wet He wilted in his tracks, sighed again, and seemed to drift placidly into a deep, soothing sleep.

Then a noise partially awoke him. His senses swam, and he thought he heard himself laughing crazily, but could not make sure whether he was laughing or only had imagined it. A man was reeling toward the remaining horse, both hands to his head, and he looked so helpless and befuddled that Hiram laughed again—or thought he did. The man groaned and mumbled, then fell flat on his face, as a baby falls in an unchecked collapse. A little while he lay there, then struggled to his feet again, and tottered toward the horse, who seemed to be neighing shrilly for the mates that had deserted him.

Why, that was what Hiram had heard, he reasoned. He had not been laughing at all. A long space of semiconsciousness. Then came the dull thunder of hoofs once more. Hiram half raised his body on an elbow. There lay Jerkline Jo, stiff and immovable in her yellow oilskins. There was no one else about. Save himself, of course, but he was so sleepy.

He fell back with a crash.

Arthur Preston Hankins

CHAPTER XXVIII

FOUR-UP FOR HELP

Bound and helpless, Jerkline Jo Modock lay on the ground and listened to the sounds of the battle raging around her. She knew that her hero from Wild-cat Hill had come with his terrorizing panther scream, and she heard curses and thudding clubs, then popping revolver shots.

She was struggling desperately to free herself of her bonds, but she only wearied herself and accomplished nothing. With her teeth she chewed at the cloth that covered her face, trying to draw it down below her eyes, so that she could at least see; but her efforts here proved futile, too. Then she began twisting her head from side to side and hunching her shoulders, which she found she could move, in an effort to loosen the knot at the back of her head, or to scrape the cloth away.

This last in time she accomplished, but it was long after all sounds of the conflict had ceased.

As the cloth came loose she moved it along by sticking out her tongue and working it from side to side, at the same time tossing her head about. At last it slipped off, and, by raising her head, she gazed about through the dark, wet trees.

She had heard the thud of horses' hoofs, but now not a horse was to be seen. Fifty feet from her, perhaps, lay the silent form of Hiram Hooker, flat on his back. No other human being save herself and Hiram seemed to be in all that dripping wilderness.

Time and again she called to the man to whom she had given her heart, but Hiram's lips remained motionless. A great fear clutched at her. Hiram was dead.

She fought down her terror, the horror of it all, and sought desperately for a way to release herself. She was bound round and round until she was so stiff that even to roll over and over on the ground was impossible, as she could get no purchase whatever for her strong, tough muscles. She began striving to bend her knees, and in this, as the bonds gradually changed position and gave a little, she was eventually successful. Once she had a start in this tiresome process, she gained more and more, and finally she could move her legs from their straight position.

She rested then, and when she began squirming again found that she was able to flop over on her side.

In this new position she looked about over the ground for something to help her, and close at hand she saw the dull gleam of steel.

As yet she had not the remotest idea of why she had been kidnaped; nor had she seen any of the persons who had perpetrated the act. Not a word had been spoken to her or in her presence before the fight. She had heard the man yelling about "the paper," though, toward the close of the battle, but no other words throughout the entire ordeal.

The blade that showed its dull steel against the soggy brown pine needles lay five feet beyond her reach. But now she could roll to it, and began to do so, flopping along like a fish in the bottom of a boat. She rested when her face was close to it, and began to study how she might make use of it.

She might be able to take it in her teeth, but doubted if she

Arthur Preston Hankins

could reach that part of the rope about her shoulders, even then. If it was a dagger, she could not think how she could utilize it, as it probably would have no cutting edge. If it was a pocketknife, it doubtless would be dull, as pocketknives usually are, and therefore useless. With any pressure that she might be able to command, a keen cutting edge would be necessary to free her from the coils of the lariat.

By now she had regained her strength, and once more began wriggling and worming until her eyes were close to the blade, half hidden by pine needles. Then she realized with surprise and a thrill of hope that the object was a razor.

How such a tool came to be dropped by her assailants was more than she could fathom. She did not try. Working her face closer and closer to the razor she took the end of the handle between her teeth, and, twisting her head from side to side, finally managed to close the blade without cutting herself by pressing it against the ground.

Then she rolled so that her face was directly over it, and took both handle and blade in her mouth, by the middle. Her brain had been active through these clumsy maneuvers; she had a plan.

Now for a tree from which suckers were growing close to the ground. The pines were hopeless in this respect, but off a way she saw the naked branches of a black oak, and toward it she rolled, the closed razor in her mouth.

It was a long, tiresome trip, and when she reached the tree there was not a sucker growing from it. She saw another black oak close at hand, and continued her flopping, seallike progress, toward it.

Here, to her unbounded delight, slender suckers grew up from an exposed root. She released the razor and chewed upon one of them until she had browsed it down to a leafless stub four inches high.

Then, working with her teeth and tongue and straining every muscle in her neck, she contrived, at the risk of slashing her face, to insert the stump of the sucker between the two halves of the razor handle.

This pushed up the blade, and it remained in a half-closed position like a threatening guillotine. Knowing now that she would not be cut, she took the end of the handle in her teeth and pulled it down as far as it would go. Still the edge of the blade remained balanced against the top of the sucker. So she rolled about until she found a pine twig, which she took in her mouth, rolling with it back to the razor. With one end of the twig in her mouth, she was able to push the blade open with the other end, and it fell back against the root of the oak, edge uppermost.

She rested again, and then crawled over the root until a coil of the rope that bound her shoulders was pressing against the keen edge of the razor blade. Working her shoulders up and down, she saw the leather strands parting clean, and soon only one strand remained uncut. She rolled from the razor and scraped this last strand against another exposed root of the oak until it parted.

Two minutes more, and she was sitting up, unwinding the rawhide lariat from her legs with hands that were free.

She struggled to her feet, and though she ached in every bone and muscle, ran to Hiram and bent over him with a little cry of anguish on her lips.

His shirt front was stained crimson, and terror seized her. She fought it off and, bending down, listened with an ear to his heart. She breathed a little tremulous prayer of thankfulness as she heard his regular heartbeats, and then tore open his shirt to find that a bullet had entered his breast, high up on the right-hand side.

As best she could she stopped the bleeding and tried to revive

Hiram. Into cold rain water, collected in a hollow of the ground, she plunged her handkerchief again and again, bathing the man's temples and chafing his wrists.

At last he opened his eyes, stared oddly at her a little, then, seeming to remember everything, strove to rise.

Probably one woman in all that country could have completed the gigantic task of getting this big, wounded man back to the wagons, but Jerkline Jo was fortunately that woman. With an arm of Hiram about her neck, and her arm about his waist, they staggered away through the rain, Hiram conscious enough to direct the way, for the girl was completely lost. It was early in the morning that their journey had been interrupted so ruthlessly, but it was afternoon before they came again to the road, and Hiram dropped exhausted in Jo's lead wagon.

Here she was able better to attend to his wound, and brandy, which she always carried, revived him greatly.

There was no course open now but to loose all the horses but four, leave three of the wagons where they stood, and drive as fast as she could with the four hitched to the head wagon, to get the wounded man to Artesian Ranch, about eighteen miles distant down on the Julia side of the desert.

Never before or afterward in the lives of the actors in this outland drama were the mountains that divided the desert to know such a drive as that. Jerkline Jo had a set of four-up checks which she carried in case of emergency, and by one o'clock four of her big whites were racing down the perilous grade, with Jo holding the four leather lines and operating the brake repeatedly, urging them to greater efforts continually. The huge wagon careened about hairpin curves, skirted precipices, rumbled from canon to canon, while the girl, always sure of herself, always sure of her horses, guided it skillfully and laughed at catastrophies that yawned at her every foot of the way.

In the middle of the afternoon they raced out on the desert and took up the long miles to the ranch. At dark they reached it, the horses badly spent, unaccustomed as they were to moving faster than a walk. There was an automobile at the ranch, and Hiram was hurried on to the doctor at Julia, while Jo worked far into the night rubbing down her trembling whites, crooning to them, and giving them short drinks of water until they were resting their weary bodies in the litter, content and quiet at last.

CHAPTER XXIX

THE GENTLE WILD CAT RETURNS

Hiram Hooker was very weak when he reached the doctor. The bullet was found and successfully removed, however, and Hiram's great physical perfection did the rest.

He was quickly on the mend, and in a month was able to take his team again.

Meantime Jerkline Jo and her four other skinners had contrived to make their customary trips from Julia to Ragtown, all of them calling to see Hiram, who was being cared for at the doctor's house, the minute they completed their west-bound trip. Jo spent most of her time with him when in Julia, and when he was well enough they talked frequently of the strange occurrence in the mountains. But they did not get down to solid work on the mystery until Hiram was on his first trip to Ragtown after his wound had healed. Then the wagon train came to a stop at the curves, and Jo and all of her skinners walked through the forest to the scene of Hiram's battle.

After a search they found the spot. Jo showed the men the razor, still propped up as she had left it, held up by the sucker of the black oak. She found the remains of the lariat, too. A search failed to reveal anything beyond the razor that had been dropped by the surprised kidnapers.

"Lord, be merciful unto me, a skinner!" exclaimed Heine

Schultz, seating himself on a prostrate pine. "Wild Cat, you say one o' these Jaspers was bendin' over Jo with this here razoo?"

"I'm sure it was that that he had in his hand," Hiram replied. "He was the second one that I soaked, and I saw him drop it."

"Boy! Boy! That musta been some fight," observed Jim McAllen. "Think of our ol' Wild Cat puttin' the three of 'em on the run! Man, how comes it I miss all the good things in this life? Jo, was they aimin' to cut your pretty throat?"

Jo shuddered. "Thank Heaven I was blindfolded!" was her grateful thought. "But how ridiculous, boys! A razor! If they'd wanted to kill me, at least one of them had a gat. Ask Hiram."

"Maybe they was just goin' to cut you loose and tell you why they'd swiped you, when the Gentle Wild Cat went wild again," suggested Gulick.

"Cut a perfectly good lariat!" Jo picked it up. "Couldn't they have untied the knots?"

Gulick took the lariat and examined it. "Thirty-five feet," he said. "Rawhide—six-strand plait Been rubbed with cow's liver to soften 'er, too. What else? Whoop! What's this?"

He was studying the honda, also of rawhide, pressed flat when soaked and riveted in shape, a plaited button on the end of the lariat proper to keep it from slipping through the hole.

"Letters cut in this," Gulick announced. "T. H.' Who's that stand for?"

All went silent for a time, thinking; then Hiram Hooker said quietly, as if what he suggested mattered but little:

"Tehachapi Hank."

All talked at once now. Not one was there that was not sure Hiram had hit upon a clew.

"And Tehachapi Hank's a bad man," said Heine. "Admitted it himself. And he's a side-kick of that cholo-faced Drummond!"

Study of the razor, now red with rust, showed the amateur detectives nothing.

"And ye saw only the face of one of 'em, Hiram?" Blink Keddie asked it.

"Only one. The others managed to keep their masks on."

"Tehachapi Hank and Al Drummond them other two was," said McAllen positively. "Too bad it wasn't one o' them you knocked the mask off of, Wild Cat."

"And you never saw this fella that you got a look at?" asked Schultz.

Hiram shook his head. "I didn't even see him well," he added. "Through revolver smoke—and the rain pouring—and next instant his face didn't look like anything much. That was a wicked old pine knot."

"I'll say she was, boy! But about the razor?" Keddie kept on.

Again Hiram could not answer.

"Why, that's easy!" laughed Heine Schultz. "They was gonta give Jo a shave!"

Jo and Hiram walked together behind the rest and talked as the party returned to the wagons. For the first time she told him of what her skinners had had to report when they were over their sickness following the doping at Ragtown. One and all, they said, they had been invited to the little cabin of the girl who ran the shooting gallery for a drink; after having fired several strings of shots and "joshed" with her out in front. From there they had gone to the Palace, and afterward, being dazed and feeling drowsy, had wandered in a group into the Dugout, a place that they seldom frequented, and could remember nothing after that.

"Why—why—do they think Lucy doped them?" cried Hiram.

Jo shrugged. "They can't remember drinking anywhere but with her and in the Palace," she said. "They got it one place or the other, Hiram."

"The Palace, of course, then. Why—Lucy—she—"

"Is a friend of Al Drummond," Jo helped him out, her red lips set.

"Did you find out whether or not Drummond was in Ragtown at the time?"

"I looked into all that I dared, but it was nine days before I got back. Oh, I had an awful time, with nobody to help me but a few green men I'd picked up at Julia—finding the horses and all. But Huber got his hay!" she added proudly. "When I got back to Ragtown, of course nobody remembered whether Drummond had been there that day or not. He goes and comes frequently, you know. And I didn't dare press questions. I told the boys to keep still about it all. I thought that best."

"Was Drummond there on your last trip in?" he asked.

"Yes."

"Beaten up? I'm sure I must have left my mark on all three of them."

"I didn't get to see him, but no one said anything about any injury."

"Much as we dislike him, it's hard to think that Drummond would be concerned in such a plot," Hiram remarked.

"Plot?"

"Of course, Jo."

"Against me? What have I done?"

"We're getting nowhere with such speculation, Jo," said Hiram. "We boys will just have to keep our eyes open and see what we can find out. There's more back of it than the idea to tantalize you because you beat Al Drummond in the freighting game. I wish I knew what the razor was for."

"Of course, they weren't going to kill me, Hiram. No need for all that monkeywork, if that had been the case."

"I only saw the man with the razor," Hiram told her, "and got busy. Of course, I didn't even know it was a razor then, but I saw steel. I thought they were going to kill you. Didn't take much time to think, at that."

"You terrible scrapper!" laughed the girl. "Who'd have thought that I'd ever have needed such a man—and got him! Hiram, you've—you've never kissed me since that night."

Hiram's face turned red as fire. "I ain't worthy to kiss ye, Jo," he said, lapsing into his backwoods drawl. "Wait'll I settle this thing that's come up for you. Wait'll I find out about 'the paper.' Then maybe I'll have somethin' to offer you."

In his great embarrassment he pointed to the ground, where were tracks and scratches.

"Ben a bob cat usin' thereabouts," he drawled.

With Twitter-or-Tweet Orr Tweet the month that Hiram had been laid up had developed a new and unforeseen situation.

He laid the particulars before Jerkline Jo and Hiram, both investors in his enterprise. The conference took place when Jo's freight outfit jingled into Ragtown two days later.

Tweet invited them to dinner in the Wigwam, a saloon and restaurant and gambling house combined, where the patrons sat on stools before a high counter which was in the nature of a continuation of the bar. The three took seats at the farther end, so that their conversation would be less likely to be overheard.

"Playmates," Tweet began, when their orders were before them, "I didn't think our Uncle Sam would go to work and hand us a package just when we were gettin' us a toehold. But that's just what he's done. I been watchin' for it to develop for some little time. Now the leak has sprung.

"You see, outside o' Paloma Rancho, every other section o' land in here b'longs to the Gold Belt Cut-off, and adjoinin' sections are government land. Maybe you c'n guess what's happened."

"Thrown open," Jerkline Jo said promptly.

"Yep—open to homesteaders. They're flockin' in in automobiles, in perambulators, on motor cycles, burros, horseback, and afoot—in everything but submarines. So far as any one can see, they're gettin' just as good land as Paloma Rancho; and the folks we've sold to are castin' dark looks at one Tweet. As if I was to blame! Two fellas that hadn't paid in much have jumped their contracts with us, and are takin' up claims. If many more pull stuff like that—say, somebody'll be in bad!

"Just the same, though, my engineers tell me there's shallower water here than any place on this ol' desert. Butte Springs proves that, too. And we got the water right on the mountain lake; so they can't get that. Riparian rights—all straight, by golly! No worry there. I don't think settlers'll have any luck striking water without big expense anywhere around us. Just the same, it'll take time to prove that.

"The settler, you savvy, has six months after he files before he's got to get on his land. Even then he ain't required to develop water; and chances are he won't. He'll put in dry crops to cover the improvements demanded by the government, whether they succeed or not—which they won't. But all this time, because nobody'll be makin' a great effort to locate water, folks will be believin' that government land is as good as ours. See the point? Paloma Rancho land will stop sellin' pronto, and our pleasant little dream will turn into a scary nightmare."

"But if the surrounding land is inferior to the rancho," said Jo, "it's only a matter of time until people will find it out. Then you'll regain your old status, won't you?"

"In time. Yeah—that's it. But time's money, little girl; and once every three months I gotta slap down six thousand filthy lucreinos, plus a neat little bunch o' interest, or—bingo! All is lost!"

"Folks that peddled me this property are gettin' on their feet again, and their young lives are one long regret over havin' had ta part with Paloma Rancho. 'Salways th' way. One dog leaves a bone, and another dog comes along and goes to work and picks her up. Then the other dog he goes to work and thinks that was a pretty darn good bone after all. Then fur begins to fly, and old ladies yell: 'How cruel! Stop it, you big heartless men!'

"So the other dogs won't miss a chance to shoot the prongs into me the moment I fail on a single payment and the interest due. They don't have to; I signed to forfeit everything any interest day that I failed to pungle up. Three days o' grace— then—boom! 'Wasn't it pretty, papa! Shoot off another one just like it!'"

Jerkline Jo sipped her near-coffee thoughtfully, and gazed

unseeingly at the menu card, a marvel of weird orthography, punctuated with fly specks and splatters of egg yolk. Jo had over ten thousand dollars invested in Paloma Rancho.

"We're not doing the freighting business that we did," she confessed, aware that Playmate Tweet was studying her face expectantly and patiently straightening a nose whose tip always left true center the moment he released it. "Lots of the smaller contractors have finished here, and are moving on to new jobs up the line, out of our reach. Ragtown, too, seems to be slowing up, don't you think?"

Tweet pursed his lips. "I hate to admit it," he said, "but I guess you're right. Still, we can expect things to be slower in winter. Then these settlers oughta help Ragtown some when spring comes along. Chances are, though, most of 'em are broke. 'Salways like that. I've been homesteadin' communities before now. No good, as a rule.

"But I ain't worryin' about Ragtown. She'll perk up. We're gonta get the yards and the roundhouse—that's a cinch. I know it now. Demarest slipped it to me. I've spread the glad tidin's, o' course, but it didn't seem to help. Folks have believed it all along, and have gone ahead on that belief—so the rush because of that feature was over before I sprung it. But Ragtown'll pick up in time. The floaters will go, and substantial citizens will take their places. It's the land contracts that we need in order to meet our payments and have a future to bank on, and they're what'll slow up and hurt us till folks get sane and see we got the only dope."

"You'll have to meet the next payment—when?" Hiram put in here.

"April first—two months off. Six thousan' dollars and interest on deferred payments."

"Can you meet it?"

"I couldn't if it was due now," was Tweet's reply.

"Well, I'll see that you meet that payment," Jo said. "That will give you three months more leeway—five months, counting from now—and by that time things should begin to look up once more."

Tweet heaved a great sigh of relief. "That's a big load off my chest," he claimed, as they left the stools.

Two hours later Hiram Hooker, apparently wandering aimlessly about the dimly lighted street, saw Al Drummond lift a hinged portion of the shooting-gallery counter and pass within. A man was in charge, and there was nobody shooting. Drummond nodded briefly to him, traversed the length of the target range, and disappeared through a door in the rear.

Three minutes after this Hiram slunk stealthily along the alley and up to Lucy's little cabin. Softly his fingers plucked at a knot in a knothole, which he had loosened that evening while Lucy was on watch in the gallery. Holding the circular bit of wood in his hand, he placed an ear to the knothole, which was hidden from those inside by a huge piece of furniture.

CHAPTER XXX

HIRAM TAKES THE TRAIL

Hiram Hooker stood motionless in the alley back of Lucy Dalles' cabin and listened intently through the knothole.

"Well," he heard Al Drummond saying to Lucy, "I see they got in again this evening."

Hiram supposed "they" referred to the freighting outfit of Jerkline Jo.

"Yes," replied Lucy, "and here it is late January, Al, and we've accomplished nothing."

"No, nothing," Drummond admitted gloomily. "And our chances look mighty slim to get at her. Every trip she's got those five husky skinners with her, and I guess every one of them is fool enough to put up a scrap for her if he knew he'd get croaked in the deal."

"We must think up another plan to separate her from them," the girl suggested.

"Confound it!" muttered Drummond. "Everything was moving along smoothly, and the next minute we'd have had the razor working; then here comes that big boob and takes us by surprise. Lord, how he swung those clubs!"

"You're afraid of him, since he beat you up on the desert," Lucy said tauntingly.

"Huh! I'll get him yet! I'm willing to admit he's too many for me in a stand-up and knock-down fight. He's a whirlwind—I never saw his like. Why, up there in the mountains he seemed to have a dozen arms, all working at once. Wild Cat is right! But I haven't been raised on salt pork and corn bread. I've lived. Just the same, when I get good and ready I'll fix his engine for him."

"I imagine he'll be around to oversee the work," remarked Lucy in a tone that probably made Drummond long to choke her.

"Well, that's not the point," she went on after a little. "What are we going to do to get at that creature known as Jerkline Jo, the four-flusher? She's crooked as a dog's hind leg, and goes around pulling the pious stuff on the roughnecks."

"You think because you're crooked every other woman is, eh? I'll say this for Jo—she's straight and a dead-game sport. She's not a four-flusher. Of course I'd do anything to get even for the way she handed it to me in the freighting game. But there's no sense in you and me running her down to each other when we don't believe ourselves."

"So you've fallen for her, too, have you?" Lucy asked sarcastically.

"Don't be a fool, Lucy! A man can't help admiring a girl like Jo."

"Thanks for your assurances, Al," Lucy said cuttingly.

"Well, well, well! Scrap all night about nothing! Forget it! Shut up! Guess who I saw to-day as I was driving over the desert."

"Who?" sullenly.

"Your dear old uncle."

"My uncle!"

"Sure—that's what you called him. Basil Filer, the crazy prospector."

"Sure enough, Al?" Lucy's tones were brighter.

"Pretty much so. Didn't seem to recognize me at all. I was at Comstock's camp, and he rambled in with his burros. Stood within five feet of me and looked right at me. Never saw me before!" and Drummond chuckled.

"Al, where on earth do you suppose he's been since you took him out on the desert and dumped him?"

"Heaven knows! Wandering about looking for a prospect, I suppose. I'd have given fifty dollars to be hidden close by when he came out of it next morning."

"Poor old duffer! But suppose Hooker and Jo or some of that bunch should stumble onto him, Al! Was he making this way?"

"Yes; but he was fifty miles up the lines. There were two or three women about Comstock's commissary tent—two of Comstock's daughters and the wife of his walking-boss. The old bird kept looking at them and shaking his head, just like he did with you. He's still hunting for his pardner's daughter. He's a crazy nut, and I guess wherever he goes he's trying to get on her trail."

"Don't you suppose he remembers me, Al? We sure had him going that night. I was Jean Prince to him, all right. And when you inked me up, and he got a look—say, he couldn't tell his story fast enough, could he?"

Drummond chuckled reminiscently. "Yes, next minute he'd

have had you scalped, kid, if I hadn't slipped him another powder. Well, if he does drift back here you've simply got to lie low and keep out of his sight. I'll tell the boys to keep their eyes open and slip me the dope if they see him rambling into Ragtown. Then you fade away till he beats it out again."

"Won't he ask about me? And try to find out where I've gone?"

"I doubt it. He's still got his precious paper. If, we'd stolen that, instead of copying it, there might be the very devil to pay. But as long as he's still got it he's too nutty to suspect. Of course, though, nobody can tell what's going on in the other fellow's noodle. I'd say, though, that if you aren't here he'll think the whole business was a pipe dream."

"I hope so. We don't want any further complications. Now when are you and Hank and that friend of his going to make another attempt to get Jerkline Jo? And how are you going about it?"

"Hank's still camping up in the mountains and spying on the outfit when it travels through the pass," Al informed her. "He's watching their habits, and taking note of just how they travel along, trying to dope out something new. He'll get a scheme before spring, I'm thinking. There's a bad hombre, kid. It would give me the creeps to know he was trailing me through those lonesome woods. Man! I wouldn't turn my back to that plug with fifteen cents in my jeans!"

"Can't we get some more of Hank's pals and simply ambush Jo's whole outfit? Collar all of them, and then get after Jo. Surely a bunch of men could take them all by surprise and put the fixin's to 'em."

Drummond snorted. "We've got to split the haul four ways as it is," he pointed out. "And that bo that helped us get Filer away—Stool—he smells a rat and is keeping an eye single to horning in on the clean-up. Lucy, I wouldn't attack Jo's bunch of roughnecks with less than a dozen men; and you can bet your young life our gang is too big as it is. Keep the home fires burning, I'll say!"

"Well, for Heaven's sake, try and get busy soon!" Lucy cried petulantly. "Goodness knows I did my part—all that any woman could be expected to do. So far I'm the only one that's accomplished anything. Why in thunder didn't Hank's friend, Pete, 'tend to the business up there in the mountains, after you and Hank had beat it? Hooker was out, this fellow said, and the girl still tied. And then he comes out of his dope and gets on a horse, and beats it like you other two quitters!"

"He didn't have the paper," explained Al. "Besides, Pete thought he was going to croak. He was laid up longer than Hooker, even, and Hooker had got a bullet. Pete's skull was cracked, and for a time it was a toss-up whether he'd pull through or not. He went nutty up there, I guess. He was lying sidewise across the saddle, unconscious but holding on for dear life, when the horse caught up with us. And Hank and I ducked out because—well, it's hard to explain. Both of us were pretty badly beaten up, you know, and there wasn't much fight left in us. Hooker had surprised us, and we were rattled. I don't know—a fellow can't explain just why he does the wrong thing in a situation like that. But knock the fight out of a man and make him groggy, and he'll bungle every time."

"Well, do something now," ordered Lucy frigidly; and Hiram heard Drummond scrape back his chair in rising.

"All right—we'll see. I'll beat it now. Up late last night playing poker. Rotten luck, too!"

"Al," said Lucy's voice, "when we get that jack, are you going to give me a fair share of it?"

"Sure—sure! Why do you keep harping on that, Lucy? Haven't I promised you I would? Good night. I'm dead tired!"

Half an hour before dawn next morning Hiram Hooker crawled from his blankets in camp and fed hay and grain to Babe, Jerkline Jo's black saddle mare. Then, leaving his companions placidly snoring, he walked briskly along the trail to Ragtown. Ten minutes after his start he was knocking on the door of Jo's tiny pine cabin.

"What is it?" finally came the girl's sleepy tones. "Who is there?"

"It's I, Jo. Hiram. Will you come to the door a second? I want to talk with you."

"You big whale! What do you mean, waking me up in the middle of the night? Anything wrong?"

"No, Jo. And it's almost time to get up. The boys will be out by the time I get back. Hurry and get dressed, won't you?"

There was a rustling and quick moving about inside, and presently the door was unlocked and Jerkline Jo poked her head out inquiringly.

"I came to ask you for a few days off," he explained.

"Why, Hiram?"

"Yes, just one trip, Jo. There isn't any more freight than the rest of you can handle just now. Won't be till spring, I'm thinking."

"Oh, I could spare you now better than later on. But—but what, Hiram?"

"And I'd like to borrow Babe and your saddle and bridle, too."

"Take them," she said confidently. "Whatever your mysterious disappearance means, I know I can trust you."

Half an hour afterward Hiram swung himself into Jo's big California saddle, and then leaned over and spoke to Blink Keddie and Heine Schultz, busy at harnessing the teams.

"I don't know when I'll be back, boys," he said. "But remember what I told you: Don't let Jo out of your sight in the pass—nor anywhere else, for that matter—and keep your guns handy all the time."

"Don't worry, Gentle Wild Cat!" Schultz assured him.

"So long, then," said Hiram, and swung Babe into the road that connected Ragtown with the line of camps which dotted the desert from end to end.

CHAPTER XXXI

A TALE OF THE DESERT'S DEAD

No land seems so delectable as the desert early on a crisp morning. The rare air causes the blood to pound through one's veins, and an unexplainable rapture seizes man's spirits.

Jo's black mare, Babe, had not been ridden for weeks, and every greasewood bush that she saw became in the weird light of sunrise a grotesque goblin ready to spring at her and devour her whole. At least, so she pretended, and as her natural weapon of defense lay in flight, she kept Hiram Hooker busy holding her down to a fast gallop.

The low-hanging tapaderos flapped loosely. Hiram's borrowed silver-mounted spurs—a reminder of Tom Gulick's cow-punching days in Utah—jingled merrily. The heavy six-gun at his hip flopped against the silver-rimmed cantle of Jo's fifty-pound saddle. The smells of the morning were sweet. Away over the vast expanse of bronze greasewood, far-flung buttes caught the early rays of the sun and took on something of the likeness of a solar spectrum, purple at their bases, the colors ranging upward through blues and greens and yellows to a spun-gold glitter at their summits. Jack rabbits loped away through the brush. Now and then a coyote, ears pricked up, trotted along, his tail dragging. Tecolote, the little desert owl, came from his hole and sat on the pile of dirt beside it, while his wife peeked out with her round head just above the ground and gave silent approval to her lord and master's querulous criticism of the rider.

Life was good—life was glorious. Life was love! The poetic heart of the man from Wild-cat Hill sang ceaselessly. He was away on his romantic quest to serve the most splendid girl a man had ever loved!

As the morning progressed and the sun climbed higher and higher, Babe bore him through many camps, both large and small. At each he drew rein and made inquiry after an old prospector called Basil Filer, who drove six burros. No one had seen such a man, however, and Hiram continued on toward the north until noon. Then he stopped for dinner and to feed and rest the mare at Demarest, Spruce & Tillou's Camp Number Two. They had come twenty-one miles that morning, he learned at dinner in the huge dining tent; and when he started out again he held Babe in, because she was soft for want of exercise.

On and on they traveled, nevertheless, Hiram making inquiry at every camp. At last, thirty miles from Ragtown, he got word of the prospector. A camp freighter who traveled to the north for supplies from Demarest, Spruce & Tillou's Camp Number Three had seen such a man trudging along with his long staff, eyes bent on the ground, behind his six burros. He had been seen about ten miles farther north, traveling south, the day before.

Hiram loped on, and now reached a strip of the right-of-way where camps were few and far between. The desert was dryer here than in the vicinity of Ragtown, and greasewood and whispering yuccas gave place to low sage and the shimmering dry lakes, which lure thirsting men on to their doom with their mocking resemblance to the life-saving water the wanderer craves.

Always, it seemed, there was somewhere within the range of Hiram's vision one of those weird whirlwinds sweeping along. Often they were so far away they seemed motionless, and looked like brown funnel-shaped pillars, wrong end up, supporting the turquoise sky. Again, they were close—sometimes six or seven in sight at once—as they spun like huge tops, sucking up everything loose in their path, and whirling it round and round with stupefying rapidity.

At last one of them overtook the horse and rider, and the mare stopped short, thrusting her head between her front legs and tucking in her flowing tail. Hiram had time only to grab his hat and throw himself forward along the mare's neck; the next instant it seemed as if a million tugging hands had hold of him and were trying to whirl him into the heavens and carry him, like a garment whipped from a clothesline, into mysterious distances.

When it had passed he sat erect once more and dug the dirt from his ears and eyes, trying to follow the twister's progress as it sped drunkenly on to find other victims.

Then it was that Hiram saw the pack train, not far distant over the desert, making ready to receive the coming whirlwind. The burros, wise little animals that they are, had huddled together, tails outward, heads down; and in the center of them Hiram saw a man just stooping for the protection of their bodies. Next instant the group vanished—was swallowed up by the wind demon.

When the old man looked up after the onslaught, Hiram was riding upon him. The prospector stood trying to stare at him from the center of his pack train, wiping his watering eyes and sand-stained mouth.

"Hello, there!" called Hiram. "It spoke to us in passing, too. How do you like 'em?"

"I got to like 'em," returned the old man. "I eat 'em—break-fast, dinner, and supper. Grub don't taste good any more 'less a twister's passed over it and seasoned it up. Who are you?"

Hiram swung his great frame from the creaking saddle.

"I'm Hiram Hooker," he announced, lowering the mare's reins and advancing until a mouse-colored burro aimed a kick at him to show him that he was a rank outsider whose company was not desired.

"Why, Muta, that ain't no way to act!" mildly expostulated the burro's master. "She's just a mite playful," he explained apologetically to Hiram. "Muta, she thinks a heap o' the ole man, ye see, an' she's always lookin' out that strangers don't mean 'im any harm."

He placed both arms about the shaggy burro's neck. "You must be more polite, Muta," he said chidingly, while the little animal trust out her upper lip and nibbled at the large horn buttons on his dusty canvas coat.

"Which way are you bound?" asked Hiram.

"South now. Just travelin'. Maybe I'll make it over to Rattlesnake Buttes"—he raised an arm toward the northeast—"and maybe down Caldron Canon way." He pointed southeast toward the mountains. "I dunno—just driftin' along, me an' the little fellas. Sometimes we drift here, and sometimes we drift there. Don't matter much, s'long's there's grub an' a little rolled barley in the pack-bags. What's the dif'rence anyway?" His red-lidded eyes looked up weirdly at Hiram.

Bent and pathetic he was, this old man of the hills and deserts—this old lizard of the unfriendly sands. In his eyes all time seemed to have written its history. His brows were shaggy and desert-colored, like the brows of the Ancient Mariner whose scrawny, clutching fingers robbed the Wedding Guest of his night of pleasure. His hands shook, and he carried a long cane; but for him the merciless desert seemed to hold no lasting terror, for he spent his life on its desert searching for the treasure that is hidden there.

"Me and the little fellas just drift along. We get work at the camps when our grubstake's gone; and then we ramble on and on—just driftin', kinda. I got a ole jack rabbit for supper, pardner. He was sleepin' under a sagebrush, and I puts out his eye with my six and twenty paces. Can you do that? But you're young—young and got a clever eye. Anyway, I got a ole jack for supper. Now, if you had a bottle on you couldn't we have a time!"

"I've no bottle," Hiram said. "I'm sorry. But, if you'll invite me, I'll help you with the jack."

"Got blankets behind yer saddle, I see. All right, my friend. Ole Filer's always ready to share his grub with a passer-by on the desert. There's water in my little tank. Burros don't drink much, you know. A taste's enough till we get to a camp to-morrow. Handy, those camps, for prospectors needin' a grubstake. Let's camp over there by that lonesome yucca palm. He looks as if he wanted company. Maybe he'll whisper where they's gold to-night—if we keep on ear awake. He-he! Oh, they whisper lots—lots—lots! But they always lie like sin!"

When the "ole jack" had paid the final price of his lack of watchfulness, Hiram Hooker and the crazy prospector leaned back and looked up at the cold stars that smiled cruelly down on the arid waste. The wind whispered mysteriously through the bayonets of the yucca palm above them. Not long would one be obliged to live and move and have his being alone on this desert before strange messages would begin to formulate in the wind's eerie whispering in the yuccas.

The burros ranged about, browsing off the desert growth. There had been barley for Babe, and Hiram had watered her at the last camp. A rinse-out of her mouth and she would do very well till morning.

And there under the scornful stars Hiram and the old man lounged on packbags and talked, with their tiny camp fire of greasewood roots between them. And gradually as Hiram told what he knew and convinced the gray old rat of his honesty, an uncanny tale of the barren lands began unfolding, a tale revolving about a little girl baby left by prospectors in a yucca-trunk corral—the tale of Jean Prince, daughter of Leonard Prince, whose bones had been gnawed by coyotes and covered by the shifting sands for over twenty years. And the baby girl, Jean Prince, was none other than the magnetic, dark-haired woman who now drove jerkline to Ragtown and numbered her admirers by the thousand—Jerkline Jo, Queen of the Outland Camps.

"They was three of us at first," narrated Filer in a shaky voice. "Three of us and Baby Jean. Baby Jean and me and Len Prince and 'The Chink.' And that makes four. But Baby Jean was only two years old.

"Hong Duo was the chink—a grinnin' yenshee hound from up beyond the Tehachapi—way up—up toward the Sierra Nevadas, in the placer country. White prospectors ner white miners don't often work with chinks. Chinks is only good for workin' tailin's when it comes to mines. But Len he'd saved Hong Duo's life in trouble in a dump in Placerville—ol' Hangtown—and the chink had clung to um like a burro to somethin' he's swiped from Camp.

"Agin' that, too, the chink had money—an' Len and me was broke. Fer a year he grubstaked us, and followed us around pocketin' up that a way, cookin' and such, and livin' for Len and Baby Jean.

"Baby Jean's maw she died when the kid was borned; and everywhere Len went after she was a year or more he took her. We drifted south—me and Len and the chink and Baby Jean.

"Up Death Valley way we got wind o' somethin' good. Days and days we makes it into the land that God forgot, and here and there we pecked out a little color. Then Len and me we gets a lead, and we leaves the chink and Baby Jean and drifts on into a country that makes me shiver yet ta think of.

"We got some gold—quite some. And me"—his voice grew low—"I was younger then, and mean as dirt. I was high-gradin' on my pardner right and left. I guess I was always mean; but I've paid the price.

"Then Len he gets onto me, but he holds his tongue. And we make it on and on into Little Hall, till the sandstorm come.

"Fer nigh onto fifty-nine years I've roamed the desert, pardner, but I've never seen another storm like that. Days and days she blowed, and sometimes you couldn't see yer hand before yer face for the flyin' sand. Someway we gets out of it, the Almighty knows how! But from that day to this I've never been able to find that place ag'in.

"There was gold there—piles and piles o' gold—and Len he'd found it. Found it out alone one day before the storm set in. And knowin' I'd been high-gradin' on him, he kep' this find to 'imself. Then come the storm, and we fought out just ahead o' death.

"Then Len he keeps tryin' to go back—wants to work long for a big grubstake, and is quiet and dreams a lot, with Baby Jean in his arms, and the chink settin' cross-legged lookin' at 'em with his glitterin' little eyes—half full o' hop, I guess. And I gets onto why Len wants to drift back there to that land o' dead men's bones, and I watch 'im, and freeze to 'im continual.

"Len he makes a bluff at this an' that an' the other—him and me and the chink driftin' from here to there over this part o' the desert, or hereabouts, scratchin' a little now and ag'in. But Len his heart ain't in it, I see; and all the time he's tryin' to shake me off, I get it. But I won't shake.

"Well, Len he ain't no more good after the awful time we went through up there in that terrible land. He never was a man ag'in after that; and he gets scared, I guess, and thinks he's gonna cash his chips. They's a queer look in his eyes, and in camp he just sets and sets with Baby Jean in his arms, and the hophead lookin' at 'em from across the fire with his glitterin' little eyes. And sometimes Len he just sets and sets and watches Baby Jean asleep, and his eyes are worried like a horse's eyes when he knows he's starvin'; and the yenshee hound he just sets and looks at Len, and Heaven only knows what he's thinkin'!

"Then we make it up along in where the Salt Lake road was buildin' then—up Barstow way—all wild them days. And one day Len and me and the chink goes out into the buttes, and leaves Baby Jean in a yucca-stump corral so's the c'yotes can't get at her, like we did sometimes. She wasn't never a yellin' kid. Give her a bottle o' canned cow, and she'd suck herself to sleep with varmints prowlin' about and sandstorms blowin'. Sometimes she'd sob if things was goin' wrong in her little world—low and heartbroken, like a woman cries. But yell—never!

"So we leaves her suckin' at her bottle, for Len he'd never broke her of it, and out we goes to scratch around some more up in Turkey Buttes.

"It was lookin' to storm and we hadn't oughta gone maybe; but we didn't aim to make it far, and could come back any time. But when she broke she broke sudden; and only once before had I seen such a blow as that. We got plumb lost five miles from camp; and all that day and all that night and all next day we wandered about in the whirlin' sand, outa water, and goin' crazier every minute. The chink he gives up, and so does Len; and I'm too crazy to make 'em keep on fightin'. I dragged out two days later, way north o' the buttes—plumb bughouse, my tongue all black and stiff as rubber. I've never been the same man since, I guess. I dream about them days and nights.

"The folks that found me they go huntin' for Len and the chink and Baby Jean t'other side o' the buttes. They find Len and the chink, both dead, their faces and tongues—But I don't like to remember that! Sometimes the yuccas they whisper about it; but I always plug my ears and begin to sing, or talk to the asses about the fun we'll have when we find Jean Prince and get the gold Len knew about up there Death Valley way.

"They turned Len's things over to me. The baby they couldn't find; but after weeks they stumbled onto the camp where we'd left her and found everything almost buried in sand. The kid was gone, and the c'yotes hadn't got her. They was a piece o' paper in the camp; but it had rained and rained since it was stuck up there, and all the writin' was gone. In Len's things I finds the paper that I'm carryin', and I kep' it to myself. I've got it now—right here"—he thumped his breast—"and for twenty years I've hunted for Baby Jean and never found her.

"They's gold up there—up where Len Prince found it. The paper tells only half o' how to relocate Len's claims. At the beginnin' it says the paper's for Baby Jean, and no one else is to have it. Len knew he was soon goin' to croak—and he fixed it for Baby Jean when he was gone. He done his best. Any one who's got the paper knows only half. Whoever's got the paper can't do nothin' without Baby Jean.

"The chink he done it. It was crazy—loco, you'll say. But what c'n you expect from a man who's suffered as he did? Lissen, pardner—the chink he done it. The paper tells about it. The chink he doped the kid—with opium, some way, I guess—so's it wouldn't hurt her, and then he tattooed the rest o' the directions for findin' the gold on the head o' Baby Jean. Cut off some hair in back, and shaved a spot on her little head, and tattooed it there. The chink he did. And then the hair grew out ag'in, and nobody ever knew!

"Even Baby Jean don't know—a woman grown up now. And years and years I've hunted for her, but couldn't find her. Cause I couldn't stick, I guess. Somethin' always kep' callin' me back into the hills, and I'd forgot. Just me and the little fellas, we understand. And we're driftin' about ag'in huntin' for Baby Jean.

"I had a funny dream. I dreamed I'd found her—a young woman grown. And in that dream she told me she was Baby Jean, and I told her all about the paper and the tattoo marks. And then it looked like I drifted into deeper sleep and I woke up in camp way out in nowhere. I'd forgot again, you see, and drifted for the hills just when I'd found Baby Jean. Or so I dreamed. But sometimes I think I wasn't dreamin', pardner. It wasn't just like other dreams I've had. I got it that I was in a place called Ragtown, and I know they's such a place, cause everybody tells me so. And I was sick after the dream. Funny! I'm drifting that a way now. I want to see that Ragtown. Was it a dream? Or was the yuccas laughin' at ole Filer ag'in? I dunno. But how come it I dreamed about a place called Ragtown, a place that really is but that I never seen?"

CHAPTER XXXII

LUCY PLANS A COUNTER-ATTACK

One who has never lived in a frontier camp such as Ragtown may find it difficult to analyze the characters of Lucy Dalles and Albert Drummond.

Less than a year before Ragtown had sprung up overnight, both had been ordinarily respectable American citizens. Lucy's crowning fault had been the lust for wealth. Added to this now was the fierce determination to realize her ambition, coupled with the complete breakdown of the moral fabric of her soul. She had been flirtatious and pleasure-loving in San Francisco, but perhaps not really bad at heart.

Drummond had been as decent as millions of other young men who pass for that in good society. A bit wild, but a man who dealt squarely with others sportsmanlike, and perhaps considered perfectly honest by himself and all who knew him.

But all this the frontier town had changed. That little semidormant spark of wickedness and criminality which is perhaps in every mother's son and daughter of us had been fanned to a flame by the lawlessness of Ragtown. The feverish night life, the chink of gold on gambling tables that were seldom unoccupied, the continual drinking of intoxicants, the doping and robbing of stiffs, which was practiced with studied, businesslike regularity, the brawls and shooting scrapes—all these had worked their insidious spell upon mentalities not forfeited by careful early training and bed-rock character.

Drummond and Lucy Dalles were dangerous conspirators now, and took a certain pride in the knowledge of it. They not only schemed for great rewards, but for the love of it. Lust for wealth and for revenge, the thrill of the dangerous and underhanded game they played, contempt for those whose moral fabric was too strongly woven to break under the strain of Ragtown, a certain vague satisfaction in their newly discovered rascality—all these spurred them on to make the most of their opportunities. One step in the direction they had taken leads so easily to another, that now they had reached a point in their moral lapse where they would stop at nothing—not even the taking of life—to win that on which they had set their hearts.

From a night spent at poker, Al Drummond, weary and half dead for sleep, reeled from the Dugout early on the morning when Hiram Hooker set out to find the crazy prospector, Basil Filer. As he slouched along the street in the cold he heard the jingling of bells and the rumbling of heavy wagons; and presently the freight outfit of Jerkline Jo rolled past, the girl and her skinners, bundled to the ears and slapping their hands against their ribs for warmth.

Drummond gave them a contemptuous glance for their honest and difficult endeavor, then took note that his old enemy, the man from Wild-cat Hill, was missing. He wondered about this, but gave it little thought until it dawned upon him that Jo's beautiful black saddle mare, which usually followed behind the wagon train with doglike loyalty, was absent too. He stopped short then and found that he was thinking of the old prospector, whom he had seen for the second time the day before.

He was worried. Could it be possible that Jo and Hiram had got wind of the mystery? For all he knew, they might have met the old man somewhere on the desert and learned his secret. It was such a usual thing to see Hiram behind his ten black freighters on every trip in or out that the conspirator could not down suspicion.

All that day he worried over it, but did not mention it to Lucy. Coming from another night of poker the following morning, having seen nothing of Hiram Hooker in the meantime, he decided to look into the matter as best he could.

He would get his car and drive up the line a way, toward the camp where he had seen Filer two days before. He could readily learn at intervening camps whether or not Hiram had ridden that way on Jo's black mare.

He had no appetite for breakfast, so he got out his touring car and drove away toward the north while Ragtown slept.

Men were at work in the third camp that he reached, and here a little inquiry brought forth the information that Hooker had gone the way Drummond had feared. Now he drove fast along the road that followed the right of way, passing rapidly through camp after camp, until he was far from Ragtown.

It was not yet eight o'clock when, far ahead, he saw a black horse galloping toward him. He had just run the car out upon the smooth, dark surface of one of the desert's famous dry lakes, where almost nothing grew. The ground was level and hard as a dance floor, so he turned from the road and drove at right angles to it across the crusted soil. He drove fast, and by the time the rider reached the point in the road where Drummond first had seen him Drummond was so far away that Hiram could not recognize him or his car.

Drummond circled now and regained the road, continuing on into the north in search of what he dreaded to discover. But not many miles had been covered before he was gritting his teeth and swearing over the knowledge of his scheme's defeat. He saw rolling toward him, swinging their packs from side to side as gently as a mother rocks a cradle, six shaggy, long-eared "desert canaries" with an old desert-colored man behind them who limped along with the aid of a cane.

Drummond drove no farther in that direction. There was no need for it. The sight of the old man drifting toward Ragtown and Hiram galloping on ahead of him showed him plainly that the cat was out of the bag, that the two had held a conference on the desert during the night just past.

Bitter with rage, Drummond turned about and drove fiercely back in Hiram's wake. He slowed down when he began to draw near to the horse and rider, and for an hour kept his distance while he waited for Hiram to reach another dry lake that was nearer to Ragtown than the first.

When the rider ahead had reached it and was galloping across if, Drummond speeded up, reached the lake in turn, and at last was able to make a wide half circle over land where no greasewood grew to impede the course of the car.

The lake was a large one, and by driving at close to sixty miles an hour and skirting its edge, he reached the road again a mile ahead of Hiram, and sped on toward home to break the news of defeat to Lucy Dalles.

At ten o'clock he reached Ragtown, having driven recklessly.

"Somebody's spilled the beans!" was his stormy beginning. "We're gypped. Got any jackass? Gi'me the bottle. I'm a wreck!"

He dropped wearily into a chair and told of what he had discovered.

"How on earth did they get wind of it?" she asked.

Drummond threw out his hands in a gesture proclaiming ignorance and despair.

"There's one thing sure," she said thoughtfully. "He saw the paper only yesterday or last night for the first time. Else why did he ride way up there to see Filer? Jerkline Jo, then, has not yet seen it. They've heard about it, though, and Hooker was sent out to hunt for Filer. So the first thing the big rube will do when he reaches Ragtown will be to travel over toward Julia to overtake Jo and report. He'll get another horse, maybe, or hire a machine. Tweet would be in on it, no doubt, and would take him in his car. So what we've got to do, my dear boy, is to see that Hooker doesn't get to Jo with what he's learned."

"What can we do? He probably made a copy of what's written on Filer's paper, so, even if we were to hold him up and get it away from him, old Filer still would have the dope."

"Of course. That means that we've got to fix that old dub, too."

"What d'ye mean fix him?"

The girl shrugged. "Stop the leak some way," she replied. "If we can destroy Filer's paper and the copy Hooker's got, then we'll be the only ones who know the dope. We'll have the only copy in existence, in other words; and even if we fail to get at Jerkline Jo and learn the rest of it, we can hold her to our terms. She won't be able to do a thing without knowing what her father wrote on the paper that Filer has."

"Lucy, it's a crazy business," said Drummond. "Sometimes I think it's all a pipedream of that nutty old prospector. They're all bughouse—these old desert rats."

"It's not a pipedream," Lucy stoutly maintained. "I tell you I saw the blue tattoo marks on that woman's scalp when I was beautifying her up for the ball that night. I wondered what they were. Of course, with her heavy hair covering them— growing right out of them, in fact—I couldn't make out anything but blue dots."

"And you didn't ask her about 'em?"

"Why, of course not, Al! Do you suppose a hair dresser would last very long in the business if she showed curiosity about a thing like that? You don't know much about women. If I'd found a knob on her nut as big as a baseball she'd never have been told that I'd seen it."

"But how in thunder has she reached her present age without knowing it's there?"

"She inadvertantly explained that; and so, when later in the day, old Filer spilled what he knew I was sure Jo had never dreamed of what she is carrying about under her hair.

"You see, she was raised like an Indian. She told me that, even when she was a little kid, she'd always been made to wash her own hair. She naively confided to me that when she came into my place it was her first time in any sort of a beauty parlor. A woman can't very well see the back of her head, can she? And she'd never be able to see the tattoo marks, even with two mirrors, with all that beautiful hair she's got. Do you know what your scalp looks like, at the back of your head, just above your ears? I guess not! You bet it's straight! And here you sit arguing about a trifle, when a rich gold claim is slipping from our fingers. Can't you—put your brain to work?"

"Well, what's to be done?"

"If that big boog starts to overtake Jerkline Jo, he's got to be stopped, and the copy taken away from him. While this is going on, Filer must be held up and the original taken from him and destroyed.

"Then when we get the copy away from Hooker and destroy Filer's original, we can throw our cards on the table and laugh at 'em. Come right out and say, 'Yes, we schemed to beat you, and we've done it. What're you going to do about it? You've got the tattooed part, we've got the only copy of the other part. Make us an offer! Otherwise, throw us in jail, if you think you've got it on us; but before we go the paper will go up in smoke!' That'll hold 'em; and we'll demand that we are not to be prosecuted, and we'll shake down half of the haul.

"But listen, Al—we'll do that only if they beat us out up to a point where negotiations become necessary. If only we can destroy the original and Hooker's copy, we can hold Hooker a prisoner till we get at Jerkline Jo and find out what's on her head. Then we can hog it all and beat it."

"Well—well, how'll we begin? You got me beat, Lucy. You're a better schemer than I am. What's to be done first?"

"Beat it in your car to the mountains and get Tehachapi and the other roughnecks. Send Tehachapi Hank up the line to waylay Filer between camps somewhere, with instructions to get the original from him by hook or crook. Leave it to Hank.

"Meantime, Hooker gets in here and starts after Jerkline Jo. It's doubtful if the thickhead will think to memorize what's on his copy, as I have done. Even if he does think to, he won't have time to do it before you nab him. He's dense—he wouldn't learn it in a week, I'll say!"

"You and Hank's friend will waylay him, then, and get his copy, destroy it, and take Hooker into the mountains as a prisoner, with Hank's friend to guard him. Then it will be up to you and me to get Jerkline Jo as she's coming back through the mountains. Yes, I'll go along! It seems the rest of you can do nothing. Leave that Jane to me! I'll get her by a method unknown to you men!

"We'll dope her, cut off her hair, shave her scalp, and get the part of the directions for finding the gold that we lack. Then, Al, why can't you and I get the stuff, beat it, and give Hank and the other jasper the ha-ha?"

"Lucy, you're getting to be a regular little devil!"

Lucy shrugged and seemed rather pleased than otherwise.

"And your ideas about that gold are of the vaguest," he continued. "You seem to think it's lying about in chunks, begging to be picked up and heaped in bushel baskets! All we can do, perhaps, is make claim filings, and get to Los Angeles and record them. Then, to realize anything, we've got to take mining engineers out there to make tests. Then the companies they represent will make us an offer—and probably skin us alive. In the meantime we'll be having all kinds of trouble with Jerkline Jo and her bunch of roustabouts."

"Well, then, we'll settle all that later," Lucy retorted. "Your first move is to go for Hank and get a toehold, as Tweet says. Don't borrow trouble! It's time to figure out our future steps when we know we hold all the trumps. And the sooner you start the better. Thank Heaven you've not gambled away your last automobile, Al! Their horses beat you before, but your last little old boat will win out now. Get after 'em, boy! It's a great game if you don't weaken!"

Five minutes later Drummond was driving rapidly toward the mouth of the mountain pass. By three o'clock he was back and following the line of camps again, with Tehachapi Hank huddled on the floor of the tonneau and covered with robes. Drummond had the good fortune to pass through Demarest, Spruce & Tillou's Camp Number Two when Hiram had stopped there for a late "hand-out," furnished by the obliging cooks. Drummond saw the black mare standing near the cook tent door, and hurried on through, elated over the knowledge that Hiram had not seen him. He at last dumped his passenger on the desert between camps, having estimated that the slow-moving burro train could not be many miles ahead.

Promising to return for Hank as soon as possible, Drummond raced back toward Ragtown, passed Hiram again—at close quarters this time—and reached the tent village ahead of him early in the evening.

Now he and Lucy settled down to wait for Hiram's coming and to watch his future movements.

CHAPTER XXXIII

POCKETED

Hiram Hooker, knowing well the story of Jerkline Jo's having been found as a baby girl in a deserted camp on the desert, had easily been able to convince old Basil Filer that she was the young woman he had been searching for so long.

They had spent half the night in planning in their desert camp. Hiram's frank, open nature tended to breed confidence in the most pessimistic of men; and when he told Filer of the wonderful character of Jerkline Jo and assured him that, despite his past rascality, he would be handsomely rewarded by her, the helpless old man agreed to all that he proposed.

Knowing that the prospector would not reach Ragtown for a long time with his sauntering burros, Hiram was for making a copy of what the precious paper contained and hurrying on ahead, to overtake Jo as soon as possible, and suggest that she make arrangements for a strip to the lost claims before starting back from Julia. To this the desert rat agreed; but when they were ready for Hiram to make a copy it was discovered that neither man had a scrap of paper, or even a pencil.

There was nothing to be done then, if the original plan was to be carried out, but for Basil Filer to surrender into Hiram's keeping the document. This, with many misgivings, Filer consented to do.

So they broke camp early next morning, and Hiram hurried on ahead with the original in his pocket. The old man was to traipse along after him, and in all probability would reach Ragtown before Hiram had overtaken Jo.

Al Drummond passed Hiram in his car as he was nearing his journey's end late that afternoon; but of course Hiram thought nothing of this, as Drummond and his car made a familiar sight about the country. Hiram had decided to ask Tweet to carry him in his machine until Jerkline Jo had been overtaken, which would probably occur between the foot of the mountains and Artesian Ranch on the other side. Then Tweet would return, and Hiram would ride on with the outfit and reveal to the girl what he had heard of the strange thing she had worn concealed under her lustrous hair since she was two years old.

Hiram knew about how Drummond and Lucy had stumbled onto the truth, which Jerkline Jo herself had not even dreamed of.

What the old prospector had told him of his "dream" convinced Hiram that Lucy had got wind of the secret and had cleverly posed as the lost child grown up, and had been able to draw Filer's story out of him. He had said that in his dream he had been shown something on the girl's scalp, under her hair, that looked like tattooing. Hiram reasoned that Drummond could have dotted Lucy's scalp with a pen and ink sufficient to convince the old desert rat that she was the girl he was seeking. Then he had told his story, but had been in some way rendered unconscious and disposed of before he could demand the clipping of Lucy's hair and the shaving of her scalp. No doubt, while he was unconscious, Drummond and Lucy had made a copy of what was on the paper.

To Hiram's great disappointment he found on reaching Ragtown late that afternoon that Twitter-or-Tweet had driven to Los Angeles on business. He hunted about for another machine, but there seemed to be none in town that he could hire. There was Drummond's, of course, but to deal with him was out of the question.

"Hello, Hiram boy!" Lucy called sweetly as he walked past the shooting gallery. "You look worried. Whassa malla? Jo fired you?"

"Not yet," said Hiram briefly. "I was looking for a machine so that I could catch up with the outfit, but can't seem to locate one."

"Not many about town this time of year," she commented. "Did you get so cuckooed Jo had to leave you behind to sober up, Wild Cat? And now you've got to chase her, eh? 'Fraid Heine or some of 'em'll get her away from you if you don't stick around—that it?"

To this Hiram smiled with cold politeness, but, made no reply, passing on down the street.

He would be forced to wait until morning. Then, provided Tweet had not returned, he would have to ride Babe over the mountains and reach Jerkline Jo at least before she had started back. After all, there was no great hurry. The gold had lain where it did for countless centuries. It would continue to lie so for a few days more, perhaps.

Tweet did not return that night, and at dawn Hiram was away toward the mountains on the black mare, the precious paper secreted in his shirt. He was ten miles from Ragtown before it occurred to him what a fool he had been in not making a copy of it. Any one of a hundred things might happen to it. Still, the crazy prospector had carried it through all the years and had lost it.

He wondered if it would not be a practical idea to commit it to memory. Why, certainly—that was the thing to do.

He was nearing such foothills as the abrupt mountain range boasted when he decided not only to memorize it, but to make a copy on an envelope which was in his pocket. It had covered a letter from Uncle Sebastian Burris, Hiram's benefactor, up there in Mendocino County. He had found it awaiting him the night before at Ragtown. He and Uncle Sebastian had kept up a correspondence ever since Hiram had come south.

Although he had no pencil, it occurred to him that he could write with the lead bullet of one of his revolver cartridges, which simple feat he had often performed in idle moments in the woods up home.

Dismounting, he lowered the bridle rein over Babe's head, and sat down on the ground. He took out Uncle Sebastian's letter, and with his pocket-knife slit the envelope till it provided him with a square of paper. He laid the worn original—a yellow piece of tough sheepskin paper—on a flat rock beside him. He took a cartridge from his belt and began to copy the reddish writing.

He had just completed the task when there came a sudden terrific roar in his ears, and before he knew what was happening a desert twister had swept down upon him in all its fury.

It passed swiftly, and through half-blinded eyes Hiram saw that the original had been whisked from the rock on which it had lain as if by magic.

Fortunately he had held to his copy instinctively; but he had not compared it with the original. He might have made some small but vital mistake. Away over the desert twisted the miniature cyclone, and he knew that, spinning around with it, was the sheepskin. Rather foolishly in his excitement he grabbed his six-shooter from its holster and slapped it down upon his copy to protect it from another such catastrophe, and, still half-blinded, vaulted to the saddle and set the mare at a dead run in the wake of the whirlwind.

Then it was that Al Drummond, who had been slowly

Arthur Preston Hankins

creeping through the greasewood bushes toward Hiram, arose with a yelp of triumph and ran to the weighted-down copy of the precious directions.

Out there in the whirlwind the original was fleeing rapidly away from the frantic rider, with the chances many to one that it would not be recovered. Here in Drummond's hand was the only copy in existence, except the one already in his and Lucy's possession. It was plain that Hiram had not previously made another copy, else why would he have stopped here on the desert to draft this one? Also, by the same token, it was plain that Hiram had not memorized the contents. Basil Filer might have done so, it was true; but, then, Tehachapi Hank would attend to Basil Filer.

Quickly Drummond stooped and touched the blaze of a match to the envelope, and in a few minutes only a crinkled bit of black, charred paper lay on the ground.

"Pete!" he called, and from the greasewood another man arose and hurried toward him.

"Look!" Drummond cried exultantly, pointing to the burned paper. "There's what's left of the copy he was making. And here's his gun—he used it to weigh down the copy when he raced away after the whirlwind. Run for the horses. We'll get after him and get the original away from him, if he gets it. Then, if Hank gets Filer—which he certainly will—we'll have the only copies in existence!"

Pete, the bosom friend of Tehachapi Hank, turned about and ran up toward the fringe of junipers that concealed their horses, brought down the day before from the mountains. Drummond, while he waited, gazed after the strange chase, and noted that the fleet black mare was steadily overtaking the moving funnel of dust which represented the whirlwind.

"By golly, if he can ride into the thing and break it, or keep up with it till it breaks itself, he'll get the sheepskin!" Drummond muttered. "But he won't keep it. He's left his gun. He's our meat now!"

Then Pete rode up rapidly, leading Drummond's mount, and next moment they were on the dead run in pursuit of Hiram.

Time and again, as they drew nearer, they saw Hiram deliberately riding the mare through the whirlwind, trying to break it. The thing seemed a devil, alive and diabolically bent on eluding him. It changed course from right to left, but the cow pony was as quick as it was; and it seemed to the racing spectators that she enjoyed the game. Hiram was so intent on his task, so frequently blinded by the whirlwind, while his ears were filled with its roar, that to ride almost upon him without his knowledge of it was an easy task for Pete and Drummond.

They were very close to him, then, when at last the mare's lunges broke the whirlwind, and a scattered cloud of dust hid horse and rider. Whether or not Hiram had rescued the paper they could not tell, but they spurred their horses on.

The dust settled, and close at hand they saw Hiram, dismounted. At the same instant he seemed to hear the thunder of hoofs, and glanced their way. He took a couple of steps and grasped his mare's bridle, and was standing unconcernedly at her head When they raced up, both training sixshooters on him.

"Stick 'em up, Hooker!" ordered Drummond. "This means business at last."

Totally unarmed, Hiram grinned and slowly elevated his hands.

Watching him closely, Drummond and Pete dismounted, and, still keeping their sixes trained on Hiram's stomach, approached him.

"Well, Hooker," Drummond said sneeringly, "we meet again,

Arthur Preston Hankins

don't we? You see, we've showed our hand at last—and it's a pretty good one, too. You're onto us, anyway, I guess, so from now on we'll fight in the open. Did you get the sheepskin?"

Hiram reverted to his provincial drawl, as was his habit in moments of great stress.

"No, she got plumb away from me," he said. "She got outa the whirlwind back there somewheres, or else she's gone on with what's left o' the twister."

"I was afraid you wasn't going to say that, Hooker," Drummond said. "Well, let me show you something. Do you recognize this gat?"

Hiram looked uneasily at a third big six-shooter, which Drummond had produced as he spoke.

"I reckon she was mine a while back," he said with a gulp.

"Exactly. And what you left it to hold down, Hooker, has gone up in smoke."

"You got—You burned—"

"Got and burned is right, Hooker. But I don't just like your tone. If you were on the stage, Brother Hiram, I think you'd get the hook. 'Hook Hooker!' the audience might yell. Don't you think I'm funny at times, Gentle Wild Cat? It's just my pleasant little way of informing you that I consider you a poor actor. 'You got—you burned' was pretty fair, Hi-ram, but not quite good enough. So we're going to search you and make sure you didn't get the sheepskin out of the whirlwind."

"I didn't get it," Hiram said sulkily. "She's gone forever."

"She is in any event, Hooker. But we have a copy at Ragtown—don't forget that. Now let go these reins and step over here. And be mighty careful, Hi-ram—mighty careful.

My friend here is a nervous man with a six-gun."

Obediently Hiram dropped the mare's reins and stepped away from her head. Drummond laid the two revolvers at some distance away from them on the ground, so that, while he was searching Hiram, the latter would have no opportunity to grab one from him and turn the tables.

"Keep 'em up," he ordered; and, while Pete trained his gun on Hiram, Drummond searched his prisoner from head to foot.

"Guess you told the truth," he said. "Still, a fellow never can tell. You're a pretty foxy guy at times. Strip, Hooker."

"I guess you did tell the truth," Drummond said a few minutes later after a thorough search had been made. "Still I'm not through yet. You saw us coming and had time to hide it, if you found it."

He stepped to the mare and went over her saddle, even turning the cheek straps of the bridle inside out, and pawing through her heavy mane and tail. He looked and felt in her ears. He held her nostrils with his fingers until she jerked up her head and snorted out a blast of held-in air.

"Guess that would have shot out any paper in her nostrils," he remarked.

"They say this Jo's a hoss trainer," suggested Pete. "Maybe the mare's a trick hoss. Look in her mouth Drummond."

Drummond did this, but found it empty. He studied a minute, his eyes closed thoughtfully, then threw off the saddle and examined the sheepskin lining, *tapaderos*, jockeys, skirts.

Now for fifteen minutes he walked about over the ground. It was hard and firm here—almost as smooth as the surface of a dry lake, with no loose sand in which the paper might be concealed and little desert growth.

Returning he lifted the mare's feet one by one, then faced Hiram again.

"Open your mouth," he commanded; and Hiram obeyed, displaying an empty cavity.

"Well, ole hoss, I guess the game's up for you folks," Drummond said chuckling. "I never thought we'd be lucky enough to get rid of the original. So now we'll leave you to put on your clothes and go your way. You may see Jerkline Jo and tell her your little story; and you two can discuss what's best to do. When you've decided, come to me and we'll dicker with you."

"How 'bout takin' 'im into the mountains?" asked Pete in a low voice.

"No, that won't be necessary now. We need him to put the case before Jerkline Jo. I'm against violence, anyway, in the main. And I'm not a hog, like a certain person I might mention if it weren't for Hooker's overhearing it. We'll let him go, and dicker later. Half suits me."

Drummond climbed into the saddle, and the two wheeled their horses and rode away.

Hiram began to dress.

"Look, Hooker!" called Drummond from a distance. "I'll drop your gun right here."

Hiram nodded and continued putting on his clothes, then resaddled the mare.

Then when the departing riders were mere specks in the distance he stepped to Babe's head, reached his fingers up one of her nostrils, and pulled out the wadded sheepskin document.

"A heap o' fellas call themselves hossmen that don't know about that little pocket in a hoss' nose," came his whimsical Mendocino drawl. "She could snort all day, but the pocket ain't connected with her nostrils." He patted Babe's glossy neck. "Li'l' black mare," he crooned into her furry ear, "le's go find Jo!"

CHAPTER XXXIV

WHILE SPRING APPROACHED

At a late hour in the evening of the day that Hiram Hooker set out to ride with the sheepskin to Jerkline Jo, on her way to Julia, a strange figure presented itself at the door of the lighted commissary tent of Demarest, Spruce & Tillou's Camp Number Two.

"Well, who in thunder are you?" exclaimed the young commissary clerk, as his eyes fell upon a set of shaggy gray brows and a dusty, bewhiskered face.

"I'm Basil Filer—ole Filer," was the croaking reply. "I jest stopped in to see if ye got a' automobile, or a hoss an' buggy, or somethin' here."

"Well, what if we have?"

"Thought maybe ye'd give Tehachapi Hank a ride," came the answer. "He's too heavy for Muta—that's my biggest burro. His feet drags and ketches in the greasewood, and Muta she gets provoked at him. He won't bother you none—Hank won't. He's peaceable. But he oughta be got to a constable or somethin'. You see, Hank he's dead."

This brought the clerk out into the night; and there in the light streaming from the tent door lay the figure of a man crosswise and face down on a burro's back.

"Ye see, I know Hank some time," explained Basil Filer simply. "And jest last night a friend o' mine he camped with me, and said Hank was up to his old devilment ag'in. So I was camped on the desert out there this evenin', and Hank he drifts in. And—well, I'm watchin', you see; and so when Hank he sidles round and I see somethin' heavylike in his hand, why, I ups and goes for my cannon. Then Hank he goes for his, and I have to let him have it from the hip. Got any ca'tridges, pardner? Hank he wasted the last one I had."

"You—you killed this man?" faltered the clerk.

"I hadn't only one ca'tridge, pardner," Filer said patiently. "And Hank he's accounted a pretty clever gunman. Well, maybe he was. Ole Filer he shoots ole jack rabbits in the eye at twenty paces with a six, they'll tell ye. Anyway ye can figger that out, here's Hank. And he oughta see a coroner er somethin'. I don't want 'im. Besides, time Muta'd packed him to Ragtown, Hank he'd spoil. Muta she never did like Tehachapi Hank, nohow."

The following day the mortal remains of Tehachapi Hank were brought into Ragtown, together with his self-confessed killer Basil Filer. The constable—for Ragtown had one now—took Filer in charge and hurried him to the county seat in Twitter-or-Tweet's machine. The burros had been loosed to pick their living on the desert.

"So that failed beautifully!" exclaimed Al Drummond to Lucy Dalles. "Who'd have thought that old rabbit would be too quick for Hank! He must have been on his guard."

Lucy shrugged indifferently. "Filer was a master shot," she observed. "Failed beautifully is right, Al—beautifully for us. It couldn't have happened better. Now Brother Hank is out of it. If you can contrive some way to shake Hank's partner, Pete, there'll be no one but you and me to whack up.

"Since Hank is numbered among the late lamented," she

continued, "I can forgive you for bungling the Hooker end of your job. With Hank's finger out of the pot, I'm content to split with Jerkline Jo. So, no thanks to you, everything has worked out all right after all. Can't you send Pete out with instructions to bite a rattlesnake, or something like that?"

"You're mighty good-natured to-day, kid," Al said.

"Why shouldn't I be? Since we know the original document and that boob's copy are both destroyed—and that before he had time to commit the directions to memory. We have nothing whatever to do but wait for Jerkline Jo to come to us and ask us what our terms are. Then if you and I aren't foxy enough to squeeze out the amiable Mr. Pete—Well, leave it to me!"

"But have you thought," Drummond pointed out, "that perhaps Filer has committed the instructions to memory?"

Lucy scoffed at this and dismissed it with: "That old lunatic? Never! He can hardly remember the story, and now and then forgets that he's hunting for Baby Jean and hikes back for the desert. Don't worry about his having committed anything to memory. He has no memory to commit it to!"

At about the time the foregoing dialogue was being spoken in Ragtown, Jerkline Jo, in her tent at Julia, was making strange remarks to Hiram Hooker, to wit, as follows:

"Hi-*ram*! It ti-i-i-ickles! Sto-op-op! Wait a minute, Hiram!"

"Huh!" snorted the unfeeling man. "Whoever heard of anybody being ticklish on the head!"

"But I am, Hiram! I just know I am! And isn't that razor far too sharp?"

"'There ain't no such thing,'" quoted the man out of the store of his masculine experience. "Now quit wiggling, Jo, or I'm liable to cut you."

"Now go slow, Hiram. And if I say it feels funny, you stop. Now easy at first! Horrors! I wouldn't be a man for anything!"

"Don't blame me," mumbled Hiram. "Now quit wrinkling your scalp, Jo. Fella'd think I was going to cut your head off, the way you dodge and shrink."

They were alone in the tent. Jo was on her knees on the ground, and behind her and over her stood Hiram with an old-fashioned razor in his hand. Beside them on a chair lay a strand of almost black hair three feet in length, which Hiram swore that he would preserve until his dying breath. On the back of Jo's head appeared a round spot, covered with hairs half an inch in length, and these the brutal man was trying to shave off with the razor. Never had barber a more provoking customer.

"Oh, I'll look like a fright, Hiram! I've always been proud of my hair."

"It'll grow out again," he said soothingly. "Besides, what I cut off didn't cover a spot an inch and a half in diameter. With hair like yours, it can't be noticed. If I'd thought it would disfigure your hair, girl, I'd have said, 'Let the old gold go!' What an idea!"

"I positively never heard of such a weird thing. And to think it's on me! And—Oo-oo-oo-oo! You cut me, Hiram! It's bleeding!"

"No, no, no! Only more lather. Don't wiggle, Jo!"

"There! It's all over," Hiram said after a minute of silence.

Four days later Lucy Dalles and Al Drummond stood behind the counter of the shooting gallery at Ragtown, and with a certain amount of nervous expectancy watched the freight outfit of Jerkline Jo grow larger and larger as it neared the journey's end.

Soon they heard the merry jingling of hundreds of bells, and next the big horses were planting their heavy fetlocked feet in the street, their glossy necks arched proudly as Ragtown turned out to greet them.

Lucy stood on tiptoe and craned her neck along the line of heavily loaded wagons. "Don't see Jo's whites at the tail end," she remarked.

And presently her companion supplemented: "Nor Hooker's blacks. Say, that's funny. There's only four teams, Hooker and the girl didn't come!"

"Oh, dear, dear! What can that mean? Al, Hooker must have memorized the directions! And—"

"Nonsense!" he exclaimed. "If he'd memorized them, why did he sit down on the desert to copy em?"

"Oh, that's right, of course! But I'm worried, Al. Something must be wrong."

Just then two men passed along the street, and a fragment of their conversation floated to the anxious pair: "Says Jo's sick at Julia—"

"Oh that's it!" Lucy murmured in relief. "And the hick stayed to nurse her. There's not so much freight to be hauled right now. See, Al—Heine and Keddie each are driving sixteen, with trailers. The extra horses are white and black—Jo's and Hiram's. I wonder what's the matter with Jo."

"Huh!" snickered Drummond. "The package we handed her is enough to make anybody sick! But I don't just like the way things look, either. By golly, aren't we to know where we stand until Jo gets well!"

Three of the wagons and trailers groaned on through the town toward Demarest, Spruce & Tillou's Camp Number One, while the fourth—Heine Schultz driving—entered the alley to reach the rear of Huber's store. Twenty minutes later Schultz suddenly presented himself at the shooting gallery.

"Howdy," he greeted Al and Lucy, touching the broad brim of his hat with a forefinger. "Jo's sick. I guess you've heard."

"Yes, so some one said," Lucy smiled amiably at the dusty skinner. "Isn't it too bad! What seems to be wrong, Heine?"

"Bad cold—settled in her lungs," replied Heine briefly. "Er—now—Jo told me to ask you somethin', miss. Either you or Drummond, she said. I don't know what it's about. She just said: 'Go see Drummond or Lucy when you get in and ask them their terms and let me know what they say when you get back to Julia.'"

Drummond darted a quick, triumphant glance at the girl.

"Oh, yes," she said lightly to the skinner, "I know what she refers to. Why, just tell her, 'Half,' Heine. That's all you need to say; she'll understand."

"Gotcha," said Heine, and lounged away, rolling a brown paper cigarette.

The outfit started back again early next morning; and eight days later it returned, still minus its two important figures. Again Heine Schultz rested his bony elbows on the carpeted counter of the shooting gallery, and spoke to Lucy, who this time was alone.

"About that business between you folks and Jo," he said, indolently filling a cigarette paper.

"Yes?" eagerly returned Lucy.

"Jo says tell you, 'Half is too much.'"

"Oh! She—she's still ill?"

Heine, shook his head sadly and tapped his chest. "Can't hardly hear her talk," he said. "It's fierce. Wild Cat's scared stiff about it. Well, what'll I tell 'er, Miss Lucy?"

"I'll have to see Al before giving you an answer," she told him. "Can't you drop around after supper, Heine?"

"Sure. I'm on the water wagon, though," he added blandly, with no suggestion of a deep meaning in his tones.

An hour afterward Drummond met Heine on the street and handed him a sealed envelope. "Give that to Jerkline Jo," he commanded shortly.

"Gotcha!" drawled Heine, and slouched on up the street.

"Confound it!" Drummond grumbled to Lucy little later. "Why in thunder doesn't Tweet put a telephone line to civilization? We're wasting time!"

"Couldn't do anything, anyway, till Jo's on her feet again," the girl practically pointed out. "Don't be overimpatient."

Eight days later Heine Schultz faced them again.

"Jo's still too sick to write," he announced. "But she's gettin' better right along. She told me to tell you that what you wrote was fierce, and that you was too greedy. That's only what Jo said. Don't take it out on me. She said she'd be willin' to let you have a fourth, over an' above all expenses."

"Well, she'll do nothing of the sort!" Lucy cut in hotly.

"Come around later, Heine," put in Drummond. "I'll have another note."

"Gotcha!" replied Heine, and picked up a rifle to sight at a target before strolling nonchalantly on.

Two miles out of town next morning Heine took out his pocketknife and slit the envelope covering the note that Drummond had given him to be delivered to Jerkline Jo.

"M'm-m!" he mumbled, reading slowly, a great calloused forefinger following the lines.

> You'll come to our terms immediately, or our copy of the instructions goes into the fire. We've reached the end of our rope, and won't monkey any longer. Take your choice, Miss Modock—or Miss Jean Prince—half or nothing. Yes, we're just ornery enough to rob ourselves to spite you.

Heine scratched his head and muttered: "Lord, be merciful unto me, a skinner! Now what'll I say to that? Guess I'll stretch this trip out to twelve days—we c'n have a breakdown or somethin'."

It was indeed twelve days before the outfit was again seen in Ragtown; and then Mr. Schultz had this to say to Drummond and the girl:

"Jo says she'll be about pretty soon now, and she'll come over with us next trip and see you herself. Says for you not to do anything rash, or anything like that. What'll I tell her?"

"Tell her to hurry up!" Drummond said angrily.

"Gotcha!" drawled Heine, and betook himself to camp.

Ten days later Mr. Schultz had this to report:

"Well, sir, Jo she just naturally had a terrible relapse. Doctor's worried blue about 'er. She can't talk, and she can't see to read. She just lays there and gasps somethin' fierce."

"What on earth has she?" cried Lucy.

Heine scratched his head. "The doc said it was a kind o' complication or somethin'. Dip'theria and appendiseetus, I think he said. Yes, sir—that's it. Dip'theria and appendiseetus."

"Ridiculous!" scoffed Lucy. "Did they operate?"

"Operate! I should say they did! They whittled that woman down to such a frazzle and when the doc goes to see her in the mornin' he has to shake the sheets to find her!"

"Heine, I believe you're a humorist," Lucy said doubtfully.

Heine grinned. "She's gettin' better now, though; and the doc says next trip she'll probably be over. Then she c'n 'tend to her business with you herself. I wish she would. I get things all mixed up."

Drummond and Lucy stared at each other when the skinner had left.

"Gypped!" exclaimed Drummond. "There's something phony about this! By George, I'm—I'm scared there's something wrong! Heine's been lying like a sailor. I believe I'll drive over to Julia tomorrow and see what I can find out."

"Sit down, Heine," invited Twitter-or-Tweet Orr Tweet, rising and lowering the window shade in his little pine office as the jerkline skinner entered.

Heine accepted.

"Well?" queried Tweet, with a look of worriment in his face.

"Ain't heard a word from 'em, Playmate, since they come in and filed, and went back with a minin' engineer," said Heine. "I'm gettin' worried myself. You see, that's a bad country up in there where they've gone. Many a man's gone in there and left his bones for the buzzards to pick."

"But weren't they fixed for an ordeal, Heine?"

"No one ever hit Death Valley better fixed," was the reply. "Jo, she hires two big trucks and takes horses and pack burros and feed and grub and water till you couldn't rest. They aimed to go as far as they could with the trucks, and then make a headquarters there, leave the drivers to look out for the camp, and her and Wild Cat was gonta make it on in with the horses and the canaries. They had a scout that knows that country from the southern end o' the Panamints to Lost Valley. Oh, they went heeled; but it's a big job and takes time. Still, they oughta be showin' up by now."

Orr Tweet heaved a great sigh. "Jo's simply forgotten all about me," he said mournfully. "Heine, I don't mind tellin' you— but if somethin' don't happen pretty soon one Tweet goes up Salt Creek. Here it's only ten days till I gotta plunk down six thousan' iron men, plus a raft o' interest money. And the mortgages o' this blame rancho are watchin' me like buzzards, ready to swoop down the minute I begin to gasp. They got me where the hair's short, Heine. I not only lose the rancho and all, but every cent Jo and me and Hiram's put into her. I ain't sellin' an acre these days. Won't till summer's here, and the blame'-fool homesteaders see that Paloma Rancho's worth ten times what the government land's worth. The work on the grade is nearin' completion, and the steel's creepin' closer every day. Every mornin', when it's still, you c'n hear the whistle o' the track-layin' engine. The camps are finishin' and movin' on, one by one. That takes trade away from Ragtown, and concessionaires are quittin', too. A month from now Ragtown will be only a memory, Heine. Not that, as Tweet, she won't build up later and more substantially, when the steel's laid and trains are runnin'. But to keep a stiff upper lip till then brings gray hairs!"

"Don't you worry," Heine said consolingly. "You just set tight and watch the spring blossoms come. Jerkline Jo never failed man nor horse nor dog in her life, and she ain't forgot you for a second. You bet your last dime on Jerkline Jo, ol'-timer— and Wild Cat, too, s'far's that goes. They'll ramble home in time to save you. I'll bet my bank roll on it!"

"Only ten days more," Tweet sighed heavily. "Oh, papa, what pretty fireworks you made! Heine, are you still keepin' Drummond in hot water?"

"Oh, yes," Heine assured him. "They're doin' very well. Guess Drummond'll be drivin' to see how Jo's gettin' along pretty soon. I guess I queered things to-day. Tried to get funny, and pretty near spilled the beans. I'll say he'd better take along about five huskies to move boulders outa the road, if he tries to make it through the pass. Them big boys just naturally roll down behind us the minute we've passed. And comin' back, we hook on and snake 'em outa the way. And then, by golly, they spring right back again! Funny rocks in this country, Tweet."

CHAPTER XXXV

THE WAY OF LIFE

Sand, sand, sand—far as the eye can reach, a sea of sand, with here and there a half-buried and bleached horned skull, and vultures circling high above in the heavens.

Away in the blinding distance five specks appear, and finally are seen to be slowly on the move. Hours after this discovery, if an observer were to remain stationary, the specks take on the shapes of animal life—two men, a woman, and two burros bearing packs. Onward they move slowly, and once more become mere specks, scarce discernible against the weird hue of the sky, then vanish altogether. Once more in all this vast, dread waste moves nothing save the vultures indolently circling in the hot dome above.

Days later a dust-covered automobile worms its way through the traffic in Los Angeles and comes to rest before a tall office building. Two as dusty as the car descend from the tonneau, and one leaves the seat beside the driver. Pedestrians stare curiously at the trio as, talking and laughing in high spirits, they cross the pavement to the building's entrance.

"Desert rats—mining folks," observes a wiseacre to his friend. "Look at the girl and the chaps! Peach, eh? That's the life! Ho-hum! Gotta get back to the old office, Bill. See you to-night at lodge, I s'pose. S'long!"

Arthur Preston Hankins

In a lavishly furnished anteroom of a suite of offices on the top floor of the building, Jerkline Jo and Hiram Hooker sank into overstuffed chairs and relaxed, while the other man, in khaki and scarred puttees, excused himself and entered the rooms beyond, carrying a suit case that tugged at his arm until his shoulder sagged. He was absent from the intercom a half hour.

"Well, boy," said Jerkline Jo, "it's all over, I guess. What an experience! I thought I knew the desert and the rough life before, but I wasn't out of my A B C's."

"It was glorious, though," said Hiram. "I wouldn't have missed it, dear, for worlds."

"Nor I, either. But I don't wish ever to return. Once is enough."

After this they were silent. Both sat with eyes closed, dreaming of the past and the beckoning future. Their dreams were finally interrupted by the reappearance of Mr. John Downer, the mining engineer for the Gold Hills Mining Co., in whose offices they now sat.

"Well," he began, smiling, "if you'll come in now, Mr. Floresta would like to have a talk with you. Getting a bit rested, Miss Modock?"

Mr. Floresta, president of the Gold Hills Mining Co., was a pudgy, pink man, carefully groomed and manicured and barbered, who radiated businesslike good nature. On his rich mahogany desk lay a row of gold specimens that glittered in the sunlight streaming in through a window. He shook hands warmly with Jo and Hiram; and when all were seated they talked of the trip for a time, and then the president plunged to the heart of the business that had brought them together.

"Knowing that you were in a hurry, Miss Modock," he said, "I called a meeting of the stockholders, and we reached the conclusion that, if Mr. Downer's report was entirely satisfactory, there would be no use in quibbling over the price you and Mr. Hooker have asked. The sum that you ask for the group of claims that you filed upon is, as you are aware, an enormous one for unproved mining properties. Still, we wish to be fair; and on Mr. Downer's glowing report we are going to take a chance. Therefore, please state your pleasure in the matter of payments, and arrangements will be made at once."

A great sigh escaped Jo, and tears welled to her dark eyes.

"Thank you, Mr. Floresta," she said. "If you can let us have two hundred thousand at once, I'm sure payment of the remainder of the million can be easily arranged to suit both sides."

Mr. Floresta bowed and pushed a buzzer button. A moment or so later a messenger was on the way to a bank with a check. When he returned he handed Floresta another check—one certified by the cashier of the company's banking house.

"Now for yours and Mr. Hooker's signatures, please," said Floresta. "I have indicated in the transfer papers that the remainder of the million dollars is to be paid in four semi-annual installments, of two hundred thousand each, with interest at six per cent on deferred payments. Is that entirely satisfactory?"

"Entirely," Jo told him, and went to his desk and took up the pen he handed her.

Five minutes later Hiram and the girl were alone in the anteroom once more. Hiram took the hands of Jerkline Jo and bent over her.

"Ma'am," he drawled whimsically, "if you'll let me, I'll kiss you now!"

Twitter-or-Tweet Orr Tweet paced back and forth in his little pine office, his hands behind his back, his brows furrowed. Every little while he grabbed his nose and straightened it savagely, but each time it reverted to its list to port again, and Tweet marched on disconsolately. It was the evening of the next to last day of his three days of grace. To-morrow Paloma Rancho, Ragtown, and all that they represented would slip automatically from his control, and he could not raise a finger to stop it.

Suddenly the door burst open with a bang, and Heine Schultz filled the little office with the roar of a behemoth:

"Oh, boy! Have you seen it? Just come in with the mail! Los Angeles papers! Here, read, man! And then get drunk! I'll help you!"

Tweet snatched the paper from him, and his steel-blue eyes bugged at the glaring headlines:

Gold! Gold! Gold! Death Valley Gives Up Another Secret. Rich Find in Little-Known Corner of Treacherous Waste. Dead Father of Picturesque Girl Called Jerkline Jo the Finder. Weird Tale of Struggles and Death and Baby Lost on Desert. Gold Hills Mining Co. Takes Over the Claims at $1,000,000. President Says Richest Discovery Since Days of '49.

"Great stutterin' Demosthenes!" exclaimed Tweet, and fell limply into a chair.

Then again the door was opened, and a boy from the post office handed Tweet a special-delivery letter. Tremblingly he tore the envelope and removed a yellow telegram. Tears sprang to his eyes as he read aloud:

"Have to-day deposited to credit of your checking account in Bluemount National Bank, Los Angeles, one hundred thousand dollars. Check against it at pleasure. Hiram and I on our way to Mendocino County for a little rest and to see old friend of his. Reach Ragtown in about two weeks if all goes well.

"JEAN PRINCE HOOKER, JERKLINE JO."

Tweet sprang from his chair, cramming on his hat.

"Lock the door and take the key, Heine!" he cried. "I'm going to Los Angeles at fifty miles an hour!"

At the same time in the shooting gallery Al Drummond and Lucy Dalles stared over the top of a newspaper at each other, their eyes tragic.

"Gyped!" exclaimed Drummond at last.

"Gyped!" Lucy echoed faintly.

Then for a time there was silence, broken at last by Drummond's weary voice.

"Guess I'll drift up to the Dugout," he said. "See you later."

Lucy made no reply, but stood staring out across the spring-scented desert, her thoughts on the tinkling streams of Mendocino and the big, kind, sheltering trees. The rhododendrons were beginning to blossom there now. Soon the redwood lilies would be scenting the air with their delicate fragrance. Gray squirrels would be scolding in lofty trees, and trout would be leaping in still, dark pools.

Lucy sat down very suddenly, and then her head fell forward on her arms. There on the carpeted counter, between the rifles, she sobbed heartbrokenly. She knew by intuition that in her quest for wealth she would not have Al Drummond to help her in the future.

Ragtown's biggest day was when old Basil Filer, having been acquitted of the charge of murder on the evidence furnished by

Jerkline Jo and Hiram Hooker, returned to hunt for his burros. This was Ragtown's greatest day because Hiram Hooker and his bride came, too.

They had spent a pleasant time with Uncle Sebastian Burris in Mendocino County, most glorious of countries in spring. Hiram had expressed the wish to see Uncle Sebastian again and to tell him all that had befallen him in driving jerkline to Ragtown. Hiram had learned a great lesson, he felt. He had left the north woods to do something less prosaic than driving jerkline, and a series of peculiar incidents had forced him back into the same old groove again. Yet the once scorned, neglected task had brought him adventures and a fortune and a splendid girl. Over all this he wished to marvel with his old benefactor and friend, and Jo had readily consented to the trip. They had returned for Basil Filer's trial as the main witnesses for the defense.

The stage brought all three into the town, and for the first time they saw the new steel and the track-laying engine beyond. Carpenters were building the roundhouse, and new buildings were going up all over the village.

Ragtown turned out in a body to meet them. The wagons and teams of Jerkline Jo's freight outfit were covered with flags, and Jo's proud skinners paraded the streets, the wagons loaded with cheering townspeople. Carried on the shoulders of men, the bride and groom were escorted to the Palace Dance Hall, where a banquet had been prepared, over which presided Twitter-or-Tweet Orr Tweet.

Far into the night they celebrated, and in all of Ragtown there was only one who did not attend. This was poor little Lucy Dalles, sobbing her heart out in her little cabin, her dream of wealth and marriage with Al Drummond gone.

It was nearly midnight when there came a gentle tapping on her door. Dashing the tears from her eyes, Lucy walked unsteadily across her expensive rug and opened the door to a crack. Next moment she found herself in a pair of strong arms, and her head lay on the breast of Jerkline Jo.

"There, there, dear! There, there! Don't cry! It's all right—all right! I know—I understand."

With her arms about the sobbing girl, big-hearted Jerkline Jo, the desert's grandest product, led the way to one of the big leather chairs and sat down. Only Lucy's sobs broke the silence, while Jo sat and smoothed back her pretty hair.

Presently the sobbing ceased, and then Jo rose and, taking her in her arms again, kissed her and smiled into her eyes.

"You must bathe your eyes now, dear," said Jo, "for Mr. Tweet is coming to see you pretty soon. He told me so. Now look your best for Tweet has something serious to say to you."

She left her then, and an hour later Tweet interrupted Jo and Hiram in Jo's little cabin on the edge of town. He came in and sat down.

"Well, Jo," he said, "it's a go. We'll go to work and get married to-morrow mornin', if the old bus will take us to a preacher. I guess I've loved her some time," Tweet added bashfully. "Lucy and me'll make nice little playmates."

Hiram rose and gripped his old friend's hand. "I'm mighty glad, Tweet," he told him. "Just too much Ragtown—that's all that was the matter with Lucy. She was kind to me up there in Frisco when I'd just come out of the woods. Her heart's warm, and that's what counts."

Tweet's steel-blue eyes twinkled. "Course nobody could blame her for makin' you spend four dollars an hour for an automobile," he said. "It was a crime not to roll you for your jack in those days, Hooker. I forgave her for that a long time ago."

Next morning Basil Filer drifted into town, driving his recaptured burros ahead of him. Silently he worked at packing the bags and throwing diamond hitches.

Jerkline Jo and Hiram stood laughing at the gurgling imps of the desert, and Jo went up to Filer.

"What does this mean?" she asked. "You're all packed up for a trip."

The weird old eyes looked up at her queerly. "We're goin'— out there," croaked Filer, a trembling finger pointing toward the fragrant desert. "It's spring, Baby Jean—and now's the time to hunt for gold, when there's lots o' feed for the little fellas."

"Gold!" cried Jo. "Why, man, you've so much money coming to you that you can't spend it in the rest of your natural life."

"Money?" he said absently. "Yes—you've done me han'some, Baby Jean. But I ain't got much use for money. Money's only a grubstake, so's you c'n buy things and go out and hunt for gold. Good-by, folks! Next fall you'll see me and the little fellas ag'in. Hi, Muta! Lead out!"

And, gripping his staff, he limped off in the wake of his long-eared companions, swinging their packs from side to side as a mother rocks the cradle.

"They're all like that," said a man. "It's the hunt for it that keeps 'em goin'. They don't know what to do with it when they get it."

The dark eyes of Jerkline Jo were full of dreams.

"Yes, we're all like that, I imagine," she said.

"And how bout *you*, Jo?" some one asked. "Now that you're rich and married and all?"

Jo looked down the street at the nearly completed roundhouse and the track-laying engine working on below the town.

"I?" she said dreamily. "Why—why—I don't just know. The steel has come, and now freight will reach here by train. We're going to New York—Hiram and I—and maybe across the Atlantic. But we'll come back soon, and—and—Oh, there'll be a new road building somewhere—another Ragtown. We couldn't quit, I guess. What's city life and all that money will buy compared with the thrill of driving a ten-horse jerkline team over the desert and the mountains? I guess, after we've looked about the Gentle Wild Cat and I will just keep on driving jerkline to Ragtown—somewhere."

She pointed over the desert to where a bent old man and six drifting burros were blending gradually into the landscape.

"He's not crazy," she said softly. "He has just voiced a great fundamental truth for all humanity. Money is only a grub-stake. The world needs gold and—and freight. Jerkline to Ragtown—that's life! Some Ragtown will need freight—some Ragtown—somewhere."

Choose from Thousands of 1stWorldLibrary Classics By

A. M. Barnard
Ada Leverson
Adolphus William Ward
Aesop
Agatha Christie
Alexander Aaronsohn
Alexander Kielland
Alexandre Dumas
Alfred Gatty
Alfred Ollivant
Alice Duer Miller
Alice Turner Curtis
Alice Dunbar
Allen Chapman
Alleyne Ireland
Ambrose Bierce
Amelia E. Barr
Amory H. Bradford
Andrew Lang
Andrew McFarland Davis
Andy Adams
Angela Brazil
Anna Alice Chapin
Anna Sewell
Annie Besant
Annie Hamilton Donnell
Annie Payson Call
Annie Roe Carr
Annonaymous
Anton Chekhov
Archibald Lee Fletcher
Arnold Bennett
Arthur C. Benson
Arthur Conan Doyle
Arthur M. Winfield
Arthur Ransome
Arthur Schnitzler
Arthur Train
Atticus
B.H. Baden-Powell
B. M. Bower
B. C. Chatterjee
Baroness Emmuska Orczy
Baroness Orczy
Basil King
Bayard Taylor
Ben Macomber
Bertha Muzzy Bower
Bjornstjerne Bjornson

Booth Tarkington
Boyd Cable
Bram Stoker
C. Collodi
C. E. Orr
C. M. Ingleby
Carolyn Wells
Catherine Parr Traill
Charles A. Eastman
Charles Amory Beach
Charles Dickens
Charles Dudley Warner
Charles Farrar Browne
Charles Ives
Charles Kingsley
Charles Klein
Charles Hanson Towne
Charles Lathrop Pack
Charles Romyn Dake
Charles Whibley
Charles Willing Beale
Charlotte M. Braeme
Charlotte M. Yonge
Charlotte Perkins Stetson
Clair W. Hayes
Clarence Day Jr.
Clarence E. Mulford
Clemence Housman
Confucius
Coningsby Dawson
Cornelis DeWitt Wilcox
Cyril Burleigh
D. H. Lawrence
Daniel Defoe
David Garnett
Dinah Craik
Don Carlos Janes
Donald Keyhoe
Dorothy Kilner
Dougan Clark
Douglas Fairbanks
E. Nesbit
E. P. Roe
E. Phillips Oppenheim
E. S. Brooks
Earl Barnes
Edgar Rice Burroughs
Edith Van Dyne
Edith Wharton

Edward Everett Hale
Edward J. O'Biren
Edward S. Ellis
Edwin L. Arnold
Eleanor Atkins
Eleanor Hallowell Abbott
Eliot Gregory
Elizabeth Gaskell
Elizabeth McCracken
Elizabeth Von Arnim
Ellem Key
Emerson Hough
Emilie F. Carlen
Emily Bronte
Emily Dickinson
Enid Bagnold
Enilor Macartney Lane
Erasmus W. Jones
Ernie Howard Pie
Ethel May Dell
Ethel Turner
Ethel Watts Mumford
Eugene Sue
Eugenie Foa
Eugene Wood
Eustace Hale Ball
Evelyn Everett-green
Everard Cotes
F. H. Cheley
F. J. Cross
F. Marion Crawford
Fannie E. Newberry
Federick Austin Ogg
Ferdinand Ossendowski
Fergus Hume
Florence A. Kilpatrick
Fremont B. Deering
Francis Bacon
Francis Darwin
Frances Hodgson Burnett
Frances Parkinson Keyes
Frank Gee Patchin
Frank Harris
Frank Jewett Mather
Frank L. Packard
Frank V. Webster
Frederic Stewart Isham
Frederick Trevor Hill
Frederick Winslow Taylor

Friedrich Kerst
Friedrich Nietzsche
Fyodor Dostoyevsky
G.A. Henty
G.K. Chesterton
Gabrielle E. Jackson
Garrett P. Serviss
Gaston Leroux
George A. Warren
George Ade
Geroge Bernard Shaw
George Cary Eggleston
George Durston
George Ebers
George Eliot
George Gissing
George MacDonald
George Meredith
George Orwell
George Sylvester Viereck
George Tucker
George W. Cable
George Wharton James
Gertrude Atherton
Gordon Casserly
Grace E. King
Grace Gallatin
Grace Greenwood
Grant Allen
Guillermo A. Sherwell
Gulielma Zollinger
Gustav Flaubert
H. A. Cody
H. B. Irving
H.C. Bailey
H. G. Wells
H. H. Munro
H. Irving Hancock
H. R. Naylor
H. Rider Haggard
H. W. C. Davis
Haldeman Julius
Hall Caine
Hamilton Wright Mabie
Hans Christian Andersen
Harold Avery
Harold McGrath
Harriet Beecher Stowe
Harry Castlemon
Harry Coghill
Harry Houidini

Hayden Carruth
Helent Hunt Jackson
Helen Nicolay
Hendrik Conscience
Hendy David Thoreau
Henri Barbusse
Henrik Ibsen
Henry Adams
Henry Ford
Henry Frost
Henry James
Henry Jones Ford
Henry Seton Merriman
Henry W Longfellow
Herbert A. Giles
Herbert Carter
Herbert N. Casson
Herman Hesse
Hildegard G. Frey
Homer
Honore De Balzac
Horace B. Day
Horace Walpole
Horatio Alger Jr.
Howard Pyle
Howard R. Garis
Hugh Lofting
Hugh Walpole
Humphry Ward
Ian Maclaren
Inez Haynes Gillmore
Irving Bacheller
Isabel Cecilia Williams
Isabel Hornibrook
Israel Abrahams
Ivan Turgenev
J.G.Austin
J. Henri Fabre
J. M. Barrie
J. M. Walsh
J. Macdonald Oxley
J. R. Miller
J. S. Fletcher
J. S. Knowles
J. Storer Clouston
J. W. Duffield
Jack London
Jacob Abbott
James Allen
James Andrews
James Baldwin

James Branch Cabell
James DeMille
James Joyce
James Lane Allen
James Lane Allen
James Oliver Curwood
James Oppenheim
James Otis
James R. Driscoll
Jane Abbott
Jane Austen
Jane L. Stewart
Janet Aldridge
Jens Peter Jacobsen
Jerome K. Jerome
Jessie Graham Flower
John Buchan
John Burroughs
John Cournos
John F. Kennedy
John Gay
John Glasworthy
John Habberton
John Joy Bell
John Kendrick Bangs
John Milton
John Philip Sousa
John Taintor Foote
Jonas Lauritz Idemil Lie
Jonathan Swift
Joseph A. Altsheler
Joseph Carey
Joseph Conrad
Joseph E. Badger Jr
Joseph Hergesheimer
Joseph Jacobs
Jules Vernes
Julian Hawthrone
Julie A Lippmann
Justin Huntly McCarthy
Kakuzo Okakura
Karle Wilson Baker
Kate Chopin
Kenneth Grahame
Kenneth McGaffey
Kate Langley Bosher
Kate Langley Bosher
Katherine Cecil Thurston
Katherine Stokes
L. A. Abbot
L. T. Meade

L. Frank Baum
Latta Griswold
Laura Dent Crane
Laura Lee Hope
Laurence Housman
Lawrence Beasley
Leo Tolstoy
Leonid Andreyev
Lewis Carroll
Lewis Sperry Chafer
Lilian Bell
Lloyd Osbourne
Louis Hughes
Louis Joseph Vance
Louis Tracy
Louisa May Alcott
Lucy Fitch Perkins
Lucy Maud Montgomery
Luther Benson
Lydia Miller Middleton
Lyndon Orr
M. Corvus
M. H. Adams
Margaret E. Sangster
Margret Howth
Margaret Vandercook
Margaret W. Hungerford
Margret Penrose
Maria Edgeworth
Maria Thompson Daviess
Mariano Azuela
Marion Polk Angellotti
Mark Overton
Mark Twain
Mary Austin
Mary Catherine Crowley
Mary Cole
Mary Hastings Bradley
Mary Roberts Rinehart
Mary Rowlandson
M. Wollstonecraft Shelley
Maud Lindsay
Max Beerbohm
Myra Kelly
Nathaniel Hawthrone
Nicolo Machiavelli
O. F. Walton
Oscar Wilde

Owen Johnson
P.G. Wodehouse
Paul and Mabel Thorne
Paul G. Tomlinson
Paul Severing
Percy Brebner
Percy Keese Fitzhugh
Peter B. Kyne
Plato
Quincy Allen
R. Derby Holmes
R. L. Stevenson
R. S. Ball
Rabindranath Tagore
Rahul Alvares
Ralph Bonehill
Ralph Henry Barbour
Ralph Victor
Ralph Waldo Emmerson
Rene Descartes
Ray Cummings
Rex Beach
Rex E. Beach
Richard Harding Davis
Richard Jefferies
Richard Le Gallienne
Robert Barr
Robert Frost
Robert Gordon Anderson
Robert L. Drake
Robert Lansing
Robert Lynd
Robert Michael Ballantyne
Robert W. Chambers
Rosa Nouchette Carey
Rudyard Kipling
Saint Augustine
Samuel B. Allison
Samuel Hopkins Adams
Sarah Bernhardt
Sarah C. Hallowell
Selma Lagerlof
Sherwood Anderson
Sigmund Freud
Standish O'Grady
Stanley Weyman
Stella Benson
Stella M. Francis

Stephen Crane
Stewart Edward White
Stijn Streuvels
Swami Abhedananda
Swami Parmananda
T. S. Ackland
T. S. Arthur
The Princess Der Ling
Thomas A. Janvier
Thomas A Kempis
Thomas Anderton
Thomas Bailey Aldrich
Thomas Bulfinch
Thomas De Quincey
Thomas Dixon
Thomas H. Huxley
Thomas Hardy
Thomas More
Thornton W. Burgess
U. S. Grant
Upton Sinclair
Valentine Williams
Various Authors
Vaughan Kester
Victor Appleton
Victor G. Durham
Victoria Cross
Virginia Woolf
Wadsworth Camp
Walter Camp
Walter Scott
Washington Irving
Wilbur Lawton
Wilkie Collins
Willa Cather
Willard F. Baker
William Dean Howells
William le Queux
W. Makepeace Thackeray
William W. Walter
William Shakespeare
Winston Churchill
Yei Theodora Ozaki
Yogi Ramacharaka
Young E. Allison
Zane Grey